TO BE LOVED

K. LASHAUN

TRIGGER/CONTENT WARNING

TW/CW: sexual assault, child sexual abuse and assault

Though there aren't any depictions or scenes involving the acts listed above, the topics are discussed and mentioned throughout.

Your emotional safety and wellbeing are priority and I understand if this journey is not one you would like to take with me.

If you choose to read this project, thank you.

Though Remedy's start might not be pretty, I hope you feel that the love discovered and healing by the end is worth it.

K.

Copyright © 2022 by K. Lashaun

All rights reserved.

No part of this book may be reproduced in any form or by any electronic or mechanical means, including information storage and retrieval systems, without written permission from the author, except for the use of brief quotations in a book review.

This book is a work of fiction. While reference may be made to actual historical events or existing locations - the name, characters, places, and incidents are products of the author's imagination. Any resemblance to actual person's living or dead is entirely coincidental.

Warning: This book contains sexually explicit scenes and adult language.

PLAYLIST

Lovely - Brent Faiyez
Like I Want You - Giveon
Down to Earth - UMI
Grateful - Mahalia
Temptation - Raveena
S'en aller - Swing, Angela
As I Am - H.E.R.
Fool For You - Snoh Aalegra
Frozen - Sabrina Claudio
My Song - H.E.R.
One Unread - Amber Olivier
I Choose You - Kiana Lede

1

REMEDY

"Underwriting, as well?"

My newly promoted VP, Jaxon, nodded from beside me, thankfully answering yet another of the interviewer's questions so I wouldn't have to.

I wished I would've popped an aspirin before this interview because the ongoing ache in my chest seemed to worsen. Hot lights and cameras surrounded us, causing my skin to crawl with irritation.

The interviewer, Laura, asked another question and Jaxon, once again, answered easily.

I respected Jaxon a lot. He was knowledgeable and a huge asset to my data analytics company, RemEx Analytics.

I'd already solidified my company's reputation and status before hiring him but he'd worked tirelessly beside me since then, fostering new ideas and taking an initiative that helped catapult REA to heights I'd never thought possible.

Though I appreciated his contribution, I treated him like I did everyone else.

Distantly.

I kept him at arm's length because I'd learned long ago that people will disappoint you once you reveal how much trust you have in them.

I'd wanted to conduct the interview in the conference room on the second floor but my secretary, Miranda, had insisted it would come off more personable if we did it in my office. If she wasn't so efficient in her job, I'd think she was a complete idiot for that idea.

The woman knew there was nothing *personable* about me.

Jaxon's easy laugh brought me from my introspection and I smiled on cue, not knowing what he'd said.

Though Jaxon had confessed his public anxiety years ago, it wasn't apparent in today's interview.

Or maybe he was like me. A hot, uncomfortable mess trapped in the shell of a robot. My outward appearance revealed none of the unease coursing through me.

The urge to wring my hands together was strong but I resisted. I needed to maintain my composure and not draw attention to myself as Jaxon breezed through the interview.

At this rate, I wouldn't have to say a word.

But I'd spoken too soon because not even a second later, a cool, blue gaze swung in my direction.

"You're so quiet, Ms. Sinclair. Let me direct this question to you."

I froze, caught off guard, before nodding stiffly.

"With the advancement of today's technology and the exponential growth in need for data analytics companies like yours, how do you put a price tag on data?"

Thank God it was an easy question.

"Well... first, we don't actually *sell* data." I conjured the control I loved, allowing it to take over and give my words the crisp, certain tone I normally held. "We put together datasets and analyze them using software that compartmentalizes the information received and packages it in a way that's consumable for our clients. We look for patterns in the data to find solutions to the problems brought to us. So, the price isn't placed on the data itself, but on the *solution* that data provides for a particular issue."

I'd thought the answer was sufficient, and it probably was, but the way the woman paused after, as if taken aback, let me know my tone had likely come across as cold rather than professional like I'd been aiming for.

Beneath my cool veneer, my skin heated under the sudden scrutiny of so many eyes. But I kept it together, not revealing the mess of emotions swirling in my chest.

I hadn't meant to come off as a bitch that time but more often than not, it was the default setting for me.

Thankfully, the woman directed the rest of the questions to Jaxon until the interview concluded.

When it was over, I smiled on cue, reaching out to shake her hand and thank her for her time before standing behind my desk, watching silently as they packed up the equipment.

I didn't miss the way the interviewer purposely avoided speaking afterwards but I didn't care. I *preferred* silence over forced, awkward conversations.

Jaxon offered to walk them out and I finally released the breath I'd been holding once they were gone.

I might be uncomfortable in a lot of places but this normally wasn't one. Here, behind this large matte white executive desk, I was comfortable, at home, and at ease.

This was my safe space, sitting behind a door labeled CEO.

Business made sense to me and running mine became as instinctual as taking my next breath.

I knew who I was here and that comforted me.

"Well, that was uh..." Miranda's words trailed as she looked down at her shoes.

I knew she wanted to say it was a disaster but was afraid to. "I told you I didn't want to do it." I defended myself.

"It was good exposure for the company, if nothing else."

I respected Miranda, too, even though I also kept her at arm's length. She was always pleasant and had a mind like a steel trap that helped make my job a hell of a lot easier.

A small creaking noise had my eyes shooting over to look at Lathan, my massive asshole of a bodyguard, who had his big arms crossed over his chest as he shifted on the small, uncomfortable chair.

When he was first hired, he always remained in the waiting area on the executive floor. But once he learned how much his presence annoyed me... he'd taken up residence in the corner of my office in what was once Miranda's desk. Within a few hours of his arrival, I had the spacious desk and chair replaced with one more suitable for a child, but Lathan had strolled in unaffected and continued sitting in that uncomfortable ass chair every day without complaint.

When our eyes met, he lifted both brows before dropping them and winking. My cheeks heated, but I narrowed my lids before looking away.

Lathan was unmoved when I ramped up the bitch to the maximum level. His half smirks and lack of response had grated over my nerves for the last two years since my childhood friend, Verse, assigned him to me.

His big, tattooed frame reared the tiny chair back onto two legs, easily rocking his bulk back and forth, producing the same squeaking noise each time he moved.

We both knew he was doing it to get under my skin but I refused to admit that he was affecting me. I'd *never* reveal that his petty antics did indeed ruffle my feathers.

Most times, he was impartial towards my attitude, overlooking me like I was a petulant child more than anything.

I *hated* him.

Well, not really.

I hated that I hadn't been able to run him off like I'd done to the other bodyguards Verse hired prior to him.

I'd received harmless threats nearly two years ago and despite my resistance, Verse had set me up with a bodyguard. The first four had come and gone before I'd even memorized their names and I'd expected the same from Lathan.

But he'd remained resilient.

Though the threat was eliminated and the guy arrested, Verse kept Lathan around and eventually I'd given up on running him off.

I'd been so lost in my thoughts that I missed what Lathan said to Miranda after I glanced away but I caught her blush and tittering laugh in response.

She had a crush on him.

I didn't like it, nor did I understand it, but I guess I could see the appeal.

He was tall, probably close to six and a half feet, tattooed, and... *thick*. Solid and sturdy, like a tree trunk. But despite his bulk, he didn't stomp around like a bull in a china shop. It was quite the opposite, actually. Lathan had a quiet grace that allowed him to sneak up on me more times than I cared to admit.

Again, his eyes flashed in my direction, boldly looking me over before swinging his gaze back to Miranda and smiling at her. While they talked, I took a moment to inspect him.

He had a smooth, caramel skin tone that was littered with tattoos. Two letters were inked under his left eye and I'd been dying to know more about them but refused to ask.

I'd never seen him wear glasses over his light brown eyes, minus the dark shades tucked in the neckline of his shirt.

Lathan had a low, tapered cut and full, thick beard that was trimmed neatly on his jaw but extended a few inches off his chiseled chin.

Physically, *I guess*, he was attractive, but I didn't look at any man with interest. *Ever.* So, to me, he was just my annoying and unnecessarily large bodyguard.

When Miranda exploded with laughter again at something he said, I cut my eyes in his direction.

"Your job is to be seen and *ignored*."

My scathing tone had wilted even the toughest men who opposed me in the boardroom but Lathan merely chuckled, flashing another wink my way before mockingly twisting his fingers over his lips and tossing away the imaginary key.

Asshole.

I stood from my seat and rounded my desk, which prompted Miranda to do the same. "Don't forget, you have the opening tonight."

I paused in the middle of the floor, face contorting in a frown before I sighed. "Can I just send a gift?"

Miranda hesitated, flashing her gaze over to Lathan as if asking for help. After so many years of working closely, she was still nervous around me. I didn't purposely intimidate her, nor could I just turn off the cold, unapproachable disposition I carried.

But Lathan took the bait, always eager to get under my skin. "One of your childhood friends is having an event to celebrate him achieving his lifelong dream. You don't think sending a gift would be impersonal?" At my prolonged silence, he scoffed. "Damn, Rem. I knew you were cold, but not *that* cold."

To him and everyone else, it appeared cold.

But to me, it was survival.

People can't hurt you if you don't let them in.

That was one of the hardest things I had to learn, and I had zero intentions of repeating the lessons that had molded that viewpoint.

But Truth was a friend from childhood. Another one of the Uptown kids who'd made something out of nothing, despite the odds being stacked against us. Though I knew I wasn't well-liked by anyone, it wouldn't be right to just *not* show up.

Truth and his ex-wife Capri had been at every major event concerning REA since its conception and it was only fair that I did the same.

"Have a dress sent to the house," I said to Miranda before moving towards the door. When I opened it and didn't hear the chair squeaking in relief after Lathan lifted his bulk, I cut my eyes back to him. He remained in the seat, arms folds, lips curved up in a smile.

"*Let's go.*"

He chuckled, getting even more comfortable, tossing one leg over his knee. "Say please."

"Go to hell." I spat instead, pulling the door open and striding through it.

God, he made my blood boil.

Why couldn't I remain as unaffected with him as I did with everyone else? He got more of a reaction than people I had known for thirty years.

My heel tapped impatiently against the white floor as I waited for the elevator.

"You should try to be nicer since I'm kind of in charge of protecting you." I heard from behind me.

Don't turn around. Don't turn around. *Don't turn aro-*

I whirled to face him, venom dripping from my tone with each word I spoke. "I didn't ask for you to protect me. I've tried to fire you. Multiple times. Go find another client. Maybe they'll be nicer to you than I am."

His big hand reached out and I stilled, not missing the way his lids narrowed. I had a weird aversion to being touched, especially without my permission.

Hands that large, scarred, and calloused were only good for one thing in my experience... hurting others.

So I watched him nervously just as he continued watching my frozen frame through thin slits before twirling one of my loose, burgundy curls around his index finger and releasing it.

"Hmm," he hummed before gesturing behind me towards the elevator that I hadn't noticed arrived. "After you."

I WAS UNCOMFORTABLE.

And thirsty.

But I had zero intention of leaving my quiet corner to venture out into the crowd.

Looking over the room, I rubbed at the center of my chest, hoping to ward off the tightness and ache that had been getting worse over the last few days.

I really, *really* needed to call my doctor to get it checked out.

But with my hectic, never slowing schedule, I had too much shit to do to be put down by discomfort, whether physical or emotional.

The opening event for Truth's cannabis dispensary was nice, but the throngs of people milling about had my skin crawling. Crowds made me uncomfortable.

People, *in general*, made me uncomfortable.

And every time I felt overwhelmed like this, my reaction was visceral. Clammy palms. Damp skin. Wild and wide eyes that swung back and forth, searching for an escape.

I squeezed the untouched champagne flute in my hand so tight, I feared I'd break the glass.

I didn't drink but had taken it anyway because I didn't want to just stand there with my hands hanging limply by my side. Hell, I *already* looked out of place.

As I continued to search the room, hairs rose on my arms when I caught several curious glances in my direction. I understood people could consider me a... celebrity of sorts, but that didn't mean I *liked* it. Though I wanted REA to be catapulted higher with success, I didn't want nor need my notoriety to grow as well.

If I could remain anonymous during that process, I would be pleased.

Hell, I don't know why I'd let Lathan change my mind about attending.

These unwanted feelings swirling inside of me were exactly why I didn't want to come. On the outside, I wore my normal blank mask, appearing cool and aloof.

But on the inside, I was losing my shit.

No one was the wiser about just how uncomfortable I felt in my skin. Too many times I'd been made to feel as if my body wasn't my own and that feeling had never left me.

I wasn't stupid enough to pretend that I hadn't heard what people called me behind my back.

Cold. Frigid. Unapproachable. *A bitch.*

The icy demeanor I gave off was enough to make polar bears shiver.

Most times, I liked the power and space my coldness provided me. I was left alone because no one wanted to deal with it.

And sometimes that became... *lonely.*

Even tonight, at an event where over half the occupants were people I'd either grown up with, known for years, or had done business with, only two had ventured in my direction.

Verse, because he was fearless and had somehow grown immune to my attitude.

And Lathan.

That was it.

"You still over here in the corner?"

Speak of the devil and he shall appear. Swiveling my head to the right, I locked eyes with Verse.

Once upon a time, I'd convinced myself that I wanted him. *Romantically.*

Standing several inches taller than my five-foot seven frame, he was definitely easy on the eyes, with his full beard and hickory brown skin.

Like always, his eye contact was piercing. Intense and probing, yet somehow... he still didn't *see* me.

Not fully.

Looking back on it, my... *feelings* for him had stemmed from the years of his protectiveness after my dad died. He'd been my best friend. My family. And he'd refused to allow me to seclude myself after my father's death. He was the only person I'd allowed in, so it was only natural that my feelings for him would grow.

But he'd never seen me as anything but Big Tim's daughter. My father had been a mentor to him and so many others in our old neighborhood of Uptown, which resulted in Verse viewing me like a sister rather than a potential love interest.

Which was fine because once I outgrew those feelings, I realized we would've been a *horrible* match.

Besides, now he was engaged to a woman I'd been avoiding for the last few weeks.

"Yep," I responded. "Why does it matter?" My tone turned cold and flat. Even though I knew I didn't need that defense mechanism with him, my brain wouldn't switch off.

"What's going on with you, Rem?"

So many things that I'll never say out loud. "What do you mean?" I asked instead.

"You've been more...."

"Bitchy?" I supplied, knowing that was the word he meant, even if Verse would never refer to me or any other woman that way.

"You know better than that." He said, shoving one hand in the pocket of his slacks, looking like a GQ model without even trying. Broad shoulders filled out his jacket, unknowingly drawing the gazes of women from all over the room.

But it didn't matter.

The most eligible bachelor in Sienna Falls was head over heels in love with Garryn Taylor, the proud owner of a well-known art gallery. And it was obvious he only had eyes for her.

"What I was going to say was *distant*."

I shrugged, avoiding his probing gaze. If I was this overwhelmed by him as a friend, I could only imagine how Garryn felt when that stare focused on her.

But beyond the surface level of his attractiveness, I noticed something else. Verse looked *relaxed* and at peace, more than he had in years.

He was in love and it looked good on him.

I gave my default excuse to his question, not in the mood to be called out about my issues. "I'm *fine*. Just thinking about work stuff."

He only hummed in response, seeming to accept my answer, which once again proved just how little he knew me.

His gaze left mine, searching the room before landing on his gorgeous fiancée, smirking when she spotted his leer and preened under his intense glare.

From my peripheral, I spotted Lathan approaching with a champagne flute in each hand.

He walked with the confidence of a man who lacked embarrassment and was fully aware of his physical attractiveness. It was weird seeing him out of his street clothes and in a suit. From the way the material fit perfectly over his solid frame, it was obviously tailored. The man was tall, ridiculously so. Almost the same height as Hakeem, who was the tallest person I knew.

Hakeem was another childhood friend who doubled as a bodyguard for Verse and Garryn while running the successful security firm that had lent Lathan and his predecessor's services to me. HB Corp was well known amongst celebrities and had even trained and assigned security detail to high-profile politicians.

I might have the emotional range of a turnip, but even I felt immensely proud seeing so many of my tribe thriving in life.

After the shit we all went through in Uptown, we deserved every bit of success everyone had achieved. Plus *more*.

Without asking, Lathan smoothly exchanged the glass in my hand with the one he held, causing me to frown. "I didn't drink the one I had already, so why the hell would you bring me an-"

"I know you don't drink, Remedy." He cut me off mid rant. "It's *soda*."

Instead of thanking him, I kept my eyes locked on his and brought the glass to my nose and sniffed. "Is it poisoned?"

"Try it and see." He shot back, playful grin in place. From the corner of my eye, I spotted Verse looking between the two of us curiously, so I averted my gaze from Lathan's and pulled out my phone to check emails.

"You can't resist, can you?" He quipped, nodding towards my device.

I really couldn't.

Work was an escape for me and I had no clue what I'd do or who I'd be without it.

"Mind your business."

"You are my business, Remedy Sinclair. Remember?"

Another *go to hell* was on the tip of my tongue, but a rough hand on my forearm robbed me of my response.

I hated that the first emotion I felt was fear. I tensed with it, going stock still, pulling on every ounce of my strength to force it back down.

All the years I'd spent perfecting my uncaring mask went down the drain from a simple unwanted touch. The initial panic I felt must've been evident because Lathan reached over, pulling me out of the man's grasp and towards him, which calmed me rather than sending me spiraling further.

"Hands off," he ordered sternly.

From this angle, I had a clear, unobstructed view of the asshole who had no sense of boundaries.

He looked vaguely familiar, like someone I might've consulted with before. But I encountered so many people in my line of work that even if I did care to remember their names, I wouldn't be able to.

"Whoa, *whoa*," the man said, holding up his hands, adopting what was supposed to be a charming smile but failing miserably. "No harm done. I was trying to get Ms. Sinclair's attention, that's all."

"For what?" Lathan's tone was still harsh.

The man frowned, looking at him, then swinging his gaze to Verse, who stood there coolly with a single brow lifted. "I'm sorry if I overstepped." He apologized, finally locking his gaze with mine. "I was just hoping to discuss some business with you. I've been attempting to schedule another consultation because I think the first time we got off on the wrong foot and I would like to start fresh. Calling your company and requesting another meeting hasn't been the most successful, so I saw you over here and used this opportunity."

The more he spoke, the more it jogged my memory until I clearly recalled our disastrous meeting.

From the start, he'd made thinly veiled sexist remarks about how I'd gotten my position before rambling on about how I would benefit from taking him as a client as if he hadn't practically begged for my services for the last six months.

Needless to say, that had been our first and *last* meeting.

"Does this look like a business setting?" Lathan countered, head tilted and hand buried in the pocket of his slacks. His entire posture screamed relaxed and unbothered but the calm blankness on his face felt scarier than if he'd been in full rage mode. "If you want to discuss *business*, make an appointment."

The man whose name I still couldn't recollect frowned, sizing Lathan up despite being several inches shorter and probably fifty pounds lighter. "Who are you? Her assistant?"

Lathan remained unfazed by the weak jab. "My title doesn't matter but my words do. She doesn't want to discuss business at this event. *Especially* with you."

He must've recognized him, too. Lathan had been in the corner of the room like always while Miranda and I had taken the meeting. He hadn't said a word or moved the entire time, so I'd assumed he'd either nodded off or wasn't paying any attention.

Clearly, I was wrong.

"Ms. Sinclair," the man tried again before slamming his lips closed when Lathan took a step forward.

"I'm speaking English, right, VP?" Lathan's tone was casual and curious as he tossed out the question.

"Last time I checked." Verse supplied, lips quirked up in a half smile.

"Then that means you're just not fuckin' listening." His voice turned sharp and cutting and my gaze locked on his profile. I'd never seen *this* side of Lathan.

From what I'd gathered since he'd been hired, he was always *Mr. Laidback.*

But he hadn't actually been in any situations where I needed actual *guarding*, so I guess it was nice to know he was capable if the need arose.

The man's frown deepened and he puffed up his chest, stepping forward and making the small amount of space between him and Lathan tinier.

Suave as ever, Verse slipped between them, likely realizing things were well on their way to getting out of hand. Charming smile in place, his palm slid smoothly in the angry man's. "Mr. Dampier, do you know who I am?"

Dampier. That was the asshole's name.

The man reluctantly pulled his gaze from Lathan's before nodding tightly, tone low and angry. "I do, Mr. Presley."

"Then allow me to advise that even if you were to get another meeting with Ms. Sinclair, the likelihood of your companies working together is slim to none." Which was true. I'd worked hard to make sure I contracted only reputable companies with REA and he was nowhere near that. "But, if you'll follow me... there's another company that I think you'll be a great match with."

The man hesitated, bouncing his gaze between the three of us before his shoulders sagged. "Thank you, Mr. Presley."

Verse's response was indistinguishable as he guided the man away from us, effortlessly getting his way.

"You okay?" Lathan asked a second before his big palm rested against the small of my back.

I stiffened this time, then nodded, hoping he hadn't caught it. But because he was Lathan, of course he fucking did.

"You got an aversion to touch or something?"

It was just a question. A simple one that shouldn't have caused a knot to form in my gut and an inability to swallow.

But it did.

For so many reasons.

And before I could stop myself, I reacted like a cornered wildcat, with claws extended.

"And why is that any of your fuckin' business? You're here to do a job and you did it. So thank you. But anything outside of *that* is above your pay grade."

Not reacting immediately, he eyed me like he was fully aware of how close I'd been to a panic attack. His warm brown eyes passed over me and he scoffed, as if finding me lacking, before looking back towards the crowd.

He hadn't deserved that but I couldn't apologize. I didn't know *how* to and because of that, I felt like shit, which was rare because I was normally unapologetic about my attitude.

I hadn't adopted it because I thought it was cute or amusing. I'd done so out of necessity and though it afforded me the distance I craved from most people, it also felt like a shackle attached to my ankle.

One that I no longer had the key to.

I felt... *trapped* inside my body.

All the emotions that I refused to allow to surface were drowning me from the inside and no one seemed to be the wiser, including those closest to me.

Even they could no longer see beyond the blank cold slate that I wore daily and I feared that would be my reality for the rest of life.

2

LATHAN

Remedy had entirely too *much damn house*.

Even after two years, that was still my first thought each time we passed the security station at the gate that surrounded her property.

Like always, stony silence came from the backseat of the SUV as I passed the large, manicured lawn and pulled up the extended driveway that ended in a loop right in front of the massive home.

Before I moved into the guest suite near the rear of the house, Remedy had lived alone in the seven bedroom, four-and-a-half-bathroom Mediterranean style two-story mansion. The oversized house came equipped with a library, media room, four-car garage, gym, sauna and steam room, full tennis court, and a massive, heated pool.

Outdoor lounging furniture was strategically placed around her patio, which made little sense because she never, and I mean *never*, had guests.

"Don't open that door." I warned once I parked the car, knowing she would ignore my words.

On cue, she hopped out of the backseat and strode towards the front door before I could stop her. With a headshake, I followed, admiring the sway of her slightly curved ass.

For Remedy to be such a stiff, *unfeeling* woman, she damn sure had a sexy ass walk.

The sensual movement *had* to be an unconscious action because Rem would prefer diving into crocodile infested waters than purposely do anything to garner someone's attention.

When she stopped and dug through her purse for her keys, I slid around her to open the door and walked inside to the familiar cold, dead silence.

Unable to stop herself, she tailed me with distrust as I did my customary walkthrough of the home to make sure no uninvited guests had slipped in during our absence.

It amused rather than annoyed me, like I suspected she aimed for.

The poor woman was incapable of letting her guards down. Even *here*.

She came across as cold and emotionless. Even I had to admit, I thought she was that way for the longest. But once I looked past the exterior and cold front she displayed, I noticed that though her expression often remained aloof, there was so much going on in the mind housed behind that cool, emerald gaze.

"You can see yourself out." She snapped once we made our way back into the foyer.

I smiled at the venomous words, watching through narrowed lids as she walked back up the curving stairway before disappearing down the hall that led to her suite.

After one last look around, I moved through the kitchen and stepped outside beneath the covered breezeway that wrapped around the side of the home and led to the guest quarters she'd so *graciously* dismissed me to.

Despite my *less than pleasant* client, who sometimes had the personality of an ice cube, this was a good gig. An *easy* one.

With the lack of excitement in her life, I was more of a companion than a bodyguard. But I wouldn't take it for granted, especially considering my past.

I was four years removed from a ten-year stint in jail. I spent the first year scrambling, trying to rebuild my life, which hadn't been that impressive before I got locked up. I went in as a twenty-one-year-old kid and emerged as a thirty-one-year-old man in a world that had moved on without me.

It had been a *hell* of an adjustment.

I'd felt weird moving back in with my parents, especially after such a monumental fuck up, so I'd bounced from couch to couch, even sleeping in my car for a few weeks when the job opportunities kept falling through.

I didn't understand how a world who shunned illegal activities continually made it hard for felons to turn their life around. Jail, though marketed as rehabilitation, was nothing more than a glorified adult babysitter for criminals.

Few of us were taught what to do when we came out, which resulted in resorting to what we knew and turning into repeat offenders.

I'd come close after nine months of freedom and only one job opportunity making minimum wage at a fast-food joint. I had family to take care of and a three hundred dollar check every two weeks would not cut it.

Luckily, before I made a stupid mistake that would send me back inside, my boy Deacon heard of a security company in need of new recruits. When I'd learned that they hired felons, I applied instantly.

The training was rigorous and intense but it'd been worth it because the monthly payout quadrupled what I made each *quarter* working the drive thru in a mass fast-food chain.

My first gig had been shadowing a spoiled socialite before being reassigned. Verse Presley, or VP, as many people called him, had grilled and vetted me thoroughly before introducing me to Remedy.

After passing their tests, her childhood friends warned me she wouldn't be receptive to my presence.

They'd *sorely* underestimated how much Remedy would resent

me following her around every day. She was still as cold to me now as she'd been on day one.

She hadn't warmed to me at all.

Not even a little.

The pay was damned good, so quitting was never an option. And as an extra incentive for not letting Remedy run me off, VP and Keem slid me a bonus at the end of each month.

And I appreciated every penny because after ten years away, I was trying to be a part of my daughter's life and make up for time lost. If tolerating Remedy and her bad attitude was the price, I'd pay it tenfold if I kept receiving the money that I forked over each month to pay for the private school my sixteen-year-old, Tessa, attended.

Kicking off my shoes when I reached my spacious suite, I went to the basement that connected from the main and guest house. Before I lived with her, it was used as extra storage, but after many rounds with Remedy and recruiting Verse to help my argument, she'd agreed to convert it into a state-of-the-art surveillance room.

I didn't understand how someone who owned as much property as she did not have proper security measures in place to keep her safe. The many blind spots and easy access points had driven me crazy for the first few weeks while everything was installed.

Now every square inch of her property was recorded on a twenty-four-hour feed I accessed from an app on my phone.

Dropping my weight onto the chair in front of the row of monitors, I flipped through the cameras like I did each time I came home.

Nothing captured my eye other than the guards at the gates switching shifts.

Grateful that everything was quiet, I stripped out of my clothes, foregoing the shower to change into my old, faithful jeans that were torn and stained from years of constant use.

They'd become my... uniform, of sorts, when creating.

Shirtless and barefoot, I was just about to go down the hall into the second bedroom where I stored my equipment, but the phone rang before I could.

My brows rose high when I spotted my baby mother's name on the screen.

"What's up, Gabbi?"

"You need to get your damn daughter," she snapped.

I rubbed my forehead wearily. I'd gotten more of these phone calls over the last few months than I cared to admit. I'm not sure what had gotten into Tessa lately, but she was going through a *wild phase* that left her mother frustrated more often than not.

"What happened?"

"She's about to drive me *crazy*." Her tone elevated, voice shaking with anger.

I sighed again, stomach flip flopping with anticipation before taking a deep, calming breath. The last time I'd gotten a call like this was less than a week ago when I'd had to fetch Tessa from a sketchy house party where her underaged ass had no business being.

"What did she do?"

"She got in trouble at school today *again* then had the nerve to ask if she could go to a *college party*. I told her young ass *hell nah* and when I got home from work, she snuck out any damn way."

"College party?"

"Yes, Lathan," she huffed with frustration. "I swear, between her, these other kids, my mama and work… I'm going to *snap*."

Uncertainty and guilt coursed through me each time I received a call about Tessa's behavior. I couldn't help but to wonder if my absence during incarceration contributed to it.

While she continued to rant, I sent a quick text to the guard who patrolled the perimeter at night. Whenever I left the property, he monitored things. Sadly, because of Tessa's antics lately, this was becoming a weekly routine for us.

"What's the address?" I interrupted, knowing Gabbi could go on for hours if I let her.

"What?"

"Send me the address, Gabbi. I'll get her."

"*IS SHE IN THERE, LATHAN?!*"

Frowning at the large brick home, I scanned the cars lining the street. "I don't know, Gabbi. I just pulled up. Let me check inside."

After parking two streets over, I walked back to the house I'd passed minutes earlier. College kids littered the lawn and up the three steps that led to the entrance of the house.

The new trap single from the popular southern rapper, Lo-Kee, blasted through the speakers as I stepped into the spacious living room. I ignored the curious glances thrown my way and scanned the semi-dark room, looking for a familiar pecan brown face.

It took nearly twenty minutes to search the first floor and the backyard. After coming up empty, I headed towards the stairs that led to the second level.

Before I could, a kid whose height nearly matched mine blocked my path. "Only the hosts can go upstairs."

I frowned before glaring at the hand he'd pressed in the middle of my chest. My skin crawled with the thought of my underaged daughter being upstairs with the *host*. I prayed this kid moved out of my way on his own accord because I'd forcibly move him if I needed to.

"I'm just looking for my daughter," I tried, holding up my hands in an innocent gesture. "Once I have her, we'll be out of here."

Again, I tried to pass, but he blocked me, this time shoving me backward. He scowled when I didn't budge and pushed me again. Though his height nearly rivaled mine, his slim, lanky build was no match for my bulk.

I scoffed, dropping my head, drawing on every ounce of patience I'd worked to build since my stint in prison. The hothead who answered every issue with his fists was in the past and I wanted to *leave* him there.

Getting arrested again because I cracked the nose of a fucking college kid would be stupid. But if he kept me from getting to my daughter, then that was a charge I'd take.

"Like I said, only the hosts can go upstairs," he reiterated before scanning me through narrowed lids. "Besides... aren't you a little old to be at a frat party?"

My jaw and fist clenched at the same time. Clearly, the little shit ignored my statement about searching for my daughter.

"Look, man... all I'm trying to do is-"

Another push hit my chest mid-sentence but this time, I retaliated, smacking his hand from me and shoving him hard enough to send him stumbling backwards on the very stairs I tried to go up.

"Are you serious?!" He snapped, scrambling to his feet, "Do you k-"

"We got a problem over here?" A cool voice offered from behind me.

"Yeah," I snapped, eyeing the asshole who wouldn't let me upstairs before turning, "Like I told your boy, I'm just tr-" My words trailed when I spotted Tessa standing right behind me with wide eyes and the guy who'd spoken arm tossed over her shoulders.

"What are you doing here?" She asked, looking around nervously.

"Who's this, T?"

Ignoring how the guy casually scanned me, I walked up to her, vibrating with the urge to knock his ass out for even addressing her so familiarly. "Let's go."

"But Daddy..."

"*Now*, Contessa." My tone offered no argument and she must've recognized how close I was to losing my temper because she sucked her teeth and shrugged off the guy's arm before walking towards the exit.

"I'll call you later, T," the dumbass called out just as I turned to follow her.

I stopped mid step before whirling back around, muscles rippling with anger.

"Daddy, let's just go." Her tone was soft and placating as she grabbed my arm.

Effortlessly, I shook off her grip, stepping right up in the kid's face, who had enough sense to look apologetic. "How old are you?"

"Uh... nineteen, sir."

I nodded, pasting on a smile that caused him to blanch. I didn't use it often but was pleased that it was still effective. "Be glad I'm leaving peacefully rather than knocking out your fucking teeth for promising to call my *sixteen-year-old* daughter."

If possible, his light-skinned face paled even more.

"*Daddy!*"

"I didn't... I... I swear, I didn't know she was..."

"Breathe in her direction again," I warned, stepping closer with lids narrowed and flattened lips. "And the two of us will have a nice, *long* talk." I kept my gaze to locked on his. "You understand me?"

When he nodded, I tapped the side of his head, smiling again. "Good boy."

My anger threatened to consume me, so I turned, sensing rather than seeing Tessa following behind.

When we made it to the car, I finally got a good look at her, which annoyed me even further.

Clearly, she'd gone searching through her mother's closet because there was no way Gabbi bought her something that short.

With her face caked with makeup, she looked older and an exact replica of her mother ten years ago.

It was scary how much she resembled her.

Heavy silence hung between us as we climbed in the car and got on the highway towards her home.

Finally, after fifteen minutes, she turned to face me. "You're not going to say anything?"

"Nope."

Her thick, drawn-on eyebrows rose high on her forehead. "Nothing at all?"

"Nope." I repeated.

"Well..." she began, eyes growing wide, "You can't be mad!"

I wanted to know why the hell I couldn't, but I didn't say that. Instead, I shrugged, keeping my eyes on the road. "Did I say I was?"

She squirmed in her seat and I knew the calmness in my tone confused her.

On the inside, I seethed, but I couldn't show that. Not yet.

I needed to regain control of my temper before I talked to her because, despite her new rebel status, she was sensitive as hell and my sometimes-harsh way of speaking hurt her feelings, which caused her to shut down.

It was a delicate balance, one I failed at more often than not.

But I was trying.

Four years after reappearing in her life, I still struggled to learn who she was and how to communicate with her because it seemed to change every day.

This parenting shit was hard and I tipped my hat to Gabbi for doing it full time with *multiple* kids.

Both of us remained quiet for the rest of the ride to her mother's house, though I'd caught her slanting her eyes in my direction the whole time.

Each time we interacted, I wished we had a better relationship but I had no one to blame for the distance but myself.

I'd gotten locked up when she was two, so her recollection of me when I got out was minimal. I'd been a virtual stranger who appeared in her life at twelve and it had been hell trying to form a bond ever since.

Once we pulled into the driveway, I parked and took a deep breath before facing her. "What's going on with you, T?"

Stubbornly, she folded her arms, refusing to look my way now that she had my attention.

"I don't want to talk about it."

I sighed, completely clueless how to handle her. "T, well what do yo-"

"I don't want to talk about it!" she snapped, shoving open her car door.

"Tessa. *Tessa!*"

A groan forced its way up my throat when she slammed the door closed and strode up to the house.

Getting out, I watched as Gabbi emerged with a sleeping four-year-old on her hip.

Time had been good to her. She was still as beautiful as she'd been fifteen years ago but exhaustion lined her face.

After exchanging low words with her mom, Tessa went inside without a backward glance. Gabbi glared behind her before coming down the steps to lean against the hood of my truck.

We'd dated on and off throughout high school and even after until she got pregnant with Tessa her freshman year of college.

Less than three years later, I was locked up for a stupid attempted robbery.

While I was in prison, she'd gotten married and divorced, giving birth to four other kids who now varied in age from four to eleven years old.

After their separation, her ex left her high and dry to raise the kids alone but because Gabbi worked a full time and two part-time jobs to make ends meet, that left Tessa to care for her younger siblings.

I know that weighed on her but it still didn't excuse the recent string of reckless behavior she'd indulged in. Though I had a nice sized nest egg built up since taking the gig as Rem's bodyguard, I wasn't rich by any means and the private school where Tessa attended was *not* cheap but I helped where I could, sliding Gabbi extra money to go towards bills or to buy things for the other kids.

Court orders had a set amount of child support I paid each month but it wasn't enough.

Not in my eyes.

Gabbi had cared for and raised my child while I'd been locked away for ten years. And when I got out, she'd let me lay my head at her place for a few months, not once judging me or holding my mistakes against me.

She'd always had my back and kept me involved in whatever Tessa had going on, whether good or bad, and I'd always look out for her in return.

"I'm so tired," she finally said. "I'm overwhelmed and... I don't know what to do with her anymore." The resignation in her tone bothered me. "I know I count on Tessa too much to help with her siblings but dammit, you *know* how my mama is, Lathan. The last thing I want is to leave them alone with her."

I understood. Ms. Gloria was mean on her best day and downright vile and evil on her worst.

And she evenly spread out her nastiness to everyone who came in contact with her, including her daughter and grandkids.

I understood Gabbi's apprehension about leaving them for extended periods with such a toxic person. She'd worked too hard to overcome the trauma her mother had inflicted on her throughout childhood so subjecting her kids to the same treatment was the last thing she wanted.

"What do you need me to do?" I asked, hefting my shoulders. "I can get her more, try to be around more but I know you need her to watch the little ones. So, tell me what I can do to make things easier."

She sighed, shrugging. "I don't know. Getting her more would resolve the Tessa issue but then it creates the *I have no babysitter* issue."

Feeling helpless, I offered what I could. "Do you need money? For childcare or a babysitter or something?"

"I *always* need money, Lathan, but I'm not going to take it from you. Our court order says we're supposed to split T's tuition at the school but you pay it in full *every* month. Not to mention, you give me extra money *all the time* and buy things for the other kids when you don't have to." Another sigh rushed from her lips. "If their dad did just *half* of what you did, I could breathe easier."

While nodding, I pulled out my phone, going straight to CashApp.

"You better not," she warned, nudging me with her shoulder. "Lathan, *no*." Seconds later, her phone dinged with the received transfer. "You don't have to keep saving me. I'll figure it out."

"I know you will. And until you do... I got you, G."

Her deep gaze searched mine and I smiled, watching as she blushed and rolled her eyes. "I wish the thought of sleeping with you again didn't make my skin crawl... I'd try it."

I tossed my head back, laughing, knowing exactly what she meant.

I loved Gabbi and always would, but we'd been better suited as friends. Romantic love just wasn't in the cards for us.

We'd tried to force a relationship many times, but it had never felt... *right*.

Thankfully, we figured that out before walking down the aisle with someone we weren't meant to spend the rest of our lives with.

I hated seeing her so stressed and overwhelmed with everything life had thrown at her. She'd been through so much and deserved the best of everything.

She'd overcome a fucked up mother, breast cancer, a locked up baby father, and being abandoned by her husband to raise five kids alone.

My heart went out to her, so I'd do whatever in my ability to make things easier.

She more than deserved it.

3

LATHAN

The woman didn't stop. She was like a *robot*.

Remedy's entire life consisted of working ten to twelve hours, then going home, minus the occasional doctor's appointment. She literally had no life and was content with it.

At least she *seemed* content.

Lately, I'd been seeing cracks in the veneer she wore. Rare moments where her authentic emotions bled through and showed her humanity. The woman was smart as a whip, fierce, and a force to be reckoned with. But when she thought no one was looking... when she believed she was alone and hadn't heard my approach, I saw *something* in her.

Something I couldn't piece together yet. But those rare glimpses had definitely captured my attention.

It was hard not to notice Remedy's attractiveness.

How could you miss the unblemished bronze skin, emerald eyes, pouty lips, and tight body? The woman was a walking fantasy.

Minus her grouchy disposition.

But because of the nature of our relationship, I ignored her physical appeal to focus on my job.

Which worked for a while, but now that I'd seen more than what she presented to the world, I was eager to dive deeper.

Learning more about Rem was like putting together the pieces of a puzzle that reset every few seconds. The aloof woman obviously didn't want to let anyone in and normally, I'd keep my distance.

I was notorious for minding my business, especially after getting involved in other's business at nineteen had landed me in jail for an entire decade.

But maybe it was the nosy ass gene I'd inherited from my mother that had me not wanting to let this go.

Whether she knew it or not, Remedy had my attention and I fully intended to tug on that thread of attraction I felt until it unraveled, eager to see where it would lead.

"I got an email this morning regarding the PCSAA auction and fundraiser."

Silence met Miranda's statement as Remedy continued typing away at her keyboard. Poor Miranda. The woman had to be a saint to put up with Remedy's coolness and still be a normal, functioning human. Prison had acclimated me to different personality types and taught me a level of patience I had never had, so I was immune to Remedy and her mouth at this point.

While Miranda shifted uncomfortably, I pulled out my phone to search for the acronym.

Prevent Child Sexual Abuse and Assault.

Based on the website, PCSAA was a foundation formed in 1998 by a woman from Sienna Falls. She'd grown up in a home where she and her siblings were subjected to sexual abuse. Once she escaped, she created the foundation which provided resources to sexually abused children or adult survivors of abuse. What started as a support group turned into a huge foundation that offered counseling, online resources for caregivers and parents of survivors, retreats, as well as legal representation.

It was an admirable cause and each year, they hosted a large auction and fundraiser to support it.

This year's event would be hosted at State-of-the-Art, the gallery that VP's fiancée Garryn owned.

"Are you going to attend?" Miranda finally squeaked out.

"Nope." Remedy said, still looking at the screen.

I snorted, ignoring the scathing glare she threw my way.

I wasn't surprised at her quick refusal. Remedy rarely ventured anywhere outside her usual trio of destinations—work, home, and the doctor—but if she did, it was always with a frown on her face.

"Okay," Miranda said softly. "Donating again?"

When Rem flashed another look in my direction, this time filled with discomfort, I sat up straight in the squeaky ass, too-small chair she'd set up, eagerly waiting for her response.

Her blunt, unpolished nails finally stop clicking against the keyboard and she huffed before nodding at Miranda. "Same amount we do every year."

While Miranda tapped away on her laptop, I kept my eyes on the woman who suddenly seemed like she didn't know what to do with her hands. She fiddled with the stapler on her desk, shuffled an already neat stack of papers, clicked and unclicked a pen before shoving to her feet.

"I'll be back," she declared, rounding her large desk and striding towards the door. The burgundy curls she liked to wear in loose waves bounced around her shoulders, as immaculate and put-together as the rest of her. The woman never had a hair out of place.

Even in the comfort of her home, though her face was devoid of makeup, she still looked put together and ready to step inside the office at any moment.

The word relax appeared to be absent from her vocabulary.

Miranda didn't notice the weirdness in her actions but I did, which instantly had me wanting to know more.

"How much does she donate?" I asked conversationally after Remedy was gone, hoping Miranda would be as forthcoming as she normally was.

Her head popped up from her task, hair falling over one shoulder as she met my gaze. "Two million."

Damn. "Every year?"

"Every year," she confirmed with a nod.

"Do you know why?"

She shrugged, swinging her gaze back to her laptop. "No clue. She donates to a lot of different causes, specifically if it concerns minorities. Most of those are for tax purposes, though, and it's usually a couple hundred thousand at the most. But this one? Even though she *never* attends the fundraiser, she donates the same amount. Two million every single year."

"Hmm."

Another piece of the Remedy puzzle was revealed but I had no clue how it fit into the overall picture of who the hell she was and what made her tick.

But that was okay.

I'd realized that this wouldn't be an easy or swift road and I was fine with it.

Getting to know the aloof woman would be worth the time it took.

4

REMEDY

I DON'T KNOW why I became panicky and uncomfortable when Miranda asked about my annual donation to PCSAA.

It wasn't like they were aware of my past.

Hell, not a single person who walked this Earth was aware of it, minus those who'd harmed me.

And I hoped their souls were somewhere rotting in the pits of hell.

But I'd felt Lathan's curious gape the second Miranda asked and my skin had grown hot with shame, as if my secret had been exposed.

So I'd given my answer and fled to the private bathroom on the opposite end of my office suite. Once inside, I bent over the sink, running cool water over my wrists, hoping it would ease the heat coursing through me.

After several minutes, my body temperature returned to normal but it had done nothing for the ever-increasing ache in my chest. I'd told myself to do it several times, but now I knew I *had* to make an appointment to see my cardiologist. Like he'd warned, the pain became more frequent if I didn't take care of myself or decrease the stressors in my life.

Little did he know, the things that stressed me the most were locked in my mind, unable to escape.

After scolding myself for being a coward and hiding out in the bathroom too long, I checked myself in the mirror, making sure nothing about my outward appearance revealed my moment of panic before walking back to my office.

My steps slowed when I heard an extra voice before stopping completely when I spotted Garryn Taylor sitting on the opposite side of my desk.

Her pretty face was upturned, head tossed back with laughter. Miranda and Lathan joined in before their smiles faded when they spotted me in the doorway.

I was used to that sort of reception but this time it caused a weird pang in my chest that had nothing to do with my medical condition.

"Garryn stopped by," Miranda supplied unnecessarily. "I'll leave you two to talk."

Her heels clicked against the floor as she left the room.

"It's good seeing you, Garryn," Lathan said, placing a big hand on her bare shoulder. I zeroed in on the contact before zipping my gaze away and striding across the floor with confidence I didn't feel.

"You, too, Lathan," she said with a smile.

His toffee gaze flashed up to mine and I narrowed my lids at the secretive smile he flashed at me.

Asshole.

"I'm ordering something for lunch. You want anything?"

My frown appeared before I could stop it.

Miranda fetched lunch for me when I got too busy to get something on my own.

No one ever *volunteered* to just grab something for me.

"Where are you going?" I asked suspiciously.

"La'Mars."

"That's my *favorite* spot," Garryn chimed in with a laugh. "I just left an hour ago. I eat there so much, I'm on a first name basis with the entire staff."

"Shit, me too," Lathan joined in and I pasted on an uncomfortable smile. Like always, Lathan saw right through it and shook his head. "So you want something or not?"

"Yes," I said, reaching for my purse in the bottom drawer, "I want-"

"I know what you want, Rem." I tensed and flashed my gaze up to his. "And I can buy the food. Don't worry about it."

I remained in the same frozen position, still searching for an ulterior motive for his sudden kindness. Usually, this would be a moment where he'd say something to annoy me or make a comment to ruffle my feathers, but he did neither.

Instead, he met my stare head on, unblinkingly allowing me to see the genuine glint in his gaze that revealed no ulterior motives.

Though it made me squirm, I thanked him, watching his broad frame turn and leave the room, closing the door behind him.

Once we were alone, I met Garryn's hazel gaze.

Though I'd only been around her a handful of times, the woman made me uncomfortable. Her supreme confidence annoyed me because I could tell that my disposition wouldn't scare her off as easily as others in the past.

"I've gotten to know practically everyone in Verse's life, *except you*. Each time we're in a room together, you avoid me." She tilted her head and healthy strands of her shoulder-length hair shifted, framing her gorgeous face. "Why is that?"

How do I explain that I resented her for stealing the heart of the *one man* I felt safe with?

Yeah, I trusted our other male childhood friends... Truth, Drue, and Hakeem. I'd even developed a bit of trust with Lathan over the last few years.

But Verse had been the only one who inspired feelings of complete safety. No matter what, I'd always known for sure that he would never hurt me like so many others had.

Once upon a time, I fancied myself in love with him but now I realized those *feelings* were more rooted in codependency rather than romantic love.

He'd stepped in after my dad died and I'd latched onto him like a leech, draining him until I remembered how to breathe again on my own.

So many people attributed my personality and disposition to my dad's death, which proved just how little attention they'd paid to me. If they had, they would've noticed my trauma had started long, *long* before then.

I'd carried that pain, shame, and a dark secret for nearly thirty years and kept it close to my chest. I trusted Verse and a few others with my life but not with this.

I didn't trust *anyone* with that vulnerability.

"I'm not a people person." I finally answered.

Her responding smile was soft and warm, totally at odds with the balls-buster Drue and Hakeem had made her out to be. "I've gathered that."

She shifted in her seat and my gaze fell to her waistline, envying her curves.

Though far from skinny, I lacked the coke-bottle figure that Garryn and so many other women possessed, including Miranda.

I had curves, but they were subtle and slight, rather than exaggerated and noticeable. My dad had been a tall, slim man and though I lacked his height, I'd definitely inherited his slender build, especially as a teen.

Lack of physical exercise and a less than healthy diet had packed on a few pounds over the last few years but it was still nothing compared to the traffic stopping curves the woman in front of me possessed.

Recognizing that I wasn't going to say more, she crossed her legs and leaned forward, resting an arm on my desk. "I've dragged my feet long enough. I've given Verse plenty of time to change his mind and he hasn't, so... I think it's time for me to actually *start* planning the wedding and I want you to be a part of it."

She wants me to... *what?*

She must've recognized the panic on my face because she laughed, "Well, not the planning... but we want you to be *in* the wedding. My best friend, Raye, is my maid of honor and I would like it if you, Gia, Krystal, and Birdie stood beside me as my bridesmaids. All of you are important to Verse, which makes you important to me and we want all of you to share that moment with us. To share in our happiness."

"Have you set a date?" I asked instead.

Her flawless face scrunched as she shook her head. "Not yet. Like I said, I've been putting it off and putting it off, but it's time." Her gaze swept over my features, softening at whatever she saw there. "So what do you say, Rem?"

My first instinct was to say no. This was out of my comfort zone.

I still couldn't gauge how I felt about Garryn but I owed Verse a lot, so *for him*, I'd do it.

No matter how uncomfortable it made me.

"Sure. I'd love to."

God, I hope I don't regret this.

A KNOCK COMING from downstairs had me pausing, frowning towards my open bathroom door.

I was just preparing to give myself a facial like I did each Sunday.

Monday through Saturday were typically full workdays for me, as well as alternating Sundays.

So I only had two true off days each month where I sat around my home and did nothing. Most people who worked as much as I did would look forward to those off days. But not me.

Idle time led to thoughts about my past and getting lost in my head.

And that place is a fucked up jigsaw I'd never task anyone with trying to solve.

Seconds later, a second round of knocks sounded off at the door.

I huffed, setting down the expensive face cream before tugging on my robe.

I hadn't expected visitors and Lathan usually kept to himself when I was home, so I didn't feel the need to be *on*.

My curls were wild and free in preparation for the deep conditioning I owed them. My face was devoid of makeup underneath the robe was the equivalent of pajamas for me—a cami with no bra and shorts that stopped on my upper thighs, mere inches below the slight curve of my ass.

A third round of knocks had me leaving the safety of my suite, moving barefoot down the hall at a brisk pace.

Maybe Lathan was in his suite doing whatever the hell he did over there and hadn't heard the knocking.

But when I descended the steps, there he was, sitting his oversized ass on my overpriced furniture, watching television in my sitting room without a care in the world. The fucker had even taken his shoes off.

"Excuse me?"

He looked over, gave me a reverse nod, then turned back to the television.

"Do you not hear the door?"

Again, he flashed a nonchalant glance my way, stopping in the middle of his movie selection. His eyes swept over me and I took a step back from the unexpected heat in his gaze. Though my robe was already tied, I tightened the ropes, hating that he'd seen me so dressed down *and* that I wasn't immune to the way he looked at me.

The corners of his lips lifted. "I'm not your butler, Rem. I believe that might be *above* my pay grade."

My face heated at his reminder of my words from the opening two weeks ago.

I'd regretted them immediately, yet had never apologized and since then, he'd found every opportunity to remind me how certain tasks I requested were above his *pay grade*.

Crossing my arms, I narrowed my lids. "What if it's a murderer or a stalker or something?"

He scoffed, crossing his sock clad feet at the ankles, gaze going back to the television. "Then they wouldn't be very good ones if they're knocking on the door to announce their arrival."

"Why are you over here, anyway?" I griped, moving towards the knocking. "Unless you've stripped everything out of my guesthouse, I remember there being several televisions."

He looked at me, one brow lifted. "Yours is bigger."

Instead of giving in to the brewing argument, I turned to open the door.

"Hi, Remedy."

My frame stiffened as I stared at the familiar face, unable to speak a word.

"Rem, who's at the door?" Lathan called out but I couldn't make myself move. "Rem?" This time his voice was closer and more concerned, likely from my lack of response.

"Do you know who I am, Remy?" The person at my door asked gently.

That nickname that I hadn't heard in almost twenty years snapped me out of my stupor and my face contorted with anger. Moments later, Lathan's heavy presence was at my back but I paid him no mind, unable to tear my gaze away from the unwanted visitor.

"What the *fuck* are you doing here?" I finally snapped.

The woman whose face mirrored mine collapsed and her lids closed a moment before she reopened them. "I know you don't want to see me but... I... can I please come in? I just want to talk."

"What do we have to talk about, Isabel?" I asked my mother, knowing hearing her first name was like a dagger in her heart. "The twenty something years of my life you missed?"

Seeing her here, standing on my doorstep, fighting back tears, I felt nothing.

Not even a faint thump in my chest.

Though she'd birthed me, this *woman* wasn't my mother.

When I looked at her, all I saw was someone who let me down. Another person who hadn't seen me.

Another person who left me to drown and suffer in silence.

I'd worn my pain on my sleeve then, just like I do now and still... no one saw it.

No one *cared* to see it because I expressed my hurt through a cold, standoffish demeanor rather than through tears, hysteria, and emotional breakdowns.

People dismissed me as a bitch. Not one person had ever truly tried to learn why I was the way I was.

Even Verse backed down when I gave too much pushback.

As if I wasn't worth the effort.

"I'm Lathan," he introduced himself from behind me, grabbing my waist and pulling me back enough for him to slip in the doorway. "Are you Remedy's mother?"

I snapped my head up. "No, she *isn't*."

His grip on my waist tightened. I tensed, realizing that I hadn't shown a visceral reaction when he'd grabbed me the first time.

Over the last few weeks, Lathan had touched me in other small ways that I hadn't paid attention to until now.

Which was a feat because even Verse and Hakeem kept their hands to themselves.

"Remy... Remedy," she corrected herself when my lips flattened. "I know I'm probably the last person you want to see right now, and you are completely justified for feeling that way. I can't undo what's already been done, baby girl, but I want to... to start over. To make amends for the hurt I caused you. You're my only child and being without you all these years, even if you don't believe me, was hard." Her smile grew sad and her head tilted. "I've already let too much time pass before making this trip. I'm not asking you to forgive me today and act like nothing has happened between us. I just want to make it right."

Even if I wanted to give her another chance, I couldn't.

I didn't know how.

Keeping people at arm's length was my way of life and letting her get close would leave me vulnerable to feelings, experiences, and emotions I needed to stay buried.

I didn't need her.

Not anymore.

When I needed people to protect me, no one had, so I learned to protect myself.

And right now, I was going to protect myself from whatever her proximity would expose me to.

"Your chance to make it right was the day of my father's funeral, when you knew I had nowhere to go. I was a seventeen-year-old high school graduate who'd just lost everything. That was your chance to step in and be a mother but you didn't. You were gone before I could say a word to you. You ran from the child you claimed to miss so much."

The tears that she'd been holding on to finally spilled over, leaving wet streaks on golden cheeks before dripping off her chin. "I'm sorry, Rem. I didn't know how. I didn't know how to approach you or what to say... so I *ran*."

"Do us both a favor and pretend like you still don't know what to do, Isabel. See yourself out and please... don't bring your ass to my doorstep again."

5

LATHAN

The silence after Remedy's mom left was thick. *Heavy.*

For a moment, I'd glimpsed vulnerability on Remedy's face as her mom spoke, but as quickly as it was there, it was gone, replaced by the cold indifference I saw day in and day out.

I didn't know much about Remedy's upbringing outside of the fact that her dad was murdered right outside of her high school graduation.

I'd always noticed when Verse talked about Remedy's father, Timothy "Big Tim" Sinclair, he'd never mentioned her mother and neither had Rem.

From what I gathered, Big Tim was a legend in the Tri-City area and adored by all, so I sympathized with Rem on losing such a huge figure.

After spending most of my life in Huntsville, Alabama, I wasn't as familiar with the comings and goings of Sienna Falls.

The only reason I'd moved here after getting released from prison was because of Tessa and Gabbi, who'd stayed local and worked at Harmony Medical Center after dropping out from Sienna Falls University her sophomore year.

But I'd always assumed that Remedy's mom had also passed away when she was young, so imagine my surprise when I'd gotten a text from the guard at the gate that Isabel was on her way up.

"*She*," Remedy began in a tone that could cut glass, "is not allowed through that gate anymore. Do you understand me?"

My neck reared. Not only at her condescending tone, but the cold statement.

"That's your *mom*, Rem." It was unfathomable to me that anyone could hold such venomous feelings for the woman who birthed them. Anne Calloway, my mother, was worthy of nothing but admiration and adoration for the sacrifices she made to keep the Calloway clan intact. I'd taken it for granted growing up but I recognized and appreciated it now.

More than she would ever know.

Besides, my dad would knock my ass out if I even *thought* about speaking to my mother the way Rem had done to hers.

"Just do what the fuck I said!" Remedy snapped, turning to face me, green eyes blazing with emotion.

I felt pity for her more than anything. On one of the rare occasions where she actually allowed her feelings to show, it was in a moment of anger.

It was a shame because she was stunning even when she carried herself like an emotionless robot.

But when she was this expressive?

The woman was jaw-droppingly gorgeous.

Too bad the nastiness falling from her lips overshadowed it.

"You know nothing about me or my relationship with my mother." She continued, "Mind your fucking business. When I need your opinion on what I do, I'll *ask* for it."

"Sometimes you say the most *fucked up* shit to people." I shook my head, humorless chuckles falling from my lips. My legs carried me to the back of the house and to my surprise, I heard her bare feet slapping on the linoleum behind me.

"Again, not your fuckin' business. You might've been around for two years, Lathan. But don't forget your place. You're an *employee* here. Remember that."

I should've kept walking but I couldn't.

Remedy's behavior went unchecked too often. No one gave her pushback.

Everyone either ignored the shit she said or took it and kept it pushing. And I was tired of doing that.

"You know... all this time, I didn't want to believe that you were *that* cruel. I'd convinced myself that your attitude wasn't *truly* out of a lack of humanity but... the way you're talking to me right now? The way you treated your mother? The way you treat everyone? I can't even make excuses anymore. You are just one fucked up individual. And it makes sense why you live in this big ass house all alone. It makes sense that, outside of your mother today, no one comes out here to visit you. And if I didn't collect a check each month for it, I wouldn't either."

To my surprise, a grimace contorted her features and she placed a hand in the center of her chest.

Probably surprised someone had finally stood up to her stubborn ass and gave her a taste of what she often dished out to others.

Deciding not to entertain it or her anymore, I turned, shoving open the sliding glass door and striking out across the concrete surrounding the obnoxiously large pool, heading towards the acre of manicured, yet unused land where I sometimes exercised when getting to the gym wasn't possible.

I'd just stepped onto the lawn when I heard it.

A low groan, followed by shallow gasping.

I stopped and looked back, finding her still in the doorway. My heart dropped to my stomach when I realized the grimace on her face was one of pain.

"Rem?" I called, hurrying back towards her. "What's wrong?"

Before I could close the distance, her golden face paled and she clutched tighter between her breasts, moaning. The sound ate at me and I started sprinting, carelessly knocking pool chairs and other decorative shit over in my quest to get to her.

"My... my... *chest*," she squeaked out before stumbling onto the patio. She parted her lips again as if she wanted to speak but her words faltered.

The grip on her chest tightened and her face contorted even more before her eyes rolled back and knees buckled.

"*Remedy!*"

6

REMEDY

"Will you quit that?"

Lathan ignored my complaint, continuing to fluff my pillows with the same expression of guilt he'd worn since I woke up in the stark white hospital room.

"Stop." I swatted at his hands when he reached for the pillow again.

Finally, he left me alone, dropping back into the moss green chair he'd pulled up right next to my bedside.

After experiencing the sharp pain in my chest, I didn't remember much.

Lathan said my eyes rolled back and I collapsed, thankfully missing the hard concrete of my patio and stumbling back into the kitchen, landing on the slightly softer linoleum instead.

The next thing I remember was waking up in this private room with Lathan seated in a chair next to the bed, eyes locked on me.

"I shouldn't have said what I did to you," he said lowly, bringing my gaze back to his. There was still a slight pain in my chest, but nowhere near as intense as I'd experienced earlier. "I apologize. I was out of line and it won't happen again."

I shrugged, knowing I should look away but unable to pull my gaze from his. "I've heard worse."

"It still doesn't make it right," he surmised, leaning forward, resting his elbows on top of the thin white blanket covering me, mere centimeters from my hip. I turned my head, finally breaking the intense staring contest we'd been in. "I *don't* know your relationship with your mother and I inserted myself into shit that didn't concern me. The only reason I lashed out like that was because yo' ass was talking to me *crazy*."

I snapped my head back towards him, frowning at his easy smile.

"I'm fuckin' with you," he teased before shrugging, "But I apologize." He leaned back in his chair, tired eyes hanging low as his tongue swiped against the inside of his lower lip, causing my thighs to squeeze together. "You forgive me?"

What the hell?

Was that a throb between my thighs?

Because of *Lathan*?

Oh, I must've hit my damn head too, because there was no way in hell I would lust over him if I was in my right mind.

"Well, if it isn't my most stubborn patient."

Lathan's eyes and mine lifted, watching the smirking man in a white coat as he entered and closed the door quietly behind him.

Dr. Huang's eyes flashed to Lathan and gave him a brief nod before he looked back at me. "Well... at least you didn't Uber yourself to the hospital this time. You had enough sense to bring someone with you." The urge to lift my middle finger at him was strong but I refrained because he was right. A few years ago, when I had an... *episode*, I'd been home alone. Earlier that day, the bodyguard Verse and Hakeem had assigned to me quit before they found a replacement.

I'd been in the middle of fixing lunch when a similar shot through my chest, sending me to my knees.

Instead of calling someone I knew, I ordered an Uber, waiting in excruciating pain for nearly twenty-five minutes before they arrived.

Dr. Huang had been my cardiologist for going on eight years, so there was a rapport between us that made him comfortable enough to chew me out for half an hour after doing something so *stupid*.

"I told you what would happen if you didn't slow down and take care of yourself," he fussed in his usual spiel.

And like always, I had zero interest in hearing it. "Yeah, yeah. When can I get out of here?"

He huffed, shaking his head as if disappointed. "It's not that simple, Remedy. And if I remember correctly, you sat in my office five years ago after your first episode and told me you would follow the plan we came up with together. *You* said you'd do what was necessary to stay healthy and based on the test results from today... you haven't been."

I rolled my eyes to the ceiling, refusing to answer.

"Lanhol's is a normally mild, *manageable* condition as long as the person with it takes care of themselves. But if they don't, these kinds of attacks can become more frequent and worsen the condition of your heart, which can then lead to more serious diseases."

"I'm sorry," Lathan interrupted, swinging his gaze between me and Dr. Huang, "Lan-*what*?"

Dr. Huang's smile was polite as he repeated the name of the condition he diagnosed me with over seven years ago. "Lanhol's Carditis." When Lathan's curious gape remained blank, Dr. Huang chuckled and continued. "It's a genetic condition that's more prevalent in women. It's like myocarditis, which is the inflammation of the muscle in the heart but Lanhol's is much milder and like I told her, *manageable* if she follows the treatment plan. Though it's not curable, some patients show absolutely no side effects or symptoms and live long, healthy lives with no issues. One or two minor episodes during their lifetime, which is what she experienced today, is normal. But if you're one of my more *stubborn* patients who refuses to listen..." he hiked his thumb at me, "They'll happen more regularly."

"So... you're saying this isn't her first one?"

At that moment, Dr. Huang's eyes swung to mine as his face

paled. "I'm so sorry... I didn't even think to ask before I started talking. Is it okay if I discuss your health information in front of or with this gentleman?"

I looked towards Lathan after the question, finding his lids narrowed in warning.

Rolling my eyes at the meaningless threat, I shrugged. "Go ahead. He's going to have to pick up my prescriptions."

"Thank you," Lathan muttered. I felt a jolt in my chest that had nothing to do with my condition.

"Yes," Dr. Huang answered his earlier question. "This isn't her first one."

"How many has she had?"

Again, Dr. Huang's gaze swung to mine, so I answered. "Six."

"*Six?*" Lathan's tone was low and lethal as he sat back in his chair. "You've had six in the last five years when one or two in an *entire lifetime* is the norm?"

"Exactly," Dr. Huang offered, still looking at the tablet in his hand, happy that someone else in the room felt the same way he did. "I've made that same point more times than I can count." The stylus he held tapped rapidly against the tablet screen before he looked up at me. "Have you been taking your anti-inflammatories?" My eyes rolled up to the ceiling again and he sighed. "I'll take that as a no. I'm going to call in another prescription and I'll be increasing the frequency to twice a day for the first two weeks. I'm going to go check the results of your EKG and I'll be right back, okay?"

The room remained silent until he left, closing the door behind him just as quietly as he'd done when he arrived.

"So... why wasn't I notified of this condition when I started? I'd think that would be at the top of the *need-to-know* list. Especially since you'd experienced five in the last few years."

I shifted uncomfortably, knowing my response was going to piss him off. "You weren't notified because Verse doesn't know." I cut my eyes in his direction. "And it's going to *stay* that way."

"Wait... Who knows about your condition and these episodes?" he asked, brows furrowed in a deep frown.

Avoiding his gaze again, I glared at the pristine white ceilings. "Me. Dr. Huang. And now, you."

"Not even Miranda?" His pitch rose with surprise.

I shrugged. "Nope."

He cursed under his breath. "Why... what... How the *hell* have you hidden this from everybody for so long?"

"It's easy when, like you said, nobody wants to visit me."

From the corner of my eye, I spotted his flinch. "Shit, Rem."

I hated the pity in his tone, so I did what I did best. "I expect what you learned today to not leave this room. Nobody knows and I want it to stay that way. If I find out otherwise, you will be in breach of contract and I will sue you for every damn thing you have."

I expected more of the anger from earlier in response to my statement but he surprised me when he asked. "When was the last episode?"

"Why?"

"Just answer the damn question."

I huffed but decided not to argue, not wanting to get myself worked up. "Eight months ago."

His entire expression contorted. "Eight *months*? No way. I worked for you eight months ago. I definitely would've noticed if y-" His words trailed and his eyes went hazy before he sighed as if a thought had just occurred. "Let me guess... that wasn't food poisoning you had last year."

I shook my head slowly, sneaking peeks at him from the corner of my eye.

I'd been in the shower that time and slipped on the tile, falling hard on my hip.

Though I hadn't lost consciousness, I'd laid there in excruciating agony, well after the water had run cold.

Lathan, knowing I was a stickler for time, had come up and knocked, asking if everything was okay.

I'd just pulled myself from the shower, resting my nude frame on the rug in front of my vanity, biting my fists to muffle my pain-filled groans, waiting until the pain in my chest eased.

I don't know where the food poisoning lie came from but I'd blurted it out and told him I would work from home. He'd tried to come in but thankfully, the door I always locked behind me had kept him from witnessing me at my lowest.

Lathan had checked on me often during my *sickness*, leaving soup, crackers, and ginger ale at my door through the day. I'd kept up the pretenses of food poisoning and ate the bland meals, placing the empty tray back in the hallway just outside my door when finished.

Three days later, though nursing a big bruise on my hip and *far* from one hundred percent, I'd returned to work like nothing had happened and no one was the wiser.

"You can't keep trying to do everything alone, Remedy."

His concern made me uncomfortable and I shifted restlessly on the stiff white sheets. "You don't have to pretend to care, Lathan. It's not in your contract. Just call Miranda, tell her to bring me a change of clothes and I'll be on my way."

One of his brows hiked as he looked at me like I'd lost my mind. "Can you just... sit *still* and just let somebody look out for you?"

I chuckled, laughing under my breath. "People only look out for *themselves,* so I'm doing the same." Again, I shuffled uncomfortably. "You can leave and I'll call you when Dr. Huang dismisses me."

Glancing towards the small table next to my bed, I stretched for a cup of water, grimacing from the pain that flared in my chest. Lathan sucked his teeth when my fingers grazed the cup and leaned over to catch it before it tipped over.

"Would it kill you to ask for help?"

"Yes."

He laughed at my short answer, pouring more water before passing it to me.

I mumbled thanks, sipping slowly from the straw under his intense scrutiny.

"Can you stop *staring*? You're making me uncomfortable."

His lips parted but Dr. Huang walked in before he could respond.

"Alright, Remedy. Let's get this discharge going." He instructed me to follow a strict diet, which I had zero intentions of doing, and to minimize stress.

Highly unlikely.

"I want to see you back in two weeks," he continued. "And if everything checks out at that visit, you can begin a light exercise regime to help strengthen your heart. But until then, take it easy. Though I know the likelihood of you listening is slim to none, I recommend taking a few weeks off to give your body time to rest."

Yeah, right.

If he thought I would actually do that, he didn't know me at all.

When I said nothing, Dr. Huang shook his head and pushed his thick-framed glasses up onto his short, cropped hair. "Are you going to force me to admit you or will you follow my instructions at home, Ms. Sinclair?"

"She'll follow them," Lathan said before I could respond. He directed a polite smile towards Dr. Huang before his narrowed lidded gaze swung in my direction. "I'll make sure of it."

"IF YOU THINK I'm going to let you see me naked, you have lost your fucking mind."

Lathan sighed, arms folded and shoulder propped against the doorframe as I sat on the edge of my bed.

All I wanted was to shower... *alone.*

The pain pill Dr. Huang had prescribed hadn't kicked in yet, so I was still weak and sore from the fall earlier.

Though I could eventually make my way into the bathroom and bathe without help, Lathan wasn't hearing it, insisting he needed to help me until I'm able to do it on my own.

Fuck *that*.

"Rem, I'm not trying to see you naked to get my dick hard. I'm trying to help your stubborn ass, that's it."

His words caused my eyes to flash towards his crotch before I whipped my gaze away, realizing what I'd done. "Well, if *that's* the kind of help you're offering... I don't need it." I countered, swinging my legs off the bed, preparing to push to my feet.

Despite his size, he was across the room and in my face before I could blink.

"Don't test me right now," he muttered, grabbing my bare legs and swinging them back around before tugging my blankets up around my waist. "It's two in the morning and I'm tired as shit."

Again, I was rendered speechless because he'd touched me in the first place *and* because of my lack of reaction to it.

That meant he was worming his way *in* and I didn't like it one bit.

"Either you let me help you... or I call Verse and tell him everything."

My lids narrowed. "You wouldn't dare."

"Try me."

Again, I thought about attempting to climb from the bed but the serious glint in his gaze and the fatigue lining his features revealed just how much I'd already tried his patience since being discharged.

It wasn't on purpose. Not this time, at least.

I just wasn't used to depending on anyone... for anything. So being at his mercy made me uncomfortable and had me lashing out, saying and doing things that I truly didn't mean, yet lacked the courage to apologize for.

"So... we getting in this shower?" His thumb hiked towards the open door of my en suite. "Or am I making a call?"

"*We're* not doing shit." I grumbled, figuring I'd buy myself time to find a way to get out of stripping naked in front of him. "I'll take one later."

I expected him to leave the room but like always, he did the exact opposite and dropped next to me on the bed, toeing off his shoes before stretching his long legs alongside mine.

"Are you out of your fuckin' mind?"

It felt oddly intimate when he rolled his head to the side, lids heavy and thick with exhaustion as he observed me.

"We both know that the second I leave this room, you're going to sneak in the bathroom."

I didn't refute his statement because he was right. That had been my exact plan.

"That's what I thought," he muttered, looking around the room. "Where's your TV? Behind a hidden wall or some shit? Rich people are weird like that."

My lips twitched with the urge to smile. "I don't have one."

I couldn't wrap my head around being in this position with him. Less than twenty-four hours ago, I would've had a hernia if he stepped foot inside my room without permission.

Yet here we were, lying side by side as if we were old friends.

"So.... What's the history between you and your mom?"

My eyes shot over to his, prepared to curse him out for overstepping, but I stopped when I caught the teasing glint in his gaze.

"None of your nosy ass business."

He chuckled, slouching further in the bed, lids lowering even more over his red-rimmed eyes.

I know damn well he wasn't planning on sleeping in here.

"So... what the hell do you do in here, Rem? No TV. No bookshelf. No crossword puzzles." I snorted at that last one, knowing he was once again teasing me. "What do you do when not working?"

"Check my emails."

"Still work," he countered through a yawn, stretching his big arms above his head, revealing a sliver of caramel, tattooed skin above the waistband of his pants.

Damn.

"I don't know." I mumbled in an uncharacteristically soft voice, unsettled by everything about this man. Maybe I was just in a weird space after what happened earlier. He'd been there when it happened, helped me, and stayed in the hospital despite my incessant request for him to leave me alone.

Maybe I was feeling a bit of tenderness because he'd looked out for me.

That had to be it because it didn't make sense that I wasn't practically drowning with the panic of being so close to him while in a vulnerable state, especially in a *bed* of all places.

"You need some fun in your life." He mused through another yawn.

"What I need is for you to get out so I can sleep."

A tired smile lifted his generous lips.

Okay... I guess I can more than see the appeal now that the faux-hatred veil had temporarily lifted.

From his rough, calloused hands, to the beard coating his strong jawline, brawny build, and chiseled muscles... Everything about Lathan Calloway screamed *man*.

"I'll get out in a second. Need to give myself a minute before I move my stuff."

"Where are you going?" I asked immediately, brows lowered in a frown.

"Down the hall," he said, nodding towards the open door to my bedroom. "I'll start sleeping here in the main house. That way, I'll be closer if you need me."

"*Absolutely not.*"

"Too bad. I've already made the executive decision."

I twisted in the bed to face him, face heating when my breasts swung unrestricted underneath the oversized tee I wore.

"Who's the employer, you or me?"

A lazy smile stretched across his tired face. "*Neither*. Verse and Hakeem sign my checks, not you. You're my responsibility, whether you like it or not. You have a condition which causes something like mini heart attacks, Rem. You're not even *forty* yet." His tone went serious, smile disappearing as quickly as it appeared. "And I've been around long enough to realize you're not going to do what you're supposed to. I'm here to do it for you." When I parted my lips to protest, he held up a hand to stop me. "I'm not going to hover over you 24/7 or invade your privacy. It'll be like now except I'll be down the hall at night rather than in the guesthouse. Nothing else has to change."

I sighed, hating he'd essentially put his foot down.

I wanted to argue. I wanted to give pushback and declare that this was my house, my body, and my life and I'd run all three the way I see fit.

But that normal ability to respond with a scathing comeback was absent.

Instead of dwelling on why that was, I blamed it on the pain pill and exhaustion from today's events before slouching further under my comforter and pulling it up to my neck, hoping he got the hint and left.

It didn't take long for him to roll from the bed, groaning as he bent to pick up his shoes before stepping quietly across the carpeted floor.

"I'm right down the hall if you need me. Goodnight, Rem."

I waited until the shuffling of his feet became faint before responding.

"*Goodnight.*"

"I DON'T THINK it's a good time right now."

My ears perked at Lathan's low tone as I quietly tiptoed down the steps, wondering who he was talking to. Moments earlier, there'd been knocking at the front door and I'd been sitting on the edge of my bed, still in my pajamas, as he'd moved past my door to answer it.

He'd ordered me to stay put but he could kiss my ass. I was feeling better already and would not be imprisoned in my bedroom just because he'd ordered it.

The urge to argue had been absent last night but it had returned full force this morning. The two of us had gotten on each other's nerves so badly I was sure we would need a mediator by the end of the day.

A woman's voice said something back and I moved quicker to see who it was.

But when I got to the bottom and rounded the corner, I found Isabel standing there, youthful face lined with stress as her gaze connected with mine.

Shit. I should've listened and stayed upstairs.

Lathan must've noticed the direction of her gaze because he turned, cursing when he spotted me in the foyer. "Dammit, Rem. Don't you ever listen?"

I shrugged and waved him off. "I'm fine."

"Are you okay?" Isabel asked quietly, bouncing her gaze between his and mine with concern.

I started to say something mean but the narrow-lidded look Lathan directed my way had me pausing.

A tight smile stretched my lips. "I'm fine." Again, his lids narrowed even further and I huffed. "I had a... *medical issue* yesterday but it's no big deal."

Immediately, she barged in, pushing past Lathan and stepping further into the foyer, words falling from her lips faster than I could keep up with. "Are you okay? Do you need anything? I can help with whatever you need."

Before I parted my lips to refute the offer, Lathan spoke up. "Actually... she *does* need help. There are things she refuses to let me help with but maybe she'll feel more comfortable with you, if you don't mind..."

"I *mind*." I snapped.

His expression was smug as he turned to face me. "I'm sure VP wouldn't mind stepping in if you don't need us to help." I narrowed my lids, sending the full force of my iciness towards him. Instead of intimidating him like I wanted, he smiled. "That's what I thought."

"I thought criminals and ex-cons had a *no snitching* rule." I fired back.

The gasp that came from Isabel proved my delivery hadn't been as light as I'd expected. So I flinched, expecting a comeback jab, but to my surprise, he laughed, *loudly*, as if he'd understood I had meant no harm with the comment.

It had honestly been a joke.

"No snitching applies to the *streets*, Rem. Not your health."

Isabel must've sensed my apprehension with having her here because she stepped forward, eyes pleading with me to give her another chance.

"My purpose here is not to cause drama. I honestly just wanted to see you again. Eventually, I know there'll be tough conversations to have, but for now, I just want to help in any way I can."

Again, I remained silent but a soft nudge from Lathan had me begrudgingly agreeing with a shrug. "It's fine *for now*, I guess." Lathan obviously wasn't giving in to my pushback but maybe Isabel would. Maybe I could convince her I was well enough to not need a supervisor for every damn step I took.

True, I'd been out of commission yesterday but Lathan was blowing this whole thing out of proportion.

I was perfectly capable of taking care of myself.

"Did you tell Miranda I would be out for three days?" I asked Lathan, facing him so I wouldn't have to look in Isabel's face. She was practically beaming with excitement after my acquiesce.

Lathan scoffed at my question. "Per doctor's orders, you will be out at least four weeks and I've already notified Miranda and Jaxon."

"You did *what?*" I snapped, taking a step towards him.

"First, calm your ass down..." he paused to look at Isabel, "Sorry for the language." Then he turned back to me. "But you will do *exactly* as the doctor said. Four weeks. If you don't want to listen to him or me, I know one person who might convince you."

My eyes narrowed once again at the threat of him holding my secret over my head.

"That's what I thought. Back upstairs," he ordered, nodding towards the staircase.

When I merely rolled my eyes and folded my arms, he walked right up to me. I took a step back before tensing when he bent until his face was mere inches above mine.

"I can carry you, if you prefer that." His threat sprang me into action and I whirled before stopping when he caught my wrist. "*Slowly.*"

I snatched my arm away but followed his instructions, frowning at the sound of both of their footfalls behind me.

"Stay here," he ordered after I sat on my unmade bed, "The pharmacy said your prescription is ready so I'm going to pick that up, grab something to eat, then I'll be back. You need anything while I'm out?"

"A ride to work." I said through clenched teeth.

He snorted again, brushing off my words. "I'll take that as a no." He adjusted the covers around my hips, fluffed my pillows, avoided my swatting hands, then turned to my mom. "Do you mind staying with her until I get back?"

Again, Isabel nodded eagerly, eyes lighting up as if this was the moment she'd been waiting for. "I have to warn you," Lathan added, hiking his thumb towards me. "She's a *terrible* patient."

"Fuck you." I seethed.

"See?" he added.

"We'll be fine." Isabel chimed, smile still in place. She was sorely mistaken if she thought doing this would endear her to me because it *wouldn't*.

I kept my eyes on them, frowning as Lathan thanked her before schooling my expression when he turned to me. "I'll be gone an hour at the most. TJ will be in the security room, if you need him." When I remained silent, he shook his head, walking towards the door. "Be nice."

Highly unlikely.

But I nodded anyway, keeping my gaze on the doorway he'd just vacated so I wouldn't have to look at the woman hovering uncomfortably near the foot of my bed.

"Do you need me to do anything?" she asked, wringing her fingers together nervously.

I started to snap back that I *needed* her twenty years ago but Lathan's last request rang in my mind and I didn't want to hear his mouth if she reported back that I'd been a bitch. So I pressed my lips together, pushing away the feelings of animosity and taking a few calming breaths before shrugging, still not looking at her. "I was on my way to fix something to eat when he forced me back up here."

"I can do that," she quickly volunteered. "Anything you want in particular?"

I shrugged. "I'm not picky."

I was, but I wanted to end this conversation and I wanted her gone. *Now*.

She nodded and turned to leave but stopped, hovering near the doorway before facing me once more. "No matter what you believe. No matter your opinion of me, I still love you, Remy. I always have and I always will."

Before I could react, she was gone, feet barely making a sound as she made her way down the steps of my home.

I wanted to feel something from those words, but I couldn't. I couldn't *afford* to.

I had to keep my heart closed off.

Isabel being here reminded me too much of my dad, which caused old feelings I'd thought had been buried to resurface.

My heart couldn't take anymore disappointment or letdown.

Between the physical issues ailing me and the need to outrun the memories that kept me going through life at full speed, that poor muscle in my chest couldn't stand another hit.

The quicker I got over this minor setback, the quicker I could get back on my feet and things would go back to normal.

I *needed* them to.

7

REMEDY

17 YEARS old

THOUGH NOT SURPRISED, it still hurt seeing that my father hadn't been in the stands when my name was called as I crossed the stage.

Uptown was a tight-knit community so I hadn't lacked cheers but there'd been only one voice I cared about and it had been absent.

But such was the life of Big Tim's daughter.

There were always people who needed him and his time that I'd grown used to sacrificing my important moments for theirs.

I loved my dad, more than life itself, but I was tired of always feeling like a non-priority in his life.

"Congrats, Remedy! I know Big Tim is proud!"

I smiled politely at the woman I didn't recognize but kept walking towards the exit, diploma in tow. That was another *perk* of being Big Tim's daughter. Everyone recognized you which was a blessing and curse at the same time.

On my way to the parking lot, I was stopped multiple times by people wanting to congratulate me.

Again, some I knew, and many others I didn't.

A loud popping noise stopped me in my tracks and I looked around curiously at the other people who'd also paused.

"What the hell was th-"

Two more in rapid succession sent the crowd running. The first one could've been mistaken for fireworks because people in the neighborhood had been setting them off all day.

But those second ones kicked in the survival instinct so many of us had developed living in Uptown.

But I didn't flee like everyone else.

Instead of running back towards the safety of the stadium, I ran towards the gunshots.

My gut rolled with nervousness as I did, hoping and praying the eerie feeling coming over me was just overactive paranoia kicking in.

Squealing tires greeted me as I made it to the parking lot before I moved towards the people crowded around someone laying on the ground.

"Let me through. Let me through!" I shoved spectators out of the way, forcing through the tight bodies before falling to my knees, recognizing the prone figure.

"Daddy?" I called, lids welling with tears.

I don't know how I'd known but I'd felt it the instant those second round of shots rang out.

He still clenched a bouquet and three gold balloons in his fist that rested against the ground. The other hand clutched at the three wounds in his chest. Whoever shot him had definitely been aiming to kill. Hitting him twice around the heart and once just a few inches lower on the same side.

"Daddy, *please*," I begged. All the disagreements and resentment I had towards him seemed petty and miniscule compared to the severity of this moment.

I'd take it all back to undo what had happened a few minutes earlier.

For a second, his hazy gaze seemed to focus as it landed on my face before searching the crowd surrounding me.

"V-" A ragged cough interrupted him and I allowed the tears to spill over my cheeks, chest aching with the realization that these were likely the last moments I'd ever get with him.

"What is it, Daddy?"

Again, his eyes searched the crowd. "Verse," he muttered, squeezing my hand.

Well... *shit*.

He'd been late to my graduation, likely because he'd gotten busy with some other task. He'd gotten gunned down right after the ceremony yet here I was, *his only child*, literally holding him in my arms as he took his last breaths... but his last words were someone *else's* name on his lips.

That shit *hurt*.

Like always, he wasn't seeing me, though I was right in front of him.

By the time the ambulance arrived twenty minutes later, he was already gone.

I hadn't cried when the time came because I felt... numb.

For once, I was grateful for the shit I'd gone through because I'd been able to go to that perpetual state of detachment I always walked around in.

I just cradled him in my arms, refusing to let go of his body until the paramedics pried me from him.

I managed to get the flowers and balloons from his grip, holding them close, cherishing the last gift I'd ever receive from him.

As they zipped the black bag and loaded him in the back of the ambulance, Verse ran up, eyes red and wet as he pulled me into a tight hug, ignoring the drying crimson stains of my father's lifeline clinging to my clothes and skin.

"Shit, baby girl," he said, voice thick.

At that moment, I realized this hug was more needed by him than me so I wrapped my arms around him, squeezing him against my chest despite my aversion to being *touched*.

I'd tolerate it. For him.

"I swear, Rem. I swear I'm going to find out who did this. I swear I'm going to make them pay... even if I have to set the city on fire to do it."

I didn't doubt his words one bit because if there was one thing I knew about Verse Presley... he was loyal to Big Tim.

"Fuck!" He snapped, big shoulders shaking with tears.

Around us, others were crying, saddened by the loss of the man who'd become bigger than life.

At my father's funeral the following week, people showed up in droves to pay their respects. Big Tim's name was linked to all kinds of social circles so it was no wonder that athletes, singers, rappers, actresses, radio personalities, reality stars and many other famous faces were in attendance.

Even the mayor had shown up and spoke about the legacy my father left behind.

To accommodate the people who'd shown up in droves, they held the home-going celebration at the exact stadium where I'd walked across the stage not even a week ago.

It was hard being here again but I kept my mouth closed, letting everyone who felt they knew him best make the arrangements.

I wanted to scream that he was *my* father. I wanted to yell that *nobody* knew him better than I did but that would've been a lie because he spent so much time gone that I barely saw him, left alone to my own devices or under the care of his friends who swore to look out for me and make sure no harm befell me in his absence..

They'd failed. *Miserably*.

So I kept my mouth closed when they had the funeral at this stadium despite the anxiety I felt each time I'd passed it since his death.

I kept my mouth closed when everyone was asked to wear white for the service instead of requesting the black and gold combination my father loved.

I kept my mouth shut when people came up to Verse and my father's other mentees, offering their condolences before giving me nothing more than a polite smile and a stiff hug.

I even kept my mouth closed when they buried him in the local cemetery rather than nearly an hour away on the other side of Piedmont like I wanted.

I know my dad loved Uptown more than anything, including me, but Uptown was also the reason he was dead and I wanted his final resting place to be away from there.

I wanted his burial site far from the city that had caused me so much pain. But Verse and my father's best friend, Christian, had insisted so I conceded, shutting down emotionally, feeling as if I was watching everything play out through someone else's eyes.

My presence for the planning was only for appearance's sake because my input and opinon wasn't truly needed.

So, I sat there on the front row of my father's ceremony, fingers linked with Verse's as we listened to tons of people go up and mention how loved my father was and how much Uptown would suffer from his loss. They spoke about his love for the hood and how he went above and beyond to look out for everyone in it.

The more they spoke, the more my resentment grew.

For three hours, I listened to people brag about how much my father had done for them while I sat on the same row as the very people who'd hurt me under his watch. Under his *roof*.

So… I remained blank, not shedding a single tear, even after we'd gone graveside to say our final goodbyes.

While everyone around me was falling out, crying and screaming as the casket lowered into the ground, all I felt was…. *numbness*.

8
REMEDY

My movements were quiet as I slid from between my sheets, skin damp with a sheen of sweat from the memory that had jolted me awake in the middle of the night.

It had been a while since I'd dreamed about my father.

Years.

Way more than I cared to count.

Not making a sound, I moved towards my closet, not wanting to wake Lathan, who was down the hall, or Isabel, who was downstairs in a guest bedroom.

Three days after her being here from sunup to sundown, Lathan had so *generously* offered to let her stay, not wanting her to continue making the long drive back into the city where her hotel was.

I didn't really care *where* she was, as long as she stayed out of my way.

There was more than enough square footage in this monstrosity not to bump into one another.

Climbing onto the stepladder I kept in my closet so I could reach the top shelf, I almost smiled, imagining the scolding I would get if

Lathan found me. He'd been like a mother hen since I got discharged, hovering and annoying the living fuck out of me.

I'd told him this wasn't my first rodeo and only needed a day or two to return to normal, but he hadn't listened, intending to follow Dr. Huang's orders exactly as he'd given them.

Reaching up on the shelf, I pulled down the old, small safe I'd had since I was a teenager.

One of things I remembered my father teaching me was the importance of having separate areas and *stash spots* to keep your most valuables. He was a firm believer in not putting all of your eggs in one basket and I'd taken that lesson to heart.

For the first time in probably fifteen years, I sat cross-legged on the floor, right in the middle of my closet before opening the safe, laying eyes on the box of memories.

The crumpled, long since deflated balloon and withered flowers he'd brought to my graduation.

The T ring he'd always worn on his pinky finger.

Photos from his youth and of him and Isabel as teenagers.

Baby photos of me when I was first born and others throughout the years. As I got older in the photos, the more and more my smile dimmed. I'd been suffering and not a single person who cared about me had noticed.

Verse and everyone else from Uptown probably had enough photos and memories with my father to fill an arena.

But all I had of him was in this box.

It was sad how a man who meant so much to everyone else had felt so isolated with his daughter. They'd revered him and put him on a pedestal, making him seem larger than life.

But Big Tim had *failed* at his most important job of all... protecting me from those same people he'd gone above and beyond for.

I'd been invisible to him most days.

He'd missed my track meets and tennis matches to attend Verse's basketball and football games.

He'd skipped my awards ceremony to fly with a local kid to a football camp in Denver.

Hell, the day he'd died, I hadn't heard from him all morning until he showed up with three holes in his chest. After his death, I'd learned he'd been elsewhere, helping several of my classmates' parents with their graduation parties.

He hadn't even *planned* one for me.

I knew my dad loved me but he never *saw* me.

Everyone else's problems were as visible to him as his own, yet I suffered in silence under his roof at the hands of those he moved heaven and earth for.

It might be unreasonable but I blamed him as much as I did them.

It was *his* job to protect and keep me safe.

Not Verse. Not Hakeem. Not Drue.

His.

And if he would've paid even a modicum of attention to me, he might've noticed and been able to save me from the personal hell I'd lived for years.

Maybe if he would've noticed, I wouldn't have ended up like *this*. A complete, fucked up *mess*.

When my heart started racing, I knew it was time to come back to the present and leave the past where it was. Rehashing over it never boded well for me, so I stuffed those memories back in the safe and replaced it on the shelf before tiptoeing out of my room and towards the stairs.

I froze when I passed the door to Lathan's room and peeked inside, finding it empty.

Some bodyguard he was.

I could've fallen dead in my room and he would've never known.

Continuing on my toes, I moved down the stairs, looking at the home I purchased five years ago with fresh eyes.

I built myself a castle. A home that millions of people probably dreamed of having, yet I felt as if I was in a cage of my own making.

My fortress not only kept others out, it locked me *in*.

Walking through the living room to the kitchen, I paused near the counter, noticing that a light was on in the guest house.

Moving closer to the sliding glass, I gasped when I spotted Lathan's big, shirtless frame move past the window.

Holy *shit*.

The man was built like a stack of bricks. In the two years he'd been here, I'd noticed how he filled out his shirts but had never seen him without one.

When he moved past the window again, I inched closer, hoping for a third peek.

I wonder if he had company. I'd only seen him bring a woman back once in the entire two years of his employment.

I had to admit; I was curious how it looked now because a year ago, he'd asked to gut one of the spare bedrooms. I hadn't cared then but now I was curious to see what he'd done to it.

"Remedy?" I heard Isabel call from down the hall.

Immediately, I fled as fast as my feet would carry me. I knew it was childish but the last thing I needed was to have another awkward conversation with her. Since arriving, Isabel had gone above and beyond, checking on me, cooking my meals, doing a small load of laundry... anything to make her feel useful.

And no matter how cold I'd been, no matter how many times I'd said vile things to her... she kept that same smile on her face and continued looking after me, no matter what.

After climbing the second set of stairs at the back of the house, I slipped back into my room, closing the door quietly.

After three whole days away, I needed to check on RemEx.

Though Miranda and Jaxon were perfectly capable in my absence, I needed the work to keep me busy.

I had to get out of here.

I was going crazy being cooped up. The lack of things to do caused me to get lost in my thoughts and that was a scary place to be.

So I climbed back into bed, closing my eyes and pretending to be asleep when Isabel came in to check on me again, concocting a plan on how I'd sneak away.

"YOU MIND if we make another stop?"

From the backseat, I frowned at Lathan. An entire week had passed since my hospital visit and I'd *finally* convinced him to let me ride with him to the store. Though he'd made me stay in the car, I'd just been grateful to see something other than the inside of my home.

Avoiding him and Isabel had kept me trapped in my room, which only made my desperation to get out more intense.

It had gotten so bad that I'd had Lathan pull the television from one of the unoccupied spare rooms and set it up in mine so I could have something to watch.

I didn't immediately fall in love with the streaming services but I had discovered a few shows I'd binged over the last few days and I was already looking forward to the new season.

"Rem?"

I jolted at my name, forgetting he'd asked a question. "I don't care," I answered with a shrug. He could drive to the moon for all I cared.

As he drove further away from the city, knots formed in my stomach as we passed familiar businesses and streets before he parked in front of a modest home less than ten minutes from where I grew up.

Uptown.

I hadn't been here in years.

"Who lives here?" I questioned, glancing around the neighborhood, allowing the nostalgia to wash over me. The abandoned building on the corner used to be an arcade and in elementary school, I used to walk there every day with Verse and Hakeem after getting off the bus. They'd gone to indulge in the video games while I'd sat in a corner reading, grateful to be away from that *house*.

"I can call Hakeem or TJ to come and get you because I honestly don't know how long I'll be."

"No," I said quietly. "I'll come."

There was no way in hell I was leaving. This was the most excitement I'd had in *days*.

His eyes met mine in the rearview mirror and it took everything in me not to shrink from the sheer force of it.

"Alright," he mumbled, climbing out and opening my door before I could.

Four kids of varying ages played in the front yard, laughing and squealing without a care in the world.

God, I can't remember a time when I'd been that carefree.

I waved back at the smallest one, fighting a chuckle when he flashed his gap-toothed smile.

Lathan's eyes raked over me with a look that had been occurring more frequently. I didn't know what it meant and was terrified to find out, so I averted my gaze and folded my arms across my chest, feeling out of place in the business attire. Though I'd known we were only running errands, wearing anything but heels and a work dress outside of the house would've felt weird, so I didn't.

It was my daily uniform and had been for as far back as I could remember.

Lathan, who wore a short-sleeved collegiate football shirt and a pair of sweats, glanced at me again then shook his head before walking up the steps.

A stern-faced older black woman sat on the porch, lips pinched together as if she'd just tasted something sour. Her eyes were dark and judging as they swept over us.

"Hey, Ms. Gloria."

She sucked her teeth at his greeting, flashing her gaze at him, then me before turning away. "You better get her, Lathan. She's going to make me punch her in her smart ass mouth."

I frowned at her words before swinging my gaze back to Lathan, surprised to see his shoulders tense and his fists clenching before he continued in the house without saying another word to her.

I followed behind quietly, wondering what the hell her comment was about.

The first thing I noticed when we stepped inside was a beautiful woman sitting at the dining table with folded arms and an agitated expression. She looked to be around my age, maybe a year or two older.

"Gabbi," he said, voice tight.

I glanced between them, wondering what the connection was.

She looked up, expression just as tense as his shoulders. "Hey, Lath."

"Where is she?" he asked, searching the room.

Gabbi's head nodded towards the hallway. "Bedroom."

"You called my dad?" A pretty teenager, who was the perfect blend of the two people in the room, snapped as she walked in, arms folded across her chest.

Her dad? I didn't even know Lathan had kids.

Was she the only one? Or were the little ones in the yard his, too?

Was he *married?*

It was at this moment I realized I didn't know a damn thing about the man who'd tailed me for two years.

"Yes, I called him. Just like I do every time you act an ass, *Tessa.*" Gabbi's tone was just as sharp as her daughter's before her gaze swung to mine. "I'm sorry. You must be Remedy."

"My bad," Lathan muttered. "This is my daughter, Tessa, and her mom, Gabbi. Guys, this is Remedy."

Tessa's mother. Not my wife or my girlfriend.

But *Tessa's mother.*

That meant they weren't together. Right?

Then again, I don't know why it mattered.

Gabbi shoved to her feet, moving past Lathan and I tensed, expecting... what? I don't know.

Maybe he'd vented to her about how big of a bitch I was. Maybe she wanted to hit me for giving him such a hard time.

I'd deserve it, no doubt.

But a tired, albeit friendly, smile stretched her lips when she was a few feet away. "It's nice to finally meet you, Remedy." I glanced at her outstretched hand, then to Lathan, before meeting her halfway, surprised at the kindness radiating from her.

"Hi," I muttered, uncomfortable with the attention on me.

Tessa remained in the doorway, looking in my direction but offered no type of greeting outside of the cursory head to toe sweep she'd done of my frame when she first walked in.

"I can step outside to give you some privacy." I offered, not wanting to intrude on their parenting moment.

Again, Gabbi smiled at me. "Thank you."

Lathan pushed away from the wall to walk towards me, slipping the keys in my hand, staring into my eyes with an indecipherable look. "You sure you don't want me to call Keem or TJ?"

I quickly shook my head, holding up the keys he'd just passed to me. "I'll wait in the car."

Before he could say anything else, I stepped back onto the wooden porch, jumping when the creaking screen door slammed closed behind me.

"You on the wrong side of town, huh gal?"

Now that I'd seen Gabbi, I knew that the frowning woman who'd spoken had to be her mother. The resemblance was uncanny, though Gabbi didn't emit the same nasty energy as the woman in front of me.

I frowned. "Excuse me?"

Her assessing eyes turned even harder before she glanced away. "You heard me."

I cut my eyes in her direction, giving her back a dose of coldness. "I grew up here." I said and her gaze swung back to me. I lifted a perfectly manicured nail, pointing towards the street. "Not far from 54th and Lennox."

If I thought telling her I was from around here would impress her, it didn't. Her face turned even more sour.

"I don't know what's going on with you, T, but we gotta figure it out." Lathan's heavy voice filtered through the screen door. "Whatever it is, let me help. Tell me what it is so we can tackle it together."

I twisted from the door, not wanting to eavesdrop but the seasoned voice at my back stopped me.

"You his new piece?"

My head whipped to the side, not wanting to say a word to the obviously mean ass woman. "Excuse me?"

"You like tryin' to make me repeat myself, don't you?"

Shifting on my heels, I tilted my head, returning her glare tenfold. "When rude ass questions are asked, yes, I do. And no, I'm not his new piece. We work together."

I don't know why I phrased it that way rather than saying he worked for me. I didn't mind reminding him of that fact but for some reason, saying it to her felt... *wrong*.

"Hmph," she mused, still judging me with her eyes. "You're not his usual type but you're pretty, *I guess*."

Oh, this old bitch was asking for it.

That adage of blindly treating elders with respect was bullshit. If an elder didn't treat me with respect, then I'd return the favor. Age got no one a pass with me.

"I told you, I don't want to talk about it!" Tessa snapped mere seconds before the door flung open.

I moved to the side just in time to avoid being mowed over. She shot past me and her grandmother, furiously wiping at the angry tears pouring over her cheeks.

"*Tessa!*"

Lathan came out right after, face contorted, prepared to chase her.

"Let her cool off," Gabbi urged from behind him. "She's only going right there to Lauren's house."

Though I felt uncomfortable as hell, I watched, just like they did, as Tessa stomped three houses down before taking a sharp left up their driveway and running up the stairs and into the home as if she lived there.

"I told you," Ms. Gloria said smugly. "Somebody needs to teach that little bi-"

"*Aye!*" Lathan barked, causing me to jump. "Why you always gotta do that? That's your granddaughter."

"Do I look like I give a fuck?" She snapped back.

"Lathan, don't." Gabbi interrupted when Lathan's jaw clenched.

His eyes flashed to hers before he huffed, turning to look at me with a scowl contorting his handsome face. "You ready?"

I flashed another glance at the woman whose nose was turned up in his direction, then at her daughter, who looked beyond exhausted.

"Yeah, I'm ready."

ANOTHER TWO DAYS passed before I could implement my plan.

For the first time since being discharged, I was finally alone.

Isabel, who *still* hadn't left, was grocery shopping because apparently that invitation to stay had been extended without my knowledge.

Lathan was out running errands with his daughter, so I saw my opportunity.

I'd ordered an Uber to get me to RemEx so I could check in on things. Answering emails, calls, and texts from Jaxon and Miranda wasn't enough. I needed to *physically* see that it hadn't burned down in my absence.

A notification popped up on my phone letting me know my ride had arrived, so I crept down the stairs in my flats to minimize noise, just in case one of them snuck back in without my knowledge.

My heels were in my oversized purse.

I'd called ahead to tell the guard at the gate to let the car through, so I had to move quickly before I got caught.

After sprinting across the floor, I shoved my phone into my purse and opened the front door, pausing on the top step.

The ride I'd scheduled, a silver SUV, was parked at the edge of my lawn and Lathan was straightening from his bent position near the driver's door, glaring at me.

My eyes bucked when he tapped the hood of the car and they pulled off.

Shit.

I slammed the door closed, pacing the foyer. I was never one to run from confrontation, so I waited until Lathan came inside, face still contorted with anger.

"Did you forget the whole place is under surveillance and connected to my phone?"

I *had* forgotten but didn't want to admit it aloud, so I kept quiet.

"And did you think the guard wouldn't tell me you'd told him to let a random ass car in?"

I bit down on my bottom lip before flashing my gaze at the closed door behind him. "It was *Uber*... not a random car."

Rather than arguing back like I expected, he sighed, stress lines and exhaustion evident on his face.

Curiously, I watched as he ran a tired hand down the side of his face and walked past me into the living room.

I should just go back upstairs since my plan had been foiled but something stopped me, keeping me in place as he dropped wearily on my sofa. Every instinct was telling me to walk away but my feet carried me next to him and I sat. "You okay?"

He lifted a brow and snorted, "Is this your attempt at being compassionate?"

My cheeks heated, instantly regretting the decision not to retreat upstairs. That's what I get for trying to be nice.

Quickly, I pushed to my feet, attempting to move past him, but he captured my arm and pulled me back down.

"I'm sorry," he said, still not letting go of my wrist and for some reason, I didn't want him to. "I'm being an asshole."

"You are."

His lips twitched at my blunt tone.

"So... are you? Okay, I mean."

He rubbed his jaw tiredly again. "Do you really care, Rem?" When my face contorted, he held up his hands innocently. "Not being an asshole this time, I swear. I truly want to know if you care or if you're just asking because you feel like it's what you *should* do."

I didn't know how to answer that.

Did I care?

I would think so. I mean, I wouldn't have asked if I didn't, right? There was very little in my life that was done because it was the *right* thing to do. Since becoming an adult, I'd learned how to be selfish and only do or say things that benefited or satisfied me. Sparing other's feelings or asking about someone's well-being just because it was the *right thing to do* wasn't my style.

At all.

And still, I couldn't bring myself to explain that. Instead, I sat there, spine stiff and expression blank as he searched my face. When my silence continued, a smile that looked slightly sad lifted the corner of his lips before he nodded. "Thought so."

I wanted to tell him I did care, but the words wouldn't come. Each time I parted my lips, discomfort crept up in my chest and nothing came out.

When he stood a second later, I did the same.

"Just stressing over Tessa, that's all."

Before I realized, he'd wrapped an arm around my waist, placing a kiss on top of my curls before letting me go abruptly. "Shit, I'm sorry." He took a large step back, leaving several feet of space between us. "I forgot about your touch thing, Rem. My bad."

I wanted to tell him I actually hadn't minded because it didn't cause stomach-curling nausea like so many others had.

But what I did was nod in response, remaining still as his broad shoulders brushed past me before climbing the stairs two at a time. Long after he was gone, I remained in the same position, unsure how to react to his display of... *affection*?

My normal aversion to having someone's hands on me was nowhere to be found. Each time he touched me, I expected familiar nausea but it never came.

At most, I was flustered. And for the life of me, I couldn't understand why.

Why him? Why now?

What had changed in the fucked up psyche of mine that made *his* touch okay?

"You okay, baby?"

I jumped and whirled, not realizing Isabel had come in behind me. I was still so caught off guard from the interaction with Lathan that I didn't check her for calling me *baby*, nor did I feel up to spitting out the venom I normally did.

"I'm fine," I mumbled, smoothing back my curls.

"Do you need anything?" Her tone was soft as she crossed the room, passing me with a smile before setting down the bags of groceries she carried.

"No, I'm fine." I turned immediately after, moving towards the stairs before stopping when she called out to me.

"Rem, can we talk?"

I pressed my lips together, watching her through narrowed lids before shaking my head. "I'm not ready."

I could practically feel her disappointment from across the room but I ignored it as I turned and once again fled up the stairs. If she left the decision up to me, we'd never have that talk.

I wasn't sure if I'd ever be ready for it.

9

LATHAN

"You like her."

"Who? Gabbi?" I deflected, knowing damn well that wasn't who she was talking about.

Dr. Tori, my *fine ass*, fifty-something year old therapist, tilted her head with pursed lips. She sat in front of me, legs crossed and hands loosely clasped together in her lap. "Let's be honest, Lathan. You haven't sat in my office for the last twenty minutes rambling about *Gabbi*."

My brows hiked. "You're supposed to be a professional, Tor," I shot back with a grin. "You're not allowed to call me spilling my most private, innermost thoughts *rambling*."

She rolled her eyes again and I laughed.

Dr. Tori Reynolds had been instrumental in me getting acclimated to life outside of prison. I would even go so far to say that if not for her, I would've been locked up again within the first six months of my release. She'd been a voice of reason and sounding board for me to vent about my pent-up anger and unresolved feelings—feelings I hadn't even known I had.

The easy camaraderie that flowed between us now hadn't been instant.

When we'd started, I'd been a stubborn client, refusing to give her more than surface level bullshit for the first four months of our court-ordered sessions.

As a condition of my early release, I was scheduled to six months of therapy and anger management.

At first, I'd attended because I *had* to be there. I'd always had anger issues as a kid and it had worsened after getting locked up.

But she'd stuck with my stubborn ass, helping me knock down every preconceived notion I had regarding therapy that still ran rampant in our community.

Now, four years after our first session, I still made my way to her downtown office, though not as frequently as I once did.

"I don't know if I *like* her." I countered, immediately hating the lie after it left my lips. I never had to do that. Not here and not with her. "Okay, maybe I do." I admitted, ignoring the knowing expression on her face. "I mean, she's unbelievably beautiful. I respect her. *And* I find her interesting." I shrugged, raking my blunt nails through my beard. "It's hard not to."

"What do you find interesting about her?" Her spirit was calming, much like my mom, which was another reason it was so easy to talk to her.

"I don't know." I paused, worrying my bottom lip between my teeth. "There's so many layers to her. She's this mystery that I guess I want to solve." Her brow lifted and I could tell she wanted me to expound on what I'd said but I had zero intentions of doing so. "I didn't come in here to talk about Rem, Tor."

She held up her hands. "Okay, what *do* you want to talk about?"

Over the years, she'd made subtle changes in the cozy environment she'd created but the constant that remained was the soft lighting and warm hues.

Several bookcases lined the walls, filled to the brim with paperbacks of many genres.

A lone candle burned on the table in the corner, sitting next to a box of tissues, notebook paper and cups of pens.

I'd thought the setup was weird but after hearing her reasoning, it made sense.

She called it the *purge corner*.

An area for clients who wanted to get something off their chest but couldn't build up the nerve to say the words aloud.

Sometimes it was just one scribbled sentence while others used reams of paper, releasing their pent-up feelings. When finished, they could hold on to it, give it to her, shred it, burn it... it was their choice.

I'd never used it because once I got comfortable, talking came easy. But right now, I hesitated with the words.

Once upon a time, the silence surrounding us would've been filled with the light scratching sounds of her pen skating across the paper as she jotted down notes for the courts.

Now, she approached each of our sessions empty-handed. She was familiar enough with me to no longer need notes.

Deciding I'd hesitated enough, I shifted in my chair, finally bringing up the reason I'd scheduled this session.

"Tessa," I shrugged, bouncing my gaze around the office, "I don't know what's going on with her."

I'd been coming to Tori long enough for her to know when I needed advice versus when I needed to just... vent.

This was a venting moment, so she remained quiet, eyes on mine, giving me her undivided attention.

"Gabbi was having a hard time, so she gave up her apartment to move in with her mom. I'm sure she appreciates the help but that woman is toxic as hell and she talks crazy to Tessa. To *all* the kids. Tessa was already being rebellious and giving us a hard time but since she moved in? It's ten times worse. I can't get through to her at all. She's so... *angry*. And if you push, she shuts down and you can't get anything out of her." I scoffed, flashing Tori a half smile. "Sound familiar?"

Her full lips turned up as she grinned. *"Very."*

I laughed, then shook my head. "But it's so frustrating. I feel helpless." My phone buzzed in my pocket, stopping me mid-thought. "*My bad.*"

"Go ahead. I know you have to be available if something happens. I don't mind."

I thanked her, then pulled out my phone, reading the text from TJ, the guard I normally left at the house with Remedy.

TJ: I think her head just did a 360 on her shoulders.
TJ: Help

I chuckled, knowing Rem was probably giving him hell.

She'd been in rare form when I left this morning, giving me and Isabel a hard time just because she was tired of being cooped in the house.

I could understand why she was going stir crazy because Rem wasn't used to idle time. She rarely took days off and probably put in more hours than her entire team combined.

It was admirable and sad.

"What's that look for?" She asked after I'd put my phone back in my pocket but still hadn't said a word.

"I just wish I had my own place for Tessa to come over when she needs to get away."

"You ever thought to ask if Tessa can come to the house? Maybe not to move in but stay a few nights. Come over on the weekends. Anything."

I snorted, shaking my head. "I haven't, because I already know the answer would be a resounding no."

"All you can do is ask, Lathan." Her warm tone matched the atmosphere she'd created throughout her office and I found myself conceding.

"I'll ask."

"Have you given any more thought to what we talked about? Pursuing your art full time?"

I rolled my eyes and slouched in the chair, crossing my arms over my chest. "Not this shit again."

"Don't get all defensive with me." Even in her scolding, her tone was soft and frustratingly calm. I rubbed the back of my neck, emitting another groan that sounded weary even to my ears. "Seriously Lathan, you're *good*."

I was ready to wrap up this session now and started scooting towards the edge of the couch, grateful when my watch beeped with the alarm I set to let me know when it was time to go.

"It's a hobby. An *outlet*. That's all it will ever be."

Before I could leave, she gripped my arm gently, hitting me with that smile that reminded me heavily of my mom.

"Don't limit yourself or box yourself in. You did your time for the crime you committed. You paid your debt to society. There's no need to keep punishing yourself for making a mistake, Lathan. Stop denying yourself a dream. You deserve to live yours out, just like everyone else."

10

REMEDY

Boredom must've finally driven me insane.

That had to be the reason why I stood outside of the guesthouse, hands frozen in the air, unable to complete the knock on the cerulean door.

I wasn't sure if he'd hear me, anyway.

Not over the sound of... whatever the hell that steady humming noise was.

I was curious about what he was doing but nerves wouldn't allow me to complete the last step, so I lowered my hand, pinching my lip nervously.

Seconds passed with me shifting uncomfortably before the door was pulled open.

Lathan stood there, in jeans, socks and... that's it.

His flawless brown skin was blemished with splashes of what looked like thick paint in sporadic places. Even his hands were covered with it.

I tensed when he slowly inspected me, waiting for his judgement of my outfit—boring cotton shorts that fell to mid-thigh, a short-sleeved RemEx t-shirt, and flip flops. That was the most casual I'd ever dressed around him.

To my surprise, it never came. "How long were you going to stand there?"

I shrugged, noticing the steady hum I'd heard moments earlier was gone.

"How's the heart?"

I rolled my eyes, getting impatient with not being let in. "It's *fine.*"

My stomach jolted when he chuckled, giving me one last once over before he stepped back, gesturing for me to walk past him.

After a moment of hesitation, I did, immediately swinging my gaze around the open layout.

Not much had changed since he moved in.

The muted blue and gray tones that filled the common areas of the main house bled over into this suite. The only noticeable difference was the photos of his daughter on the end table and the food on the kitchen counters.

His walk oozed confidence as he passed, disappearing down the hall that led to the bedrooms.

Again, I hesitated before following, curious when the sound of thumping filtered down the hall. I rounded the corner, stopping at the first door on my left.

The carpet had been ripped up and replaced with linoleum flooring. All the bedroom furniture was gone, replaced by a full wall of shelves that held containers and clear bins filled with supplies.

The blinds had also been removed, leaving only a black curtain that was pulled to the side, letting in loads of natural light.

In the center of the room, he sat on an elevated stool in front of a long, plain wooden table. He held what looked like a scalpel in his hand, carving away bits of clay from a sculpture in front of him.

The way the light filtered through the window and hit his broad shoulders was photo worthy. Lathan himself looked like a work of art.

He glanced up briefly before setting down the tool and grabbed what looked like a hair dryer but was clearly more industrial strength from the loud, steady hum it emanated.

Soft jazz was barely audible over the sound and I was surprised at his music selection.

Lathan was an artist?

Jesus. What *else* was this man hiding?

"Do you sell these?" I asked, walking along the shelves, looking at other completed pieces.

I was taken aback by his talent.

The quality of the work belonged in an art showcase, *not* in a makeshift studio in my guesthouse.

I stopped in front of one of his larger sculptures, immediately recognizing his daughter. It was beautiful and a replica of the young lady I'd seen the other day.

When he didn't answer right away, I looked back towards him. Sweat beaded between his brows as he focused before he finally shrugged. As if the amazing artwork in front of me was no big deal. "Nope. Don't have time for that."

I started to argue but pressed my lips together, noticing the concentrated frown on his face as he worked on the large, obviously humanoid sculpture in front of him.

I watched with widened eyes as his large hands molded the clay, shaping it before spraying it with water.

It was a meticulous process, rhythmic and intentional, but he did it with ease. My lips parted on a sigh as he pulled another chunk out of the white basin near his feet, squeezing and molding it between his powerful hands before pressing it against the base of what he worked on.

He would drop his hands every so often, staring at the structure with an artistic eye that I didn't possess before he starting up again.

I abandoned my perusal of his previous work to stand just behind him to glimpse his latest inspiration.

Once I got a clear view, I sucked in a quiet breath. "Is that..."

"You?" he finished for me, never looking up. "Yep."

Again, my mouth parted. Forgetting all about my close proximity rule, I advanced until his bare, clay-stained shoulders brushed against mine.

The details in my imitation were intricate, revealing his ridiculous skills and attention to detail.

The sculpture definitely looked like me, but he'd made me look more elegant and... *regal*. There was even a tiny crown on my curled head, one that looked more suited for a child's princess party than a grown woman.

But then something else caught my gaze.

I moved closer, squinting before looking back at the shelf where the other human sculptures he'd made had one distinct feature that mine was missing. "Where are my eyes?" They were blank slates, as if I was sightless. No eyelids, irises, pupils. None of that. Just smooth textured skin housed on the stern face that echoed the one I saw in the mirror each morning.

"I don't know what your eyes look like."

My head swiveled to meet his gaze, frowning when I realized how close we were. Still, I didn't retreat. "What are you talking about? You see my face more than any other person I know. You, of all people, should know *exactly* what my eyes look like."

Again, he shook his head. "Not really. I know what *those* look like." He pointed towards my face. "But I wouldn't call them eyes. They're shields. Your guards." He grunted. "They show nothing of the woman inside. I've been working for you for two years and I still don't think I've even tapped the surface of who you really are."

My throat constricted and hope foolishly flared to life in my chest. "And the crown?" I asked.

"For the little girl in you." His tone was soft, unusually so. "The one I believe had her heart broken so thoroughly that she turned into the woman standing in front of me. That little girl is at the core of who you are. No matter how much you've tried to stifle her. She deserves a voice too."

His words had stolen my voice.

No one else had ever made the same observations that he had.

While I stared at him, his head tilted, sweeping his gaze over me in a way that made my skin tingle with discomfort and... *something*.

Something that I had zero experience with so I couldn't find the name for it.

Staring in his eyes, I felt myself leaning closer and he did the same.

But his ringing phone had us jumping apart.

Holy shit.

Had I almost kissed *Lathan?*

What the hell was going on?

"Can you grab that while I wash my hands?"

I nodded stiffly, grabbing it and answering without checking the ID. "Hello?"

"Uh... Ms. Sinclair?" I recognized the voice of Clarence, the guard who normally worked the front gate to my property.

"Yes?" I said, tone cold and chilling.

He hesitated and I grew impatient. I was just about to snap at him for wasting time when the phone was plucked from my hands. Lathan stood just behind me, not bothering to take a step back as he looked directly in my eyes while answering the call.

"Send her up." He said with a frown after listening.

I parted my lips, prepared to ask who the hell was about to be sent up to my home when he shook his head, fixing me in place with a stern glare.

"Not *now*, Rem."

11

LATHAN

As a parent, it was always hard to see your child upset, no matter how old they were.

So when I opened Remedy's front door and found Tessa standing there, eyes red and face drenched with tears, my heart clenched.

She didn't give me a chance to say a word before she slammed into me, burying her face in my chest.

"How did you get here, sweetheart?"

"The bus."

I frowned, wanting to question her decision to take the bus all the away across town but again, I didn't get the chance.

"I can't stay there with her." She snapped, tightening her grip around my waist. "I *hate* her."

I sighed, already knowing who she was referring to.

Ms. Gloria.

"Come in, T." I urged, guiding her through the foyer and closing the door behind us.

Her damp eyes went wide as she took in the magnificence of Remedy's home. I'd gotten used to seeing it but I can only imagine how it looked to someone who was visiting for the first time.

When we entered the kitchen, Rem stood at the large island. Curiosity was evident in her pretty features but she said nothing, watching silently as I guided Tessa to the bar stools.

"What happened?" I asked crossing my arms and propping up against the island.

Her dark gaze flashed over to Rem before she shrugged and started speaking so fast, it was almost hard for me to keep up.

"I got into it with Grandma again. She's so *mean*. And she keeps calling me fast. Telling me I'm going to end up like my mama... with all those kids and no man." Her colorful nails clenched into a fist as her right leg shook with agitation. "She tried to hit me, Daddy. And I didn't even do anything this time. You told me not to be disrespectful and I wasn't. But when I tried to walk away, she kept following me. Taunting me, trying to get me to react. So I *left*." My gut clenched at her words. Again, I felt like a failure. My child, my *teenager,* was living in a house where she was being antagonized and I felt helpless. "I don't know how mom puts up with her but I can't. *I can't.* I'll run away before I go back to that house."

I couldn't blame her for feeling that way. I'd seen firsthand just how nasty and vile Ms. Gloria could be. The woman didn't have a nice bone in her body.

"Can I stay with you, Daddy? Stay here?" Though her question was directed to me, her eyes swung to Rem who still stood quietly near the island, arms folded across her chest, eyes locked on us.

Dammit. I hate this conversation played out in front of her.

"We'll... we'll talk about it later, T."

With one last glance at Rem, I guided Tessa to the guest house, convincing her to rest in the bedroom. I made sure she was comfortable before going back to talk to Rem.

When I got back to the kitchen, she was still in the same spot, drinking casually from a bottle of water.

"Look, Rem," I began, scratching the back of my head. "I... uh... I don't... I mean... Gabbi's mom is..."

"You don't have to explain," she interrupted. "I met her, *remember?*"

I'd forgotten she had.

I'd been so concerned when Gabbi called me the other day about Tessa acting out that I hadn't thought twice about Rem sitting outside with the wicked witch of the south.

"I know it's asking a lot but... can she crash here for a few days until I can work something else out? We can stay in the guesthouse. She'll stay out of your way and not mess with any of your shit, I'll make sure of it."

Remedy waved off my words. "She's fine. I don't mind."

I looked at her curiously. She'd agreed way too easily. "What's the catch?"

"Excuse me?" Her tone was cool, expression carefully blank and I fought the urge to smile. She had no clue how appealing her coldness was.

She was gorgeous even when she gave nothing away.

"You think there's a catch?" My humor quickly faded when her normally flawless tone cracked. "Your daughter needs you. Regardless of how much you may dislike me, I'm not going to tell you she can't stay here when she has nowhere else to go." Her tone turned biting and sharp as her face contorted with anger. "I'm not a *complete* bitch, Lathan."

My shoulders deflated and the humor I'd just experienced was gone almost as fast as it had appeared.

She was being kind, opening her home to my daughter when she didn't have to and I was throwing it back in her face.

"Rem, I'm sor-"

"It's fine," she said, waving off my apology. "You can tell your daughter to make herself at home. She's welcome to whatever she wants. I'm going upstairs."

I tried to stop her again but she ignored me, slim hips swaying in that sexy ass walk as she left the room.

"*Shit.*"

12

REMEDY

Watching Lathan sculpt became my pastime over the next few days.

He'd apologized after what he'd said and because I wasn't used to apologies, I waved off his words, unsure what to do with them.

His daughter, Tessa, floated through the house like a ghost, not speaking to anyone and keeping mostly to herself in the room she'd moved into next door to Lathan in the main house.

He'd insisted on them bunking together in the guesthouse but I wouldn't hear of it.

It just didn't make sense when I had so many damn rooms that were sitting empty.

Even though I'd agreed to it, I still couldn't wrap my head around being considered a recluse to having *three* people living in my house.

A moody teenager who barely said a word to anyone including her father.

My mother who I'd been estranged from for nearly twenty years.

And my bodyguard, who was getting on my nerves less and less. It was to the point that I sought him out, looking for his company rather than avoiding it like I'd been doing before.

"What are you doing this weekend?"

"Working, if you'll let me."

His big shoulders bounced with laughter. "Not happening."

I rolled my eyes. "Then you know I'm not doing a damn thing."

"Come with me."

My gaze switched from his moving hands to his handsome profile. "Where?"

He didn't answer right away.

Instead, he used his scalpel to scrape away a thin slice of clay on the indistinguishable glob he currently worked on. Once finished, he eyed his work a moment before turning on the stool, widening his thighs so they rested just outside of my hips.

I immediately recognized the intimacy of our positions but didn't want to step away and make it obvious. Or make things any more awkward than they already felt.

So I cleared my throat, crossing my arms, for once, struggling to maintain my aloof expression.

"The Calloway's are having a family reunion."

I maintained my position, lifting one brow. "And you're telling me this because?"

"Dr. Huang has cleared you for travel and exercise. And clearly, you're obviously bored if you *keep* seeking me out." His lips twitched when I rolled my eyes. "I'm inviting you to my family reunion, Rem. Just for the weekend. I think you'll enjoy it."

One of my brows immediately shot high in the air.

He thought I'd *enjoy* it?

Me?

The least friendly person he probably knew? The woman who hated crowds with a passion?

Yeah, right.

That sounded more like *torture* than a good time.

"Before you say no, if you turn me down, I'll be forced to tell Verse or Keem about your condition so they can send a repla-"

"You're going to milk this shit, aren't you?" I interrupted.

He laughed again, completely unapologetic about blackmailing me. "Absolutely."

Reluctantly, I agreed to go because... well, he was *convincing*.

"Come here," he urged after we fell silent.

I looked down at the mere inches of space separating us. "How much closer do you want me to get? I'm practically in your lap already."

Another amused snort rushed out before he jerked his head in a reverse nod. "Closer, Rem."

With folded arms, I scooted close enough for my hips to brush the inside of his thighs. "You okay with me grabbing your waist?"

My eyes jerked from where our legs touched up to his intense gaze. "What, why?"

He kept his unblinking gaze on me. "To position you in front of me. That's if you don't mind getting your hands a little dirty?" When I hesitated, his gaze softened. "You're safe with me, Rem. You know that. But I won't do it without your permission."

I don't know how he knew I needed him to *ask* for my permission but I was grateful he did without asking any uncomfortable questions.

He'd recognized my discomfort and respected it without making me feel... weird or stupid.

And I appreciated that.

So I nodded, pretending not to see the way his lips turned up in a grin that caused butterflies in my gut.

His grip was gentle as he turned us to face the table with me planted firmly between his strong thighs. Even with me standing and him seated on the stool, he still was a few inches taller.

His big arms surrounded me as he positioned us in front of the mound of clay he'd been sculpting. What had started as an indistinguishable glob had begun taking shape into what appeared to be the early stages of a womanly, curvy shape.

Hints of the silver wire he'd used as a frame for the shape peeked through the pieces of clay that hadn't been layered yet. I'd been paying attention as he patiently answered my questions the last time I'd been over here. He'd explained the wire frame, called an armature, was used to give the sculptures form and stability.

He'd told me they were for the smaller projects that had a tendency to bend or break during the molding process.

Bending, he grabbed more clay from the white basin and placed it in my hands.

"What do you want me to do with it?" I asked, squeezing it.

"Bend it." I did, watching as it curved until a crack formed down the middle. "That means it's too dry. Spray it." I grabbed the bottle from the corner of the table and followed his instructions. "You need more than that, Rem. Get it wet for me."

My head whipped around to meet his gaze, barely missing his nose.

His lips were twitching and his eyes lit up with mirth. "I'm talking about the *clay*."

My cheeks heated. "I *know* you meant the clay, Lathan. What do you *think* I thought you meant?"

He shook his head, still fighting a laugh. "Add more water, Rem."

I rolled my eyes and turned back to the table, doing as he said before following the rest of his patient instructions.

"Rotate it in your hands to work the water throughout."

"Envision what you want the piece to look like before adding it to the structure."

"Use more pressure with your thumbs to make it smoother."

His tone was soothing and relaxing and I found myself enjoying the process, even though I'd colossally fucked up the neat structure he'd been working on.

What started as a sleek womanly frame now appeared to be botched by bad surgeries. It was lumpy and uneven but I felt the beginnings of a prideful smile forming, anyway.

Art had never really been my thing so I avoided it like I did everything else I didn't care for.

I respected the skill and talent it took but knew that hadn't been a path I wanted to take.

But this was... *fun.*

"Did you start doing this in prison?" I tensed as soon as the question left my lips. I hadn't meant it to be rude and I hope he didn't take it that way.

"I did." He answered easily, speaking directly in my ear while gently brushing my hands aside to smooth out the imperfections I'd created in the piece. My hands rested loosely on his, not contributing much. "I'd always been able to draw and make shit with my hands but I didn't take it seriously until I got locked up. It was an outlet. A form of therapy." He paused as if contemplating his words. "I guess it's still an outlet and more of a hobby now."

Since he'd taken over, I found myself looking back at him more than I was looking at the clay in front of me. His hands continued to move and his gaze remained forward though his lips kicked up in the corners.

"I know it's hard to look away from a face as handsome as mine but you might want to actually *look* at the clay to see what you're molding."

I flushed, turning back to the sculpture, stiffening my spine when his chuckles fanned his cool breath against the back of my neck.

It was several seconds before I figured out a response.

"*Shut up.*"

His chest shook against my back with quiet laughter.

I think I was ready to admit to myself that Lathan was getting to me.

And I had no clue what to do about it nor did I know how to feel in response.

This was foreign territory and I was lost on how to navigate the terrain.

It was bumpy, unpaved, and rough... so unlike the safe, smooth path I took that kept every single person I knew at arm's length.

But I needed to figure it out.

Soon.

13

REMEDY

Tessa hadn't said more than ten words to me or her father the entire six-hour ride to his hometown.

I'd been surprised when she'd been waiting downstairs near the truck. Dark shades covered her youthful face while pink bluetooth headphones covered her ears. Her arms were folded and her head facing the opposite direction, not speaking even after her father and I greeted her.

The first words she'd said had been three hours in when she asked him to stop so she could grab a burger.

After that, she'd fallen silent again, huddling in the backseat while I'd been uncomfortable in the front.

Once we arrived at the park where the picnic was held, she hopped out as soon as he killed the engine.

My eyes trailed her as she rounded the hood of the car before swinging my attention to Lathan who watched her also, shaking his head as if exasperated.

She stopped only when greeted by an older black woman with a short, natural fro.

Tessa hugged her tight, saying a few words to her before taking off.

The short-statured woman then turned to face us, holding a hand up to her forehead, blocking the sun.

"That's my mom," he began. "She has a.... *way about her*."

My head whipped back to him. "What do you mean?"

"She has a gift. Like she just knows things. Things you've never spoke aloud. Growing up, it had been creepy but I've grown to appreciate it."

"So she's... what? A psychic??"

The waiting woman lowered her hand from her forehead to her hip, showing her impatience as she waited for us to get out of the car.

"She doesn't like to limit her gift with a title. She doesn't consider herself a psychic, a prophet, or an evangelist... nothing like that. She just says she has a gift from God that she uses when He tells her to."

If I'd felt anxiety before meeting her, hearing that ramped it up even more.

"You ready?"

"No."

He laughed. "Don't get nervous. She's the sweetest woman you'll ever meet, I promise. I only warned you so you wouldn't feel weird if she makes a comment."

Despite my protest, we got out of the car. When we met near the hood, his fingers linked with mine and I pulled on his strength to keep my nerves from taking over.

"Hi, mama."

My eyes swung to Lathan's, bucking at the sheepish grin he bore.

This man. This six-and-a-half-foot wall of a man was a *mama's boy*.

It was evident in his tone and the way both of their faces lit up.

"Hi, baby!" She squealed, launching herself at him. He caught her, lifting her off her feet and squeezing her tight. "I missed you so much."

The obvious display of their affection made me uncomfortable so

I glanced away, focusing on the throngs of people milling about near the picnic tables and grills.

Everyone wore matching gold and red t-shirts with shorts, capris, or pants.

I felt out of place and overdressed in my maxi dress and heeled sandals. Now, I was regretting not packing more casual wear.

"Rem, this is my mom, Anne Calloway. Mom, this is Remedy." He introduced us after putting her down. "You got an extra shirt, mom? I don't want her to feel out of place."

"It's fine," I said, even though it wasn't. "Besides, I'm not a Calloway."

"You are today." She countered, patting her giant of a son on the shoulder before moving to stand in front of me.

Like with Gabbi, I tensed, unsure of the reception I'd receive but a gentle smile stretched her lips. Wisdom practically seeped from her pores and the longer we maintained eye contact, for some reason, I felt like bursting into tears.

But I sucked it up, smiling stiffly before sticking my hand out for a handshake.

Ms. Anne looked down and tsked, moving into my space. "Oh no, baby. We hug in this family. Come here."

Before I could stop her, she enveloped me in a vanilla scented hug.

A soft grunt met my ears before she whispered words that made me gasp. "My *goodness*. So much pain. So much hurt and anger."

Immediately, I tensed and tried to pull away but she stopped me. "It's okay, baby." She soothed me, squeezing me tighter when my shoulders started trembling. "It's okay to let go of the anger. You've held on to it for so long that *you're* hurting yourself more than the memories are."

When I tried to pull away, she stopped me again, letting me back just enough for our eyes to connect. Her tone took on an airy, melodic quality, like a soft lullaby. "You have a beautiful soul. One that deserves to be shared with those who care about you." To my surprise, her eyes grew watery and her lips trembled as she said words I'd longed to hear my entire life. "You're special. And a *blessing*. You are not invisible. Your pain isn't unworthy of mention. *I see you*, honey and all that you encompass."

My shoulders curled over, chest caving in as if I'd taken a physical blow.

Jesus Christ.

Who was this woman?

What was this woman?

Lathan's soothing hand came to rest at the small of my back and that seemed to snap his mother out of whatever that hell that was.

As though she hadn't just dropped a bomb on me, Ms. Anne released me and smiled brightly. "Let's go get you a plate, baby."

HOURS LATER, I was still reeling from the words Ms. Anne had spoken to me.

Despite Lathan's warning, I hadn't been prepared.

Not for that.

How could anyone prepare for a virtual stranger to speak on their deepest wounds? Their insecurities?

I'd tried to keep my distance from her since then but that hadn't deterred her one bit.

She'd come over multiple times, checking on me, asking if I needed anything and just being *nice*.

Everyone else hadn't been as receptive and I could respect that. I was aware my disposition put off quite a few people. They hadn't outright said it but I could recognize the look in their eyes.

I'd been introduced to more people than I could keep up with but I had learned that Lathan's mom was a high school teacher who'd been teaching for 25 years.

I bet none of her students got away with anything. Not with a gift like that.

Right after she'd dropped that bomb on me earlier, we'd gone to the grills where Lathan's dad and uncles held domain.

Mr. Calloway was a tall, quiet man who'd been married to Ms. Anne for almost forty years.

To my surprise, Lathan was an only child but had enough cousins to fill a stadium.

One in particular, Venus, who I learned was an online ESL instructor, eyed me closely, as if sizing up my worthiness of her cousin.

Because I wasn't on neutral ground or in my domain where I felt comfortable, I held my tongue and endured the curious gapes and glares.

"You just gonna sit over here being standoffish all day? Not saying anything to anybody?"

Tessa's alto surprised me and I jumped, nearly spilling my coke that I'd just taken a sip from.

Placing the red plastic cup next to my heeled feet, I shifted in my chair, adjusting the oversized *Calloway Family Reunion* shirt I wore before finally responding.

"Yes. I am." With narrowed lids, I sized her up. "Besides, isn't that the pot calling the kettle black?"

She eyed me weirdly before a bright smile lifted her lips and she sat back in her metal chair, mimicking my cross-armed position. "I like you, Ms. Remedy."

The words were so unexpected that I sputtered over a response, unsure of what to say back.

She *liked* me? What the hell was wrong with this child?

Nobody liked me. Especially someone I'd barely exchanged two sentences with.

"Why?" I asked, hiking one brow, fighting a smile when she did it back.

"Why do I like you?" At my nod, she shrugged. "You're beautiful." She said simply, eyeing me.

Meh, irrelevant. Looks eventually fade.

"Confident."

It was all a front. A *lie*.

"Unapologetic."

Okay, that was true.

"Blunt."

She's got me there, too.

"You're a *badass*, Ms. Remedy and I think I want to be like you when I get older."

I don't know what I'd done to inspire this random idolization but the last thing she should want to be is like me.

And I told her as much.

Instead of taking my warning seriously, she smiled, sweeping her eyes over me quickly then once again mimicking my ramrod straight posture.

"I think my Daddy likes you." When I snorted, her smile brightened. "Do you like him?"

"Um... we uh, I, uh..." I lifted the coke to my lips once more to save me from having to respond.

"Are you sleeping with him?"

This time I did choke, spewing the brown liquid out in front of me. Before horror could contort my features, Ms. Anne's voice rescued me. "Contessa Anne Calloway, get your meddling ass away from that woman before I tell your daddy!"

Tessa giggled mischievously, looking awfully similar to her father when he purposely got under my skin.

"*Get!*" Ms. Anne warned again, swatting her bare shoulders with a folded towel.

Laughter trailed Tessa as she darted out of her grandmother's reach. I expected Ms. Anne to chase her like she'd done with many of the other kids and teens in attendance, but she didn't. Instead, she came and sat next to me, occupying the seat Tessa had just been in.

"I'm sorry about T. Sometimes she forgets what a child's place is."

"It's fine," I muttered, hating how subdued my tone was.

She must've noticed because she turned to face me. "Did I freak you out too bad earlier?" When I tensed and remained silent, she sighed and nodded. "I apologize about that. My husband and son always tell me I come on too strong but when the words come up, they come out. Lord knows I have no control over them when they do."

Again, I said nothing.

"Are you enjoying yourself, Remedy? I hope I didn't ruin today for you."

Though freaked the fuck out and uncomfortable, I didn't want her blaming herself for it.

That was practically a default setting for me.

"I'm fine," I said. When her lips upturned in a way that said she knew I wasn't being honest, I couldn't help the small chuckle that rushed out. "Okay, you... *caught me off guard* but I am enjoying myself. *Truly.*" I insisted when she still looked unconvinced. "It's been years since I've been to a family reunion. It's fun seeing family interact this way."

She nodded, eyes sweeping over many people who shared her ancestry. "It's been too many years since we've had one. Nearly a decade, I believe. Maybe longer." She paused, sighing deeply before looking over at me once more with that disarming smile I'd watched her use to get her way with all the men in the family, young and old. "Do you need anything, baby?"

Again, I wanted to decline but something was nagging me and I had to ask her. "Why are you being so nice to me?"

Ms. Anne's head tilted, assessing me. "I reckon anyone who tries so hard to push people away has something to hide. Something that hurts them terribly and they're trying to protect themselves from it. It's not my place to judge you for how you choose to protect yourself. My job is to show you and everyone else kindness, no matter what. I trust that the longer you're around us today, the more comfortable you'll feel. You'll thaw eventually." She ended her statement with a playful wink.

My chest tightened, disbelieving that a woman I'd met three

hours ago already recognized something that people I'd known forever didn't. I felt *seen*.

"Now come dance with me." Her hand held suspended between us as the classic *Cha Cha Slide* rang out, bringing people from all over to the open ground that served as a makeshift dance floor.

"Oh.... no," I protested with a firm headshake. "I don't dance."

"You've seen me in action today, haven't you? The way I interact with my family?" At my slow, confused nod, she winked again. "Then you know Ms. Anne don't take no for an answer."

14

LATHAN

Remedy was laughing.

Not snorting with sarcasm or chuckling under her breath.

But full-blown laughing at something my Uncle Lester yelled out on the dancefloor.

He could lower even the most closed off person's guards without even trying. The man had the comedic timing of some of the all-time greats and kept the family in stitches at some of his outlandish actions and comments.

With her head tossed back and eyes closed in humor, Remedy appeared relaxed. Carefree.

And she never looked more beautiful.

I'd been surprised my mom coaxed her onto the dancefloor. Then again, Anne Calloway was *notorious* for getting her way.

I'd almost gotten up multiple times to rescue her when her discomfort seemed to ramp up.

Thankfully, Tessa and my mom seemed to notice because they flanked her, dancing far enough to give her space but remaining close enough so no one else could slip between them.

That had worked until Tessa walked off with my cousin Venus's thirteen-year-old daughter, Essence.

Uncle Lester had slipped right in place, cracking jokes, and making borderline inappropriate comments that seemed to ease Rem's discomfort rather than increasing it.

"Lathan, you better come get your girl before I steal her!" Lester called out, dropping in a dip and swaying his hips from side to side with his tongue extended.

The man was a fool.

When he dipped further, hovering inches above ground, doing a move I hadn't seen since Don Cornelius hosted Soul Train, I cracked up. His wife would *definitely* need to bring out the ointment tonight. He was *showing out* and his arthritic ass would pay for it later.

After Lester's taunting, Rem turned to face me, eyes locked on mine as she followed along to the line dance perfectly.

Her hips were fluid as she effortlessly mastered the steps on the uneven terrain in her wedges.

Gone was the stiff, prim and proper woman who could freeze water with one look.

This version of Remedy was warm and open. Inviting.

Her guards were down and I couldn't resist the urge to see it up close.

Keeping my gaze on hers, I closed the distance between us until I stood right in front of her, bottom lip slipped between my teeth.

The wind in her hips subdued but she kept moving, never breaking my stare.

"Awww, shit," Uncle Lester exclaimed, glancing between the two of us. "I know what that look means." When Lester pretended to spank the air, my mama swatted at him with the towel she always carried.

"Get your mannish ass..." Her words trailed as she chased her older brother, fussing the whole time he roared with laughter.

"You good? How's the heart?" I questioned, cupping her elbow gently. I paused, assessing her reaction to my touch before pulling her against my side when she didn't recoil. Her arm loosely wrapped around the small of my back and I played it safe, tossing mine around her shoulders.

"I'm fine."

I eyed her skeptically, realizing that term was a favorite of hers, even when she *wasn't* fine.

"Really, I am. No pain or anything. I'm having *fun*." She admitted in a quiet tone.

"I'm glad you're having fun. You deserve it."

Her head snapped up to stare at my profile but I kept my gaze forward, walking us further away from the remaining family who still hadn't left the dancefloor.

We walked in silence until we reached the lake at the center of the park.

Ducks could be heard quacking in the distance along with the random splash of fish that popped up to grab lingering food floating on the surface.

There were feed centers stationed throughout where small bags of duck and fish food were available to purchase for a dollar.

"It's so peaceful." She said once we stood at a picnic table near the water's edge. "I could stay out here forever."

"Me too."

She gathered the material of her skirt to sit but I stopped her, grabbing her hips and lifting her on top of the table and sitting next to her before she could protest.

"This was my spot growing up." I sighed, breathing in the warm, fresh air. Though Sienna Falls was still in the south and had similar weather and humidity like Huntsville, there was nothing like home. "When I got in trouble, when I got mad, when I was sad... when I was hurt or disappointed... this was where I came. Every problem I had seemed... *miniscule* when surrounded by all of this beauty. It made my thoughts clearer, you know? My decision making was *easier*. I just needed a place to settle and balance me."

"And now?"

"Hmm?"

"Where do you go now to achieve that?" She worried her bottom lip between her teeth. "When you're not here, how do you... find that clarity? That peace of mind?"

I had the feeling she was asking more for herself than me.

"Therapy. Sculpting. Talking to my mom or my boys." When those answers didn't seem to satisfy her, I nudged her with my shoulder. "I'm here to listen whenever you need to talk, Rem. I'm in your corner, babe."

Her tongue swiped against her bottom lips nervously before she bit it. Several seconds passed before she opened her mouth.

My entire frame tightened with the anticipation of whatever she was about to say.

"Lath!"

I flinched at the voice calling behind us, groaning when I spotted her once open expression close off to her normal blank slate.

Dammit.

I was so close.

So damn close to having a moment with her.

Annoyance was evident on my features when I turned, watching as my cousin, Lennie, Lester's eldest son, walked over.

"What's good, Len?" My tone was dry but like his father, Lennie didn't pay it any mind. "Cuz, we're heading to this new spot tonight. They opened a few weeks ago. Want to know if you and your lady would like to come? I got VIP passes and everything."

Lennie was a sketchy ass nigga sometimes. We'd grown up like brothers and I loved him to death, even though he was never completely on the... *up-and-up*.

He must've recognized my skepticism because he smiled, gold caps gleaming. "I swear it's legit. I'm not on no *bullshit*. Even Venus and Deac are coming."

I wasn't surprised. My best friend and cousin were usually down for anything.

I glanced at Rem, finding her eyes bucked as she glanced between the two of us. I had to admit, curiosity had me wanting to see what spot Lennie was talking about but I knew Rem wouldn't be up to it. "Naw, I think we're gonna pass."

"We can go."

Lennie and I both whirled to Rem, surprised she'd spoken and agreed.

"Rem, we don't ha-"

"You're home to spend time with your family. You shouldn't be stuck babysitting me. Besides, I think it'll be fun." Her tone was lackluster at best.

"Are you sure?"

She flashed another uncertain glance at Lennie, then the water before looking back at me. "I'm sure."

15

REMEDY

I should've never agreed.

Going out to a nightclub was *so* far out of my norm.

But I'd recognized that Lathan was about to turn his cousin down because he knew I'd be uncomfortable. And I didn't want him to miss out because of me so I agreed, regretting my decision instantly but not speaking up about it.

After Lennie agreed to meet us, we enjoyed a few more hours at the picnic before checking in the hotel to change.

Tessa was spending the night with her cousins so it was just Lathan and I in the two-bedroom suite.

Less than two hours later, we walked through the doors of *Greed*.

The club looked large from the outside but that didn't translate to the inside. The dance floor and booths seemed cramped compared to the massive structure it was housed in.

My hackles rose each time someone bumped into me or brushed against my arms.

This was another reason I didn't do the night scene.

The forced close proximity.

Lathan must've sensed my discomfort and pulled me close, practically engulfing me in his arms.

"Kind of crowded, ain't it?" Lathan said to Lennie who smiled mischievously.

"Just wait, cuz. This shit is *lit*."

I met the eyes of a woman standing near the bar before averting my gaze. The lights were dimmed low enough that I felt confident no one would recognize me. I was well-known but not *famous* like Verse.

The man couldn't walk to the local coffee shop, Common Grounds, without having his photo taken.

Lathan's grip on my hand tightened as we continued following Lennie towards the back of the club until we reached a red door.

There, Lennie held up a card to the camera above the door. Seconds later, it swung open.

"What the fuck?" Lathan muttered under his breath, echoing my exact thought. He flashed a look towards me once more before tightening his grip on my hand as we followed Lennie further down the rabbit hole.

A long, dimly lit hall went on for what felt like forever before we stepped into another nightclub that was set up similarly to the one we'd just left but was much more spacious and elegant.

On my first glance around, I didn't realize what I was looking at.

Then, the chorus of moans met my ears.

"Did this nigga bring us to a fuckin' *sex club*?" Lathan muttered, eyes as wide as mine.

On cue, Lennie turned, gold-toothed grin in place. "This place is lit, right?!"

"Boy, you're *wild* for this." Lathan's friend Deacon laughed, bouncing his gaze around the room.

Everywhere I looked... there were writhing bodies.

Some fully clothed, some half-dressed. Only a small group in the far corner of the room were as naked as the day they were born, tangled up in a ball of so many limbs that I forced my gaze away, not wanting to stare too hard despite their lack of embarrassment.

My brain seemed to short circuit after the first glimpse around the red and black themed room.

This area was much less crowded than upstairs, maybe forty to fifty people at the most, including us.

People were kissing and touching everywhere.

And there was... So. Much. Leather.

"Lennie, you couldn't have warned what we were about to walk into?" Venus snapped, shoving him in the back.

Lennie shrugged. "I knew y'all uptight asses would've turned me down."

Directly to our right, a woman kneeled between a man's thighs. Her head bobbed enthusiastically as he passionately kissed the woman next to him.

What. The. Fuck.

This was... *a lot*.

"I'm in this bitch at *least* three times a week," Lennie rambled, completely oblivious to our discomfort. "Y'all are in for a treat tonight. Every Saturday belongs to Envy."

"Who the fuck is Envy?" Venus asked, slightly swaying her ample hips and tiny waist to the sensual beat flowing through the speakers.

Lennie's grin turned salacious. "You'll see."

With my past, I thought I'd be struck with terror from being in here but surprisingly... I wasn't. After getting over the initial shock, I realized that the writhing bodies and out-in-the-open sex inspired... *curiosity* more than anything.

I'd never seen sex like this.

Consensual and pleasurable for *both* parties.

For twenty years, I'd avoided sex and any variation of it like the plague. Even porn.

I was too afraid of how it would make me feel. I was afraid of... *spiraling*.

But now, seeing this... this *freedom* piqued my interest.

"We can leave." Lathan offered in a soothing tone, rubbing his thumb across the back of my hand.

"No," I answered quickly. Probably *too* quickly because Lathan's eyes swung to mine and bucked. "I'm fine." When one of his brows hiked, I gave him a shaky smile. "I promise. It's okay. I don't mind."

His grip tightened and he tucked me in close, preparing to lead me further into the room but Lennie stopped him.

"Hold up," he said, reaching behind him to grab a plain wicker basket that contained simple, colored wristbands. "Pick your color. Black means you're down for everything. Red means you're willing to play but you have limits. Blue means you're open to flirting but not sex."

"And the yellow?" Deacon prompted regarding the last color in the basket.

"In a nutshell, yellow means leave me the fuck alone, I'm just here to observe."

"*Yellow*." Lathan, Venus, and I all called at the same time, causing Lennie to flash that gold-toothed smile.

After our wristbands were on, our eyes flashed over to Deacon who shrugged. "Give me a black."

"*My nigga*." Lennie chortled and grabbed two of the dark bands before passing one to Deacon.

Moments later, we split up.

Deacon and Lennie headed further in the establishment, citing they were going down the hall to visit the kink rooms.

Venus was waved over by an old classmate of hers—*who wasn't in the throes of passion*—and left us alone, still standing near the entrance.

Lathan led us over to the bar and ordered drinks—him, a Hennessey straight and me, cranberry juice—before quickly ushering me to a quiet corner where everybody near us was fully clothed.

"Ladies and Gentlemen," an impossibly deep voice bled from the speakers, drowning out the R&B music that played moments earlier. "Feast your eyes on... *Envy*."

Deep red curtains that I initially thought were for decoration parted near the rear of the room.

Masked and seated on a throne of the same blood red color was a woman.

Red boots and a diamond-lined thong with matching tassels on each nipple was all she wore.

"Bad Girl" by my favorite R&B artist, Gideon, poured from the speakers as the crowd whooped with excitement as she remained seated, allowing everyone in attendance to ogle her voluptuous frame.

"Why choose to be good when you can be my bad girl..."

As the sensual beat continued to play, she finally moved from her seat.

Each movement was like a seduction that had every man and woman in the crowd mesmerized. As song after song played, she danced around the room.

She *controlled* the room.

Her sensuality was powerful as she spread her thighs near a man's head, encouraging him to taste before tossing her head back in ecstasy when he did.

Lord knows I would never have enough confidence or courage to work a room the way she did but I couldn't pretend that I didn't envy her.

Her poise.

Her liberation.

Her *freedom*.

I envied how she owned her sexuality in a room full of people.

She held it in her palm, sharing it when she wanted before snatching it back when *she* declared they'd had enough.

Nobody took it from her.

Nobody forced her to do a damn thing.

Envy owned her body while owning the room and I couldn't help but to wonder... what would that feel like for me?

16

LATHAN

Watching Remedy experience... *something* next to me had me hard as a rock.

I'd expected her to run from the room screaming the second she laid eyes on what was going on. But again, she surprised me.

Instead of fleeing, she looked... *intrigued*.

Sitting next to me now, her lips were slack, eyes hazy as she watched the main attraction, Envy, move about the room like a woman who knew she was in control.

Envy was attractive, I'd give her that.

But my attention couldn't stay on her because I couldn't pull it from the woman whose thighs tightened beneath the sensible dress she wore.

The woman whose heels brushed against my pants leg each time her crossed legs swayed back and forth.

The woman whose nipples strained against the fitted top half of her dress.

Fuck.

It was this damn club.

This environment.

It had to be.

I couldn't find any other explanation for this sudden surge of uncontrollable lust.

Sex surrounded us in the spacious room and I'd been abusing my hand like a horny teen for the last few months because I wasn't interested in casual flings.

I was getting too *old* for that shit.

I wanted a connection with somebody.

Not just sex.

But my raging libido didn't seem to get the memo as my dick stiffened even more when she leaned over me, placing a hand on my thigh, peeking to watch Envy as she lowered herself into a man's lap, gyrating on him sensually.

Move your damn hand, Rem.

I hoped she understood the message I was conveying with my eyes but she didn't. Instead, she leaned even further, now watching as the woman of the hour gave commands to a couple, touching them with encouragement, ordering them in different positions while rubbing her own body sensually.

"*I can't see.*" She muttered, straining her neck.

Her hand slid further up my thigh, brushing against my dick as she balanced her weight on the palm.

"Fuck." I groaned.

Reaching over, I plucked her from her seat, depositing her in my lap.

A moment of panic overtook her features before she scanned her eyes over my frame, as if to remind herself this was *me* before she relaxed, settling back against my chest, content with her now unobstructed view.

I'd originally positioned her in the corner, hoping to shield her from most of the activity in the room.

I hadn't expected her to *want* to see.

One of my hands settled in the middle of her back while the other rested on her upper thigh, just below where her dress ended.

My eyes remained on her as she looked down at my hand then back at me with her bottom lip tucked between her teeth.

"Don't look at me like that."

Her eyes darted away before returning to mine. "Like what?"

Instead of responding, I conveyed what I meant through half-mast lids, refusing to blink until she looked away.

Taking advantage of another rare moment where her guards were down, I placed my hand in the center of her chest, asking my customary question. "How's the heart?"

She let it remain there for a few moments before swatting it away, frowning back at me. "It's fine." Her eyes roamed over me again before turning back to the entertainment, mumbling under her breath. "That's not the part of me in crisis right now."

I could tell the moment she regretted her words because she tensed.

"What I meant was..."

"What part of you is in crisis, Rem?"

A shiver moved through her shoulders as my fingers on her thigh twirled in a teasing circle.

"Maybe I can help with it."

Again, her gaze swung to mine. I expected a resolute no to fall from her lips but again she surprised me, working her bottom lip between her teeth as if in contemplation.

Fuck.

If this woman told me yes...

Suddenly, the blank mask that had been absent for much of the day shuttered over her features, closing her off.

Now, despite having her entire ass planted in my lap, she seemed far away.

Unreachable.

"Can we go?"

I cringed at the coldness that had seeped into her tone.

I don't know what caused her to revert to this but if it was something I said, I'd take it back in a heartbeat.

I'd give anything to see more of the unfiltered Remedy that had been more alive than I'd seen from her in two years.

"Now?"

Her gaze swung back to Envy, watching the beautiful woman in action with another couple before a resigned sigh left her lips and she stood from my lap.

"Yeah. I'm ready now."

17

REMEDY

Things between Lathan and I felt... *weird* after leaving *Greed*.

Something had shifted between us and I didn't know what to do about it.

As soon as we'd hit the door, I hopped in the shower, not giving him a chance to address what had happened between us at the club.

I'd felt... Arousal. For *him*.

And I might be ignorant to most things about sex but I'd recognized the thick lust coating his tone as he'd made me an offer that I briefly considered.

I thought about giving in.

I thought about telling him I wanted him, *needed* him to help ease the ache at the core of me.

But then I remembered.

I remembered who I was. What they had done to me.

Sexual liberation like Envy displayed tonight was a pipe dream for someone like me.

I'd never get to experience that.

That chance had been taken from me the second my innocence had been stolen.

I was resigned to a life of fear and celibacy, no matter how tempting Lathan's offer was.

With my shields and guards firmly in place, I exited the bathroom and toweled off in my bedroom, listening to the sounds of his shower running.

Once I'd moisturized, I slipped on underwear before donning the thick robe I'd brought with me and padded barefoot into the common area in search of a late-night snack.

I paused when his door opened seconds later and he emerged in boxer briefs and... nothing else.

Instantly my eyes skated over each inch of him and I sucked in a breath, more than impressed by the powerful body on display.

His bulk had always made me assume he was strong but not chiseled. Not like Verse who was sculpted like an athlete but more similar to Hakeem with the natural bulkiness of a linebacker.

But I'd been wrong.

Underneath the casual clothes he wore every day was a sculpted physique that was a masterpiece.

His arms were thick and corded with muscle that he carried easily.

His torso was hard and ripped before trailing down to those deep cuts on each side of his pelvis that disappeared in the waistband of his boxers.

His thighs were like tree trunk, thick and study.

I remained frozen in my doorway as he crossed the room, not sparing me a glance as he moved to grab a bottle of water from the mini fridge. He took several deep gulps before he paused mid-swig, finally realizing my eyes hadn't left his frame.

"You okay?"

My lips parted to snap back that I was fine but all that emerged from my lips was a pitiful sound that had him turning to face me.

"Your chest hurt, babe?" He asked, concern etching his features as he closed the distance between us.

My eyes fell to the increasing bulge tenting the front of his boxers and another pitiful sound rushed past my lips.

This time he recognized I wasn't in crisis, at least not in the way he thought, and his lids hooded.

"You see something over here that you want, Rem." His tone was husky, brimming with the thick tension that swirled between us.

All I could do in response was buck my eyes in surprise.

The water bottle he carried was carelessly discarded on the end table as he continued to close the distance between us.

"I hope you see something you want. Because I damn sure do."

The front of his boxer briefs held my gaze hostage and I couldn't muster up the energy to swing it away.

Finally crossing the room, he hovered over me, filling the tiny space we occupied with his distinctly masculine scent that reminded me of the sandalwood aromatherapy candle I used to burn faithfully.

It was rich and earthly. Exotic and hypnotizing.

It was... *Lathan.*

"I'm about to kiss you, Rem." My eyes bucked, not only in surprise but... anticipation. "If that ain't something you want or if it makes you uncomfortable, let me know."

Still in a state of shock, I nodded slowly.

"Words, Rem."

"O-okay." I stuttered out, already licking my lips in anticipation.

He smirked but didn't call me out on my eagerness.

I hadn't ridden a rollercoaster since my school trip to Sixx Flags over Georgia when I was thirteen.

That anticipation was unmatched as the coaster rounded the last curve before mounting up the tedious tracks, climbing the highest hill, teasing you of what was to come.

I remember my stomach tightening and skin tingling, heart fluttering with nervousness as adrenaline shot through me in preparation.

Those few moments of waiting for Lathan to place his lips on mine felt eerily similar to that.

I struggled to control my breathing and slow my erratic heartbeat as I waited at the height of the last drop, adrenaline spring to life in my veins.

Then his lips met mine and I fell over the edge.

Hard and fast.

Someone had stolen too many of my firsts from me before I'd even been old enough to fully comprehend what had happened.

So I was granting myself a do over. A clean slate. From this day forward, I would consider *this* as the first time I'd had a man's lips on mine.

It was fitting because every woman deserved to experience a first kiss like this.

Lathan's lips moved against mine with the same unhurried patience that he used in his everyday life. Normally, it worked my last nerves because slowing down wasn't in my vocabulary.

But today I appreciated it.

I savored it and melted into the kiss, finally closing my eyes after a few moments and relinquishing a bit more of my control. For some reason, I instinctively knew that it was safe in his hands.

A squeal left me when he lifted me in his arms and I instinctively curled my legs around his waist. I tensed, waiting for the crippling panic that didn't come.

Instead, inch by inch, the tension seeped from my entire frame until I was completely lax in his arms, staring up at him as he carried us into my room. He gently deposited me on the bed and I reclined, eyes wide and unsure as he smiled down at me.

"Can we take this off?" He thumbed the plush robe still hiding more than half of me from his view. When I didn't answer right away, his lips lifted in a smile. "You're allowed to say no."

When he gave me that choice, it solidified my decision and I started roughly tugging at the belt I'd double tied around my waist.

Before I could get it undone, his hands gently rested on mine. "Let me."

Steady hands accomplished what I couldn't before he parted

each end. A low groan pushed past his lips when he found me in a plain pair of black, cotton underwear and... nothing else.

Immediately, I flushed, realizing he was probably expecting lace and frill and all the other sexy underwear that women wore. But the groan that left his lips, the lust that surged to life in his dark orbs as he observed me made me feel... desirable.

"You're so damn beautiful, Rem. You know that?"

I didn't get a chance to respond to the surprising compliment because his lips pressed against mine at the same time his fingers deftly grabbed the waistband of my panties, easing them over my thighs and down until they slipped off my ankles to the floor.

He leaned back, scanning his gaze over me, savoring the first glance he got of my nude body without a stitch of clothing attached.

"Fuckin' perfection."

I felt him moving between my legs, slipping his own boxer briefs off until they pooled on top of my discarded pair.

This time when he leaned down to press his lips against mine, the bulbous tip of his shaft pressed against my entrance and I instantly stiffened.

I realized a second later what I'd done and tried to relax but it was too late.

His watchful eye didn't miss a thing. "Been a while?" I didn't enjoy lying so I merely averted my gaze. Big mistake.

"Rem... Are you..." He shook his head as if clearing cobwebs. "Are you a... a *virgin*?"

My cheeks heated in embarrassment, immediately pushing his chest, wanting him off. "Get off me."

He obliged, looking stunned as he rolled next to me, still not saying a word. When I reached for my robe to cover myself, his hand shot out to grab mine, stopping me. "I'm not tripping or anything. You just should've told me. You had me thinking you were ready but I can't just go in like that. Not for your *first* time, babe."

His words caused a boulder to sink in my gut and I averted my gaze, staring at the closed curtains that led to the patio outside my room. Despite him and Tessa having to share, he'd given me the master suite with the full bath and patio attached.

"I'm not a virgin."

His face contorted as if in disbelief. "Then what is?"

"Can we just finish this?"

Skepticism rolled off him in waves but he nodded, rolling back over me once more. This time when he tried to kiss me, I turned my head away. "Just put it in."

Again, he eyed me like I'd lost my mind but he obliged.

Well, he attempted to.

Though his movements between my thighs were gentle, I was stiffer than a pile of bricks as he eased his thickness up and down my slit, coating it with the evidence of my arousal before attempting to slip inside.

The change from me focusing on what we were doing to trying to keep from falling into the darkness of my memories was so swift that it took me off guard.

I tried to remind myself that this was consensual.

That I wanted this.

I gave him permission to do these things to me.

But none of that mattered because my body was locked with fear. I couldn't convince my mind otherwise and a tear slipped over my cheek.

Lathan immediately stopped, probably not even a full inch inside, still hovering over me. "I'm not sure what's going on but if you need me to stop, I will, Rem. Nobody's rushing this shit. It's at your pace." When I remained silent, he cupped my cheek, caressing his gently with his thumb, swiping away the second tear that chased the first one. "If you want to put your clothes back on and kick me out, we can do that too. I'll go back to my room and stay there until we leave tomorrow."

"No, I don't want to do that." I muttered, squeezing my eyes before opening them and glancing back up at his face. "It's just... you're too big..."

Immediately, his eyes fell to where we joined. "I appreciate the compliment but..."

"No, not like *that*!" I snapped, cheeks heating.

His lips curved up in a smile which caused my embarrassment to deepen. "Seriously, Rem, what's wrong? Talk to me."

"*You're* too big," I repeated, gesturing towards the broad shoulders and chiseled chest hovering just above me. "I feel small and helpless and... trapped. You smother me and I can't *breathe*."

Though he was doing nothing but hovering over me, his size reminded me of a time when I was small. And helpless. And trapped in a situation that I couldn't get out of.

It brought up dark memories that would consume me if I let them.

But the second my last word fell from my lips, Lathan reared back on his knees, completely removing his weight off me and I sucked in a deep breath even though I hadn't lacked air in the first place.

My mind wanted to protect me and I felt that familiar numbness creeping up. I didn't want it to but couldn't help myself. It was a defense mechanism that had been in place for far too long.

"Don't check out on me, babe." His rumbling tenor jolted me out of the trance I'd been slipping into, forcing my eyes up to his. "You don't have to talk about it, Rem. Everything is at your pace. Your comfort level. Don't push past your boundaries for me. If I'm overstepping, let me know. *Check* me. I'm a big dude, I can handle it, babe." My lips remained pressed together, despite my eyes desperately searching his for... something. What it was, I wasn't sure but whatever he recognized on my face had him groaning and rolling next to me on the bed, tossing his forearm over his eyes. "Wanna watch a movie?"

"No." I said quickly after finding my voice. "I want to have *sex*."

His head whipped towards me. "Rem, I just said if you're not ready, for whatever reason, don't push yourself."

Frustrated tears sprang to my eyelids and I slammed them closed, willing away the weakness. I didn't cry. I *never* cry. So doing so twice in one night was unacceptable.

"I *want* to do this but... I don't know how to without thinking about *that*."

I could practically see the wheels turning in his mind, wanting to know more about the *that* I'd referenced.

But I couldn't explain further. If he thought I was spiraling now? Forcing me to talk about that would likely have me sinking into the dark place at the deep recesses of my mind that I never acknowledged.

I hadn't lost it in a very long time and was afraid of what it would look like with so many emotions I'd buried for so long finally bursting free.

"Do you have any triggers, Rem?"

"What?" I asked at the unexpected question.

"Areas that are definitely off limits. Clearly me being on top of you is one but are there any others that you're aware of? Certain words? Body parts? Positions? Anything that might trigger you?"

"I don't know." I responded in a low voice.

Triggers. I'd never thought of them that way. I just attributed my aversion to certain things as another fucked up part of my psyche that I tried to hide from everyone. I thought irreparable damage had been done to me mentally, physically, and *emotionally*.

"You trust me?"

I hated that question.

Trust was fickle and meant nothing. Just because you placed your trust in someone didn't mean that they couldn't still fuck you over. As a matter of fact, all the people who had hurt me were people I'd placed my trust in. So trust held zero weight in my eyes.

"Why?"

"You clearly have triggers but don't know what they are. Obviously sex is at the root of the problem but you still want to do this so... let's... start slow. Touching, a little kissing... *discovering*."

Lingering anxiety had me wanting to turn down his offer but the dampness between my thighs had me readily agreeing.

He rolled to face me, placing a gentle hand on the curve of my waist, watching me through thin slits, gauging my reaction. After seeing that the panic from before was absent, he pressed his lips against mine, easing his tongue past the barrier, gently intertwining with mine.

I rested my hands against the hard planes of his abs and groaned into his mouth, eager for more contact. It was several moments later that I realized his hand hadn't moved from his position while mine roamed so freely over his chiseled torso that I could sketch each slope and curve from memory.

"Touch me." I demanded after breaking the kiss that had me feeling intoxicated. Not an ounce of alcohol had ever passed my lips but if this was what being drunk and intoxicated felt like, I understood why so many imbibed.

"Where do you want me to touch you, baby?" He asked in a low rumble that had my thighs squeezing together, hoping to ease the ache at the center of them.

"I don't care," I said with an urgent desperation that I'd probably regret tomorrow. But for now, I embraced it, grabbing his hand and yanking it from my waist and placing it on my breast. "Here. Anywhere. Just *touch* me."

A low keen rushed from my lips when he obliged, tweaking my nipple between his thumb and forefinger. My thighs squeezed together so tight than an ache echoed through them but I ignored it, shoving my chest further into his hands.

"Looks like you need my hands somewhere else."

His words barely had time to penetrate my brain before he abandoned the stiff peaks and moved his hand down the plane of my stomach.

"Still good?" He asked, pausing just above the small patch of curls I now wished I'd trimmed.

But I hadn't expected this. Any type of grooming I did was for hygienic and convenience purposes only. I'd never expected anyone to see me intimately again.

I nodded before pressing my lips together when his lids narrowed, remembering his demand for my *words*. "Yes. I'm good."

"Good." His long fingers tapped at my thighs for entry and I instantly parted them, looking between us with awe.

Jesus.

This was too much yet... I didn't want it to stop. I needed this because I didn't know if the nerve and courage coursing through me at the moment would disappear come morning.

His eyes remained locked on mine, stare unwavering as his fingers penetrated my folds, gliding up my damp slit.

The most perfect groan fell from his generous lips and finally he broke our stare, looking where his fingers played between my thighs with furrowed brows.

"Prettiest little pussy I've ever seen," was muttered so low that I thought I'd misheard him.

"What?" I questioned, widening my thighs more when his thumb began a swift up and down motion on my clit that sent shock waves of pleasure racing through me.

"You heard what I said," he shot back, still not lifting his gaze, too focused on driving that little bundle of nerves crazy. "As beautiful as you look right now, that's not how I want you to cum." My brows dipped in frustration when he pulled his hand away before spiking on my forehead when he rolled to his back and pulled me on top of him.

"Still good?"

That question hit me right in the solar plexus like it had the first time.

I was better than good. Great, even. I felt more relaxed at this moment than I had in years. I was experiencing pleasure, without fear. I was being touched intimately without my stomach clenching with nausea.

I never wanted this moment to end.

"Still good."

He nodded, settling his hands on my hips before easing my body forward. He bypassed the stiff rigidity that jutted out from his pelvis, pulling me up his torso until I straddled his shoulders.

I resisted that last nudge, widening my eyes down at his handsome face.

"What wrong, babe?"

"*What's wrong?*" I snapped, flinching at the coldness of it before gentling my tone. "What the *hell* are you doing?"

"Trying to get you to sit on my face."

He was *what*? "Why would you do that?!" I screeched back, staring down at his smug expression. He'd tossed that out like it was no big deal when it fact, to me... it was a very big deal.

He laughed at the elevation of my voice, massaging my hips with gentle movements that eased me instantly. What the hell kind of magic did he have in those fingertips?

"I want to do it because it'll feel good for you... *and me*."

I couldn't muster up a response, so I fell silent, nibbling my bottom lips nervously.

The brief humor fled his expression and he tilted his head, increasing the depth his fingertips traveled into my fleshy hips. He squeezed and rubbed at it, molding it in his hands as his eyes never left mine.

"Hard limit?"

That wasn't a familiar phrase to me but I had enough common sense to surmise what it meant in relation to our current predicament. "I don't know." I said with a headshake. "I've just never... *done* that before."

"I'd be honored to be your first." He said with a smile before his face went serious. "Seriously, if it makes you uncomfortable, we can do something else or... that offer of stopping completely and watching a movie still stands."

I knew for a fact that stopping was not what I wanted.

Not at all.

Besides, I was up here now. And I had to admit that I was curious.

I was nothing if not committed to seeing something through to the end so I scooted forward and he smiled, assisting me until the only thing peeking from between my thighs was his bushy brows, wide expressive eyes, and the tip of his nose.

I was wound so tight, I felt like my body would snap in half at any moment.

"Relax, baby," He muttered and I barely resisted the urge to cry out when his cool breath fanned my damp center. "I promise to make it good for you."

My hands lifted to the headboard and forced the tension from my frame. His eyes fell closed just as his tongue slipped through my folds.

Oh. *Oh.*

"Damn, that's good." He moaned.

My grip tightened on the wood slat, and I widened my thighs, instinctively rocking back and forth on his face as he gave me tentative licks, flicking with enough speed to give pleasure but not enough pressure to send me fully over the edge.

I gasped when he slurped my clit and folds into his mouth, sucking hard. I keened like a kitten, arching my back painfully, moaning as his hands moved from my waist to my ass, using the mounds to shove me further into his mouth.

His tongue flicked against my clit with urgency now.

"Oh, *fuck*."

I had no idea it could be this good. I didn't want it to end.

I wanted to wrap it up in a box and store it in the closet with all of my other memories so I could hold on to it forever.

I wanted to keep it close, keep it safe so no one else could ever rob me of that experience.

This experience belonged to me. And I was glad it was with him.

His actions between my thighs turned noisy, filling the air with sloppy, slurping sounds that had me digging my heels into the bed, humping frantically at his face.

My heart felt like it was going to pound out of my chest and that panic set in.

"It's too much. *It's too much.*" I cried, trying to retreat from his lips.

"Relax, baby. Breathe." His hands abandoned my ass to tug on my wrist. I released my painful grip on the headboard, allowing him to lock our fingers together, resting them on my parted thighs.

My head fell back when he groaned against me.

I felt a twinge in my core and I vocalized it, desperately grinding against his face as he sporadically muttered encouraging words against my flesh.

"Cum for me, Rem."

I did. *Hard.*

I tightened my grip, rocking against him so hard that the entire bed shook, tapping the headboard lightly against the wall.

Before that orgasm could end, another began from his incessant suckling. Again, I cried out, trembling with the effort it was taking to remain upright.

When my flesh became too sensitive, I snatched away, slamming my thighs closed before sliding off and falling next to him on the bed with a harsh grunt.

I was spent.

Soft chuckles met my ears a second before he kissed my shoulder, wrapping an arm around my waist and tugging me against his side.

Several minutes of silence ensued and I started to drift off into the world of slumber before feeling selfish after remembering the hardness jutting from between his thighs. He'd given me two orgasms, the least I could do was give him some relief.

So I rolled to face him. His eyes were closed and one of his arms was folded behind his head, rigid penis jutting upwards in the air.

It was so hard that it looked *painful.*

I scooted down until my face was parallel with his pelvis before reaching for it. I'd done this before and had successfully shut off my brain each time. I could do it again to repay him for what he'd done for me.

Before I could, my wrist was grabbed and I was tugged back up the bed.

"But..." I protested, "You need..."

"I need you to go to sleep. We've done enough exploring today. If you're still interested tomorrow, we'll continue what we started. But for now, go to sleep."

I glanced down again at the hardness bobbing in the air. "Doesn't it hurt? I can just..."

"It's uncomfortable at best. I'm fine, Rem. I'm not trippin' on it. I'm a grown ass man that knows how to control himself. *It'll go down.*"

18

LATHAN

I was wide awake.

Hours had passed since Remedy curled up against my side and fell asleep after our *exploration* session.

Since then, sleep had evaded me and I couldn't rest.

Not after that.

Not after so many pieces of the Remedy puzzle had fallen into place.

I wasn't the smartest man in the world but context clues over the last two years plus her cryptic words tonight was enough for me to piece everything together.

Her aversion to touch.

The brief flashes of panic I thought I'd imagined whenever too many people were around.

The way she instinctively sidled up to me when unknown men were near.

Little puzzle pieces that once looked like they'd never fit together started making sense, giving me a full, unobstructed look behind her walls rather than my normal quick peeks.

Because of it, I wouldn't be the same.

After tonight, my life was irrevocably changed.

Since getting out of jail, I'd lived a muted existence. Simply going through the motions and floating through life, constantly trying to make penance for previous mistakes made.

And outside of being Tessa's father and looking out for my family, I hadn't thought about what my life's purpose was.

What was the one thing I was put on this Earth to do?

After tonight, I think I found it.

Ensure that no other harm or danger came to this complex woman.

Someone had broken Remedy's trust. They'd taken advantage of her and violated her in ways I still didn't know the full extent of. But based on her words, it was severe enough to cause the behavior I once thought was standoffish.

But she was a fucking warrior. One whose strength I admired now with new appreciation.

But she didn't have to be strong anymore. Not on her own. She had me to share that load with now.

A low noise drew my attention to her serene face.

I'd recognized Rem's beauty day one but ignored it because I had a job to do. But now, after watching her come apart so beautifully for me... After watching her push aside that ever present mistrust and open up for *me*, I couldn't help but to admire it.

Admire *her*.

Remedy had trusted me with something exquisite tonight, something so precious that I needed to handle it delicately.

She'd trusted me with her. Her body. Her essence. Her pleasure.

Despite wariness in her eyes, she'd placed it in my care and for as long as I lived, I'd do whatever I could to cherish it.

I had no clue what was next for us or if she'd even be interested in continuing this—*whatever the hell it was*—when clarity struck in the morning.

But she had my loyalty and that wasn't something I gave freely. But if Rem wanted it, it was hers.

Just like the rest of me.

19

REMEDY

It was still dark outside.

From how deeply I'd slept, I expected the sun to be beaming through the half-opened curtains.

I groaned and started to roll from the bed but stopped when I realized there was a thick forearm tossed across my waist, keeping me from moving.

My head whipped over my shoulder, finding Lathan's handsome face lax with sleep and all the memories from the night before came rushing back.

Us kissing.

His fingers playing between my thighs.

Me straddling his face.

And his *lips*... his tempting lips and tongue down *there*, driving me crazy.

I already wanted more.

Rolling under his arm, my eyes immediately fell, lifting the cover to peek underneath. The dick he'd said would go down was still at half mast, resting against his powerful thigh.

Though fear had won out last night, I couldn't help imagining how it'd feel inside of me. Would it be as painful as the experiences from my childhood? Or would he make it good for me, like he'd done last night?

I ran my hand up and down the length of his side, freezing when he jerked before continuing once he settled again.

I'd never been with a man outside of... *that*, so I'd never had an opportunity to do this. To explore freely, without fear.

After another quick glance at his face, I slipped my hand down until it rested near the base of his penis hidden underneath the thick white cover.

"You go any lower and I'm gonna return the favor."

I jumped, so engrossed in what I was doing that I hadn't realized he was awake.

His head had quietly turned towards me. Lids, thick with sleep, were barely parted and I just barely make out the whites of his eyes in the darkness.

"When did you put this on?" he asked, tugging at the hem of the white shirt I wore.

I shrugged, not remembering the exact time. Sleeping naked was not something I was comfortable with and probably never would be.

He rolled to his back and I thought he was going to turn away but he flung the cover to the side, leaving him completely bare and exposed.

"Go ahead, explore your little heart out. I'll keep my hands to myself."

My eyes bucked with excitement.

Unlimited access to explore *him*? I couldn't resist.

The first thing I did was skate my fingers down his abdomen again towards the penis that was stiffening before my very eyes.

"Wait." I paused at his soft command, eyeing him with lifted brows, hoping he wouldn't stop me. "I still promise to keep my hands to myself but can you take that off?" He nodded towards the t-shirt I wore. "Let me at least look at you while you're trying your best to drive me crazy."

I glanced down, then reached for the hem, pulling it off then tossing it aside.

Not giving him a chance to stop me again, I leaned forward, grabbing the base of his shaft and lifting it before circling my tongue around the plump, mushroom shaped head. My eyes flashed back up to his when he cursed, smiling to myself when he shifted in my grip but like he'd promised, he kept his hands to himself.

I did it again, enjoying the reaction I got from him before popping the entire head into my mouth.

"Dammit, woman." He groaned again. "Just go in for the fuckin' kill, why don't you?"

I chuckled, enjoying the soft velvety skin that brushed across my tongue as I took more of him in.

After a few minutes of easing him in and out of my mouth, though I didn't grow tired of his grunts and soft curses, I felt... unfulfilled.

I was satisfying my curiosity, freely, but also... I wanted his hands on me. So I reached for the fist he clenched behind his head, pulling until it rested between my thighs.

Instantly, he uncurled his fingers, pressing them against my throbbing core.

"You sure?" he asked.

I nodded and leaned over to plop the head of him back between my lips. I sucked with vigor now, moaning around the thickness as he brushed the pads of his fingers through my slit. When that teasing stroke turned firm and intentional, I abandoned what I was doing, resting my forehead against him and moaning as he brought me pleasure.

"Maybe I should've kept my hands to myself. You're neglecting my dick now that you're getting your shit off."

A breathless chuckle exploded from my lips at the same time he trapped my clit between two fingers and squeezed, sending more pinpricks of pleasure racing through me. "I'm *sorry*."

His hips lifted in front of my face and I took the hint, slipping him back inside my mouth, resuming the up and down motion as I fought the urge to collapse again.

Damn, he was good at this.

For the next half hour, Lathan let me explore and use him like a science experiment, stroking and sucking, driving him to the brink but not allowing him to fall over the edge.

I'd expected him to complain but he hadn't. Each time, he'd grown tense, body tightening to the point of snapping. Harsh breaths rushed from his nostrils and his lids slammed closed but he hadn't complained once, not forcing me to finish him off.

Meanwhile, his teasing fingers sent me orbiting into orgasmic bliss twice.

"Fuck, Rem." He groaned. That familiar tightness spread throughout his body as his head fell back and he curled his toes, preparing for another letdown.

Not this time.

This time, I wanted to wrap up what I started. I needed to see him finish. I craved the image of him falling over the edge, wondering if it was as appealing and sexy as he looked at this very moment.

I tightened my right fist on his shaft and jerked while my right cupped his balls, squeezing them with the exact amount of pressure to drive him wild like he'd shown me earlier.

My head bobbed and my tongue swirled around the tip, alternating before licking and sucking.

"You might want to move, babe."

I ignored him, increasing my pace, stomach tightening with anticipation. His hands had abandoned my core, now gently cupping the back of my head, guiding me down to his thrusting hips.

I didn't mind.

He'd given me so much pleasure in such a short amount of time that I wanted to return the favor.

Besides, doing this, watching him creep closer and closer to an orgasmic end had arousal coursing through me. My core throbbed in tune with my moving hand and I wondered if I could cum from this.

I wasn't sure if it was possible, but it damn sure felt like it.

"Last chance." He said through clenched teeth.

Again, I ignored the warning, watching with rapt attention as the first spurts of his release jetted from him.

"Ugh." He groaned, tightening his grip on my hair. "Just like that, baby. Squeeze my shit."

More cum than I thought possible sprouted from him and I eagerly continued my up and down motion, unable to tear my eyes away.

"*Shit, Rem.*" He groaned. I flashed my eyes up to his face, watching his expression contort as if in pain. His torso jerked and again, from the corner of my eye, I spotted his toes curling tight.

With just my lips and hands, I'd reduced this man to a wriggling pile of flesh.

I understood why Envy had walked around the room earlier as if she'd owned it.

This moment felt like an awakening of something that laid dormant for too long.

It felt like pleasure, unlike any other.

It felt like *power*.

"You've gotta stop, honey. I *can't*." He complained in an uncharacteristic whine. Moans fell from his lips faster than I kept up with but I continued what I was doing, watching him with rapt fascination.

If the sensitivity he felt was anything like what I'd experienced when he kept stroking my clit after I'd cum, I understood completely.

So I took mercy on him, releasing him from my grip, then squealing when he yanked me up his body.

His hand smacked my ass and I yelped. "You tried the fuck out of me." My face contorted with confusion but he continued, undeterred. "Had me in here moaning and whining like a *bitch*. What's wrong with you, Rem?" I pressed my lips together, fighting the urge to laugh. "Oh, that's funny to you?"

Those same hands pulled me further up his body, putting me in the position that had alarmed me the night before but now had anticipation coursing through my frame.

"Keep laughing." He muttered, arranging me until I straddled his face. "Payback's a bitch."

His tongue darted out and swiped through my folds, less gentle than he'd been last night. Moans clawed their way up my throat and I gave myself over to the pleasure he provided again.

If this was his form of payback, I needed to test his patience more often.

AFTER ANOTHER ROUND of *exploration* when we woke up this morning, Lathan and I peeled ourselves out of bed and packed before checking out of the hotel and heading to his mom's place to pick up Tessa.

I'd expected to wait in the car while he went in and said his goodbyes before we hit the road.

To my surprise, when we pulled up to the brick home, cars littered the driveway, front yard, and street in front of the house.

"Is this part two?" I asked, eyeing the people on the front porch howling with laughter at something Uncle Lester had said.

"Nah." Lathan chuckled, reaching over and placing a hand on my thigh with a familiarity like he'd been doing it all along. I eyed the contact and flushed, hating that my thoughts immediately went to him slipping it a few inches lower and toying between my legs like he'd done so many times since last night. "Mama likes to do a big breakfast before everybody leaves."

"Oh."

He squeezed my thigh one more time then climbed from the car. Before he rounded the hood to open my door, I was already standing on the grass with arms folded.

I was unsure how to act around him right now.

What went down between us in the hotel room had been intimate and belonged to us. But now we were back in the real world, so I was in limbo.

Clearly not feeling any of the dilemma that I was, he tossed an arm over my shoulders and tucked me against his side, guiding me up to the house where his cousins were.

"That shit was lit last night, right?" His cousin Lennie called to us as we walked up. His smile was big, mouth full of golds on display.

"That's why I don't fuck with you." Lathan shot back. "You always on some shit. You could've warned us first, man."

"Like I told Venus," Lennie countered, hiking his thumb at the woman in question, who looked at her cousin with upturned lips. "If I told y'all where we were going, you would've turned me down. Be glad I exposed y'all to some *new shit*."

"He took y'all to see Envy?" Uncle Lester piped up from his position on the porch swing.

Venus's face scrunched as she looked between her cousin and his father. "You took your Pops to a sex club?"

The grin that spread across Lester's face was sly as he tossed an arm over the back of the swing. "Best damn birthday gift I've ever had." His eyes darted to the closed front door before looking back at Lathan. "When I got home that night, I wore y'all Auntie *out*."

His words brought a chorus of groans and complaints from the group around the porch.

"Daddy, nobody needed to know all that." Lennie frowned while Venus held up her hands and walked off, muttering under her breath.

I pressed my lips together to keep from laughing as Lathan shook his head, maneuvering us around his family to go inside.

As soon as we did, Tessa greeted us with more enthusiasm than I'd ever seen from her. "Hey, Daddy. Hey, Ms. Rem." Her smile was bright, cheeks creased with dimples. She looked light and happy and I couldn't help but wonder if the distance between her and that witch of a grandmother caused it.

If not having the responsibility of looking out for her younger siblings allowed her to shed those walls and act her age.

"Hey, baby girl." Lathan greeted her, releasing me long enough to pull her into a hug and kiss the top of her head. The blatant affection between them both intrigued and made me uncomfortable.

Even the few times my dad had been around, obvious affection like that hadn't been given, especially as I got older. Life in Uptown had made him hard and though he had a heart of gold that was extended to everyone he knew, simple affection for his daughter had been asking for too much.

"Your bags packed?" Ms. Anne asked, coming out of the kitchen. Like always, her trusty towel was tossed over her shoulder, ready to be swatted at anyone who irritated her.

"Yes, ma'am. I just need to bring my bag down."

"And your charger?"

Tessa's eyes bucked before she sighed. "Forgot it."

"Um hmm."

Tessa said something in response that had her grandmother laughing but I missed it, too busy focusing on Lathan's lips as they pressed against my forehead. My eyes widened even more when he tugged me against his side, fingers toying with mine. From the corner of my eye, I spotted the curiosity in Tessa's gaze as she slanted a quick glance over her shoulder before she ran back up the stairs. When I turned back to Ms. Anne, she just smiled knowingly.

"Let me go check on these biscuits."

"What are you doing?" I whispered when Ms. Anne retreated into the kitchen. Lathan merely hiked a brow, waiting for me to clarify. I glanced around again, making sure we were still alone before huffing. "You're being... touchy with me right now. In front of your family. In front of your *daughter*."

That same brow remained raised as he gripped the front of my shirt, tugging me back into his arms. "Less than two hours ago, I had my mouth all over you. Now you want me to treat you like a stranger?"

I shook my head. "No, that's not what I want." When he continued waiting in silence, another frustrated sigh left my lips.

I wasn't familiar with this. *Any* of this. I didn't know or understand how this shit worked.

Shouldn't he continue treating me as his client around his family before she got any ideas about our relationship status? Shouldn't he try to shield our newfound connection from his daughter so he'd have time to explain it to her first?

I was lost in what to do and how to react and it was making me panicky.

"Relax." He urged, skating his thumb across my cheek. "*Breathe.* Stop overthinking shit. We enjoyed ourselves last night. We're going to enjoy ourselves this morning eating breakfast with my family. And I plan on enjoying the hell out of you later at our next *exploration* session, babe."

"Son, help your Uncle Lester pull the cooler out of his truck before he throws his damn back out." Ms. Anna ordered, reappearing in the doorway.

Lathan chuckled and nodded. "Yes, ma'am." Before walking off, he tucked one of my stray curls behind my ear, watching me with tenderness in his gaze that I hadn't expected. I couldn't recall ever being on the receiving end of a look like that. "Relax, okay?" I nodded and he smiled, pressing a kiss on my lips that had my eyes bucking wide.

"Well... that's quite a change from yesterday, hmm?" Ms. Anne asked from behind me after Lathan was gone.

My cheeks heated as I whirled to face his mom. I expected... nastiness or judgment in her brown gaze but I found neither. That same unbridled kindness was directed at me as she smiled. "Can you cook, Remedy?"

Though I hadn't made a meal for myself in years, I knew how to. I'd learned by spending time with Ms. Charlotte, one of the maternal figures back in Uptown. She'd been someone who looked out for the kids in the neighborhood and continued to be a staple in our lives well into adulthood.

She used to come to my home, just like she did Verse, and

prepared meals and cleaned for me. But driving so far out of the city had become too difficult for her, especially since she now had custody of her grandkids.

So, I'd told her she didn't need to come out anymore, even though I still slipped that same salary into her account each month. Each of her grandkids had a high six-figure balance in accounts I'd set aside for them that they'd gain access to at eighteen.

It wasn't necessarily for college because I understood that wasn't a path everyone wanted to take. I understood the importance of not getting into debt early because it could take years to pull yourself out of it.

Not enough of *our* kids had the resources to give them a head start in life that so many of their counterparts did, so I wanted to combat that.

They could travel, go to school, start a business... do whatever they want without having to ask for a dime from anyone.

"I'll take your silence as a no." Ms. Anne said with a chuckle, startling me from my thoughts.

"I'm sorry." I apologized, eyes falling to my hands. "I know how to cook."

Her smile brightened as she loosely looped her arm through mine. "You mind helping me in the kitchen, baby? All the time those kids of ours spent in the kitchen growing up and not a single one of their asses learned how to cook." The way her lips pursed as if in displeasure had me fighting a laugh. "It's *embarrassing*. They can't even boil a damn egg."

She huffed, guiding us through the house into the kitchen where the sweet scent of the icing she'd poured over cinnamon rolls filled the air. "I've been the head of the kitchen committee at my church for thirty-five years, Remedy. I won at the best dessert contest nine years in a row."

My eyes stayed fastened on her face, unable to look away at the woman who spoke to and treated me like just another member of the family.

"It would've been ten years but that Bernice Roberson won last year." She sniffed indignantly, slanting a side eye in my direction. "I know that bitch bought a cake from that dessert shop on 34th Street and pretended it was hers. There's no *way* Bernice's non-baking ass made a pound cake that damn moist."

I had no clue what she was talking about or who the hell Bernice Roberson was but the animation with which she told the story had me pressing a hand over my lips, fighting off a giggle.

Her eyes crinkled in the corners with amusement as she laughed at herself before waving a hand in the air. "I said all of that to say... cooking is in my blood. It's in my sister's blood. It's in my brother's blood. It's in my husband's blood. And not one of them sorry ass nieces and nephews of mine... or my child knows their way around the kitchen. I don't know how the hell that happened but I promised my grandbaby wouldn't be like them. That girl can throw down in the kitchen."

My brows hiked in surprise but again I remained silent.

"You don't talk much, do you?"

"*Nope.*" We both turned to find Tessa strolling in, this time with her phone and charger in tow. "Getting her to engage with you is like pulling teeth with tweezers." My cheeks heated at the observation from the teenager who'd only been around a week but already had me pegged. "But I don't mind," she continued, shrugging her shoulders. "She's cool and I talk enough for the both of us."

"That you do." Lathan offered as he walked in with a cooler in his hands. Lester wasn't far behind, face contorted in a grimace as he rubbed at his back.

"Lester, go sit down. You haven't done shit but get on everybody's nerves."

Chuckling at the insult from his sister, he straightened and crossed the room, peeking over her shoulder at the feast being prepared. "What's taking so long for the food, Annie?" I'd questioned the nickname when he'd called her that yesterday. Lathan had explained it was from childhood and only Lester still used it to aggravate her.

Rolling her eyes, she pulled the towel off her shoulders, twisting it around until it formed a thin rope. "If you want to complain about how long it takes, you oughta come *help*."

Lester chuckled, tossing an arm across his sister's shoulders, ignoring her grimace. "No thank you. It'll be a mass funeral instead of a family reunion if I cook."

Just like yesterday, watching this family dynamic, being witness to the way they interacted, was fascinating.

I enjoyed seeing family like this and could only imagine how fun each generation's childhood was if they'd been close back then.

"You still helping me, baby?"

Ms. Anne's polite question drew me from my introspection and my eyes sprang up to meet hers. Piercing brown eyes surveyed me with expectancy and I smiled, joining her at the stove.

Unable to resist, I flashed one quick glance at Lathan over my shoulder. He stood in the doorway, engaged in conversation with Tessa and Lester. His head tilted towards them, indicating he was listening but his gaze remained on me.

"I got started early, so there's not much to do." Ms. Anne said, flipping the towel back over her shoulder. "If you can fry these last few pieces of bacon and scramble the eggs, then we'll be finished in no time. You okay with that?"

Again, I glanced over my shoulder, finding the handsome man's gaze locked on me and his mother.

Almost imperceptibly, his tongue peeked, swiping slowly against the inside of his bottom lip before a slow wink had me sucking in a low breath.

Needing to shake the effect he had on me, I turned back to his mother. "Yes, ma'am."

20

LATHAN

She was so damn beautiful.

When we'd called my mom to let her know we'd made it back to Sienna Falls, she'd gushed over Remedy and how well Tessa had taken to her.

I was both surprised and pleased by that revelation, too. Tessa wasn't overly friendly and didn't take to strangers easily.

But Remedy, who did nothing to make herself palatable to others, had somehow earned her trust.

And despite that, the woman still saw herself as unlikable.

I'd noticed the way she'd tensed before I introduced her to people, as if preparing herself for their immediate dislike or scorn. She'd conditioned herself to expect dislike in every situation and I couldn't help but to feel sad for her.

This woman deserved so much more than the cards she'd been dealt.

Obviously, she'd experienced something traumatizing and had coped and protected herself the best way she knew. She didn't deserve to be punished for it.

What she deserved was the smiles and laughter that had creased her cheeks and lifted her lips in Huntsville.

She deserved to feel comfortable and take part in harmless teasing with people who liked her, frown and all.

She deserved everything that would make her days peaceful.

And though I wouldn't go far enough to guarantee anything, I'd try my hardest to give her what I could.

As if she sensed that she was dominating my thoughts, a frown disturbed her sleep and she shifted before relaxing.

Like clockwork, I'd gotten up early to take Tess to school before coming back here and slipping in bed behind her.

Before her incident with her heart, Rem was always up before the crack of dawn, getting ready to head into work way earlier than necessary. But now, since she'd been on a forced hiatus, she was sleeping in more, *actually resting*, which I was grateful for because she'd needed it.

If her heart hadn't slowed her down, I was sure exhaustion would've caught up with her eventually.

Leaning over, I pressed a kiss against the curve of her shoulder, smiling to myself when she moaned in her sleep.

Last week, when we'd been in the hotel in Huntsville, she'd told me she was too uncomfortable to sleep naked. Yet, here she was, snoring lightly, with not a stitch of clothing on like she'd done every night since we'd returned from the family reunion.

And at the end of each night, when Tessa was settled in the bedroom at the far end of the hall or staying with her mom, this was where I ended up, in bed with her.

In just the five days we'd been back, I'd seen progression with us.

Remedy was less reserved with me. More bold and vocal with what she wanted.

We still hadn't graduated to penetration and I wouldn't push her before she was ready. I enjoyed seeing her come into her sexuality during this exploration and would gladly stay in this phase with her as long as she needed me to.

I reached out, prepared to ease her onto her back so I could wake her in her favorite way... with my head between her legs.

Before I could, my phone rang on the nightstand. Irritation flooded me at the terrible timing and I briefly considered letting it ring.

But I was a parent, so that wasn't an option. I always had to be available.

"Hello?"

"Mr. Calloway?"

I frowned, not recognizing the young, spirited voice on the other end of the line. "Yes?"

"Hi, I'm Brooke. I'm calling from the administrative office at T. L. Heights Academy." I rolled my eyes at the name of Tessa's school. If she'd gotten into some more shit, I was going to be livid.

"Okay."

"There was... an altercation in her first period class and we were wondering if you were available to come up to the school to speak with the principal regarding this incident?"

"*An altercation?*" I cut my eyes back to Rem, who'd shifted in her sleep but still hadn't woken up. I guess sucking my dick like a pro last night had worn her out.

"A um...." The woman's words trailed and she cleared her throat. "A physical altercation."

"Is she okay?"

"Oh, yes. Tessa's fine." She said before clearing her throat. "It's the... other student that I'm more concerned about."

I sighed. So Tessa had beaten some kid's ass.

Jesus, this child of mine was trying her *best* to send me to an early grave.

After thanking Brooke for her call, I rolled from the bed, padding around the bedroom barefoot, just as comfortable in here now as I was in my own space.

After getting dressed, I sat next to Rem on the side of her bed, admiring her once more before tracing my hand down her side. This time her eyes fluttered open, glancing around the room before settling on me with a smile that hit me right in the chest.

"Hey." She whispered; lids still heavy from the sleep I'd disturbed.

"I've gotta go."

"Um hmm." She mumbled, lids dropping closed once more.

I smiled. "I have to go up to Tessa's school to deal with something. Might swing by Gabbi's on my way back, okay?"

She nodded, peeking her eyes open again. With that heavy-lidded look, I knew that Rem hadn't processed a damn thing I'd said.

Not wanting to disturb her further, I leaned over and pressed a kiss against her lips, hating that I had to pull away moments later. After making sure I had what I needed, I glanced back in her direction, finding her watching me with a soft smile.

And at that moment, I wanted nothing more than to climb back into bed with her. But I couldn't. I had a wayward ass child I needed to check on.

Dammit, Tessa.

21

REMEDY

"Have you ever been in a fight?"

I froze in the middle of putting away my clothes, not expecting to hear Tessa's voice behind me.

I hadn't heard them come in after Lathan left to get her from school and assumed I was still alone but the pitchy voice from behind me proved otherwise. My eyes were wide as I tracked her across the room, watching as she dropped her bookbag near the door as if she'd done it hundreds of times.

Then, she kicked off her shoes before climbing right in the middle of my bed, making herself at home.

Since our moment at the family reunion, she'd sought me out often, drawing me into reluctant dialogue, easily dominating the flow of our conversations, which I didn't mind.

"Have I what?"

"Ever been in a fight, Ms. Remy?"

I still didn't understand why she'd decided on the childhood nickname rather than the three-letter version of my name but again... I didn't mind. Tessa seemed to be the exception to a lot of my rules.

Much like her father was.

"Nope."

"*Never?*" she asked incredulously.

I shook my head again. "Fighting normally has a prerequisite of actually talking to and interacting with people and I don't enjoy doing that."

Her carefree laugh trickled out and I smiled, turning back to the clothes on the bed, sorting them in neat piles. Several minutes passed before I glanced up at the teen, who hadn't said another word, disturbed by the frown on her face.

"What's wrong?"

"Nothing."

I pursed my lips, knowing better than most that *nothing* spoken in that tone most definitely meant something. "What is it?"

Her gaze dropped while she toyed with her fingers, mumbling in a tone so low I had to strain to hear. "I love my dad and my mom but... they don't see me."

I felt a jolt in my chest from the familiarity of those words.

From what I've gathered, Tessa was a teen who'd lost her father for nearly a decade and was raised by a mother stretched so thin that she often got lost in the shuffle.

Now that her father's back, she just wants to be seen. By him, by *anybody*. Much like I had.

I'd wanted my dad, Verse, Hakeem, Gia, my neighbors, my teachers... *anyone* to see my pain and help me through it.

But no one ever did.

"My mom... she... I love her and I know she's overwhelmed with my sisters and brothers but... I'm not their *mom* and sometimes I feel like I am. I'm sixteen, Ms. Remy. But I spend more time with them than she does because she's always working. I want to have fun and I feel guilty because she needs my help."

"And your dad?"

"He's overcompensating." Her words were coming faster now, less hesitant, as if the seal had been broken and she couldn't stop them from spilling out. "He's so busy trying to make up for the time lost that he's missing out on who I am now. He doesn't *know* who I am now because he's still trying to be a dad to the baby I was when he got locked up."

Her words trailed but I remained quiet, sensing she was gathering her thoughts.

"I know I've been acting out and making things harder on them but... I'm *angry*. All the time. I want my mom to know that I'm not just a live-in babysitter and I want my dad to see that I'm sixteen. Not *two*."

"And your grandma?"

"I don't want shit from her. She's a witch."

"*Tessa*." I scolded, biting my lip and fighting the urge to laugh.

"You met her. You know I'm not lying. She's evil."

At that very moment, I saw so much of myself in her.

I'd never considered myself a role model, nor have I ever wanted to be one. The only children I'd been around were Verse's nephew, Junior, and Truth and Capri's kids, Savannah and Zaire.

But even then, it was only for birthday parties and special events where I felt obligated to show my face. Because of my... *personality deficiencies*, none of the kids had truly taken to me. Not like they'd done to the others in my circle. The kids were always polite and respectful. Hell, they even called me Auntie Rem, but that familial bond they'd developed with the other people in my tribe had always been absent when they interacted with me.

And though I'd never told a soul, it bothered me. A lot, even if I knew I caused it.

So having this teenager who I didn't even know existed a month ago take to me so quickly and want to be near me despite being fully aware of my disposition softened my heart towards her.

"So what should I do?" She asked hesitantly, still toying with her fingers.

"Be honest. Tell them the truth. Don't hold it in." I gave her advice that I wish someone would've given me. "Holding it in hurts and will eat at you until it consumes your entire life." I forced a smile, hoping to lighten the moment that was growing too heavy. "Tell them how you feel, Tessa. If you don't, you'll end up like me." I said with a laugh, though I was completely serious.

I thought that was the end of the conversation, so I turned to my dresser, placing my underwear back in their color coordinated slots.

"I wouldn't mind ending up like you, Ms. Remy." She said in a soft tone that made my heart skip a beat. "You're not so bad."

22

LATHAN

I'd taken Dr. Tessa's advice and worked on taking my ego out of interactions and conversations with Tessa.

She didn't respond well to being yelled or fussed at, so I'd switched up my approach, hoping it would make her more comfortable sharing or being open with me.

"Children aren't a monolith." She'd informed me in our last session, voice as calm as ever. *"Just like adults aren't. Forcing a certain parenting style on a child just because it's what you were used to, or it's what you responded to growing up doesn't make it right. Your job is to learn your child, be in tune with her emotions and figure out which parenting style is comfortable for both you and her so the lines of communication can stay open. Being too forceful with a sensitive child or being too lax with a wild one can be the quickest way to lose them. Don't let your pride and ego ruin your second chance with her."*

"Can we talk?" I finally broke the silence Tessa and I had sat in since she'd come downstairs from Remedy's room. Whatever conversation that passed between them seemed to have lifted the solemn mood she'd been in when we returned home with a three-day suspension letter in hand.

The entire ride from her school, neither of us had exchanged a word.

I expected her to say no like always whenever I wanted to talk but shock momentarily rendered me speechless when she nodded.

I schooled my expression to hide my reaction before diverting us past the foyer and through the large living room until we entered the kitchen.

"Hey, Ms. Isabel." Tessa said softly as we passed her coming from the laundry room.

The woman Remedy had gotten the bulk of her beauty from smiled back, reaching out to tug on a lock of Tessa's hair playfully. "Hey, sweet girl." Her soft gaze swung to mine and her lips twisted up ruefully. "Hey, Lathan."

Returning the smile, I greeted her before ushering my child out the back door to the patio before she got distracted by the aroma of the food Ms. Isabel cooked.

I'd barely had time to get comfortable in my seat before Tessa spoke. "Sometimes I don't know how to feel around you."

My brows shot up, surprised she'd broached the subject without me having to nudge her into it. My planned topic was getting to the bottom of why she was fighting in school but if she wanted to start with the issues that had been plaguing us for so long, I was game.

"Really?" I reclined in my seat, hoping the relaxed posture made her comfortable. It was hard to diminish six and a half feet of bulk and muscle but I hoped the calmness I felt internally was enough to rub off on her so we could have this conversation.

She sucked her teeth, struggling to find the right words. "Like... I *know* you're my dad. And I love you, I *really* do. But... sometimes I remember how it felt when you were out of my life for so long. Even though you're here *now*, I still have moments where I remember what it felt like when you weren't. So I get angry and I lash out. Or I act out. And if someone says something to pis-" She paused when I lifted a brow before she smiled sheepishly. "I mean, if they make me mad, I tap into that anger and lose it or make bad decisions. That girl today was picking on me but not bad enough for me to put these paws on her. But I couldn't *help* myself."

The urge to smile or laugh was strong but I resisted, dropping my head so I wouldn't have to look at her silly ass.

"Tessa." I warned, finally feeling composed enough to meet her gaze.

"It's okay, Daddy. You can laugh. I *know* I'm funny."

This time, I couldn't resist a chuckle.

I'll be damned if this girl wasn't Gabbi 2.0.

Before life, love, and relationships had worn Gabbi down, the feisty spirit housed in the teen sitting across from me was the same one that had drawn me to her mom.

Gabbi had been a firecracker and kept me on my toes.

Motherhood, a divorce, and age had calmed that spirit but I knew it was still there.

Not wanting to get too far off the subject, I repeated the statement she'd spoken before her joke. When she nodded, glancing down with guilt, I leaned forward, cupping her chin across the table until her eyes met mine.

"It's *okay* to be angry with me."

"But I shouldn't." She fired back. "You're here now. What do I have to be mad about? My grandma told me I'm an ungrateful brat and I should be glad my dad is in my life at all because some don't even have that. And she's right. So, when I remember that, I feel guilty for being mad about something that happened so long ago."

God, if there was a way I could make sure Tessa never has to spend time with Ms. Gloria again, I would.

She was a vile human, one who thrived on belittling and hurting others. I don't know what happened to her in her past to make her that way but it was ridiculous how little she cared for the emotional wellbeing of her daughter or grandkids.

"Someone else's misfortune is not a reason for you to diminish your own feelings and emotions. There is always going to be someone worse off than you, but that doesn't mean the way you feel isn't valid, Tessa. *It is.*" Her face contorted as if she didn't believe me so I continued. "You want to vent because you broke a nail, do it. You want to be upset because your favorite tv series got canceled, do it. You want to cry or be angry because your father made a stupid decision that got him taken away and locked up for ten years, then *do* it. Don't hide your feelings or hold stuff in because of someone else's opinion. Besides, those feelings about me being in jail? They're not going to go away overnight, even if I *am* back. It's going to take time to work through that. Hell, I still struggle with it myself sometimes."

My hand swiped across my mouth, waiting for her to lift her gaze from the tabletop before I continued.

"But what I want you to do when you feel that way is to come talk to me. I understand having a *rebellious teen phase* and all that," I laughed when she playfully rolled her eyes. "I had one too but putting yourself in dangerous situations can't keep happening, Tessa. That *has* to change. That and the fighting."

She nodded but I could still see that shaking the conditioning of Ms. Gloria's words wouldn't to be that easy.

"Let me make this clear for you. I made a mistake and was locked up for it. I left *you*. You didn't leave me, so any guilt in this situation is solely on *my* shoulders. You shouldn't feel guilty for something you didn't do." My fingers drummed against the tabletop. "My goal is to raise you to be the healthiest, happiest, most whole human being you can be. So if there's anything that I'm doing to hinder that, let me know. I'm not like your Grandma Gloria. I don't believe a child should be *seen and not heard*. That's bullshit. You have feelings and emotions just like I do, and I want you to trust me with them."

Another nod was the response I got but this time, my words seemed to penetrate. I allowed her to work through her thoughts, choosing to keep silent as a rolodex of emotions crossed her face. This went on for several seconds before I tensed after spotting that sneaky ass smile I've come to be leery of. "What, Tessa?"

"Can I ask you a question?" At my tight nod, she leaned forward, planting her elbows on the table and whispering conspiratorially. "What's up with you and Ms. Remy?"

Ignoring the way my gut flip-flopped, I leaned forward and mimicked her position, using a phrase Rem had tossed at me multiple times. "None of your nosy ass business."

She burst into laughter and I couldn't help joining her, enjoying the unfiltered joy on her pretty face.

"A'ight, Daddy." She said through her laughter. "You know I'll find out."

Keeping my expression blank, I stretched, hooking the legs of her chair with my feet, and tilting it far enough to give her a scare.

"*Daddy!*"

I chuckled, letting it back down, yanking my legs back to my side of the table, barely missing the vicious kick she sent my way.

"Play too much," she playfully scolded. "But I like Ms. Remy." She added.

My brows lifted. "You do?" Saying Tessa was slow to warm up to people was an understatement. She preferred keeping her distance which was why I'd been so shocked when she sought Remedy out so often since we got back from Huntsville.

"Yep." She said as we stood. I waited, watching her lift her book bag from the concrete to swing it over her shoulders. "I like the way she speaks. I like how... when she says something, it's not just to appease me because I'm a *child*. She's extremely honest and blunt and I like her. I like her for you too."

I tensed. Though I hadn't been actively trying to hide my new... *situation* with Rem or my feelings for her, I also hadn't been openly flaunting it in Tessa's face either. The last thing I'd wanted was to cause confusion for her during such a difficult time.

"And you're okay with that?" At one point, when I was first released, she'd wanted Gabbi and I to reconcile and had become even more angry after learning that wasn't going to happen.

"Why wouldn't I be?" She shrugged. "She's a baddie. She's dope. She's rich." Her gaze turned sly and I tensed in preparation of the wild shit about to leave her lips. "She can elevate you, Daddy. Lord knows you need it." Offense contorted my features as I stopped in the doorway, staring at her back.

"She can *what?*"

"Elevate you. *Upgrade* you. Ms. Remy is a *boss*, daddy, so if you're trying to be with her, that means you can't half step. You've gotta meet her on her level. *Period.*"

I cringed when she sang the last word in a high pitch.

I can't believe she tried me like I was *corny*. Telling me I needed to be upgraded and elevated.

Who the hell did this kid think she was?

"Don't be mad, Dad." She continued in that sing-songy voice. "Elevation is a good thing. Leave your dusty past behind and get with the winning te—" Her words broke off into reams of laughter when I made a move to grab her, managing to grip only the dangling straps of her bookbag before losing my grip.

I was going to strangle that girl.

23

REMEDY

"Forty-eight hours is all it takes..."

My fingers stopped twirling around my curls and I lifted a brow, turning my head towards Lathan, who quietly sang along with the music Tessa had connected to the car's speaker.

For the past ten minutes, we rode in Lathan's souped-up black on black Jeep, heading towards an unknown destination.

Well, it was only unknown to me and Tessa, who sat in the backseat quietly.

When Lathan normally chauffeured me around, he drove one of the inconspicuous black SUVs parked in my four-car garage.

Today was my first-time riding in his personal vehicle and I had to admit that I was enjoying the experience. The Jeep was lifted several inches higher off the ground than normal, so I'd needed help climbing into the passenger seat. Once settled, my eyes took in the black and chrome interior that looked like one of the vehicles on those popular car renovation shows.

Tessa was used to riding in it, so she'd hopped in with ease, immediately leaning between the front seats to plug her phone into the charger port.

Since leaving my house, I'd alternated between trying to figure out where we were going and watching him. He seemed so at ease, maneuvering through the streets in a slightly slouched position that only increased my attraction to him. His left arm rested on the door, propped up so his hand had easy access to toying with his beard. The other was tossed lazily over the top of the steering wheel, using the bottom of his palm to navigate rather than his fingers.

Sensing my eyes on him, he looked over, lips lifting in a smile that caused an inferno down below. Turning back to face the road, he had the nerve to chuckle.

The asshole was fully aware of what he'd caused.

To me, the progression of our relationship felt swift and I still hadn't had enough time to settle into it.

One moment, I was doing my best to remain distant and the next thing I knew, I was riding his face in a hotel in Huntsville.

After our *sexual* relationship began, I eagerly gave into the lust, feeding a physical need for release I'd denied for so long.

But this attraction I felt for him now was... *different,* because it had nothing to do with the ache between my thighs that flared to life each time he was around. This ache firmly lived in my chest and it was such a foreign feeling that I feared speaking or even thinking about it too much would jinx us.

God, I was terrified of what I felt.

I did nothing in half measures, so when Lathan cracked open the safe around my heart and snuck in, the immediate feelings I experienced were too big, too soon, and overwhelming.

Times like these, I wish I hadn't pushed away every single person I cared about because advice about how to navigate this shit would be so helpful right now.

I was in uncharted territory.

Or *up shit's creek without a paddle,* as my grandma used to say.

"You okay?"

His voice jerked me from my introspection and I turned from the passing scenery I hadn't been paying any attention to. "Hmm?"

"You okay?" He repeated with hiked brows. "You look like something's on your mind."

It was but I wasn't ready to reveal that yet. Any of it.

Especially with his nosy teen in the backseat, hanging on to our every word.

"I'm fine."

Instead of satisfying him, my words deepened his frown. I forgot he now knew that my customary *I'm fine* was bullshit. Normally, he'd call me on it but our captive audience in the backseat had him pressing his lips together and nodding.

His eyes lingered on mine as he waited for the light to change. Without him saying a word, I knew he was conveying he'd bring it up later when we were alone.

I damn sure wasn't looking forward to that conversation.

When he eased the truck through the green light, I switched my attention back to the passing scenery, focusing on Sienna Falls as it woke up.

It was still early in the morning, not quite eight, so traffic was light on the road.

Though a self-proclaimed morning person, the time I'd spent away from work had made me lazy and not wanting to get up early unless I had an appointment scheduled. Unless Lathan's head was buried between my thighs, since my medical hiatus, I didn't rise out of bed a minute before ten.

Tessa and I both had been grumpy as hell when he'd woken us up before seven and told us to get dressed.

"Where are we going?" My partner in crime asked for the third time.

"You'll see." He said cryptically.

My first two attempts to find out had received similar unhelpful responses, so I'd given up, trying not to obsess over it.

"Ms. Remy?" Tessa asked, turning her attention on me. She'd been so quiet for much of the ride that at times, I'd almost forgotten she was back there.

"Yes?"

"What are you?"

I glanced at her over my shoulder at the same time Lathan did, lifting my brows high at the random question. "What... *am I?*"

"Um hmm." I didn't understand what she was asking, so I tilted my head, waiting for her to elaborate. "Are you mixed?" She asked before correcting herself. "Biracial, I mean. Or are you black?"

"Jesus Christ." Lathan muttered, shaking. "Who *raised* you?"

"You." She shot back easily and I pressed my lips together to keep from laughing at the annoyed expression he shot her in the rearview mirror.

"I'm black." When she merely narrowed her gaze, I answered the unspoken question. "My mom is biracial." I supplied, hoping that answer would suffice. But of course, because this was Tessa and she was Lathan's daughter, it didn't.

"And your dad?"

"My dad was black." I said in a much quieter tone.

"Was?"

"*Tessa.*" Lathan's tone was a warning.

Instead of heeding it, her eyes bucked and her shoulders lifted as if she was prepared to argue, so I laid a calming hand on his forearm. "It's fine." Again, I turned to give her my gaze, barely resisting the urge to smile at the blatant curiosity in her expression. "He died when I was seventeen."

There was a long bit of silence and I thought that might have been the end of her line of questioning.

I was wrong.

"What happened to him?"

"*Contessa.*"

"He was shot." I said softly, flashing her a weak smile before Lathan could scold her further.

"So..."

"No more questions." Lathan said shortly. "Besides, we're here anyway."

Both of us whipped our heads around and frowned, disappointed at the huge empty parking lot of a shopping center.

He got us up at the ass crack of dawn for *this*?

"What are we doing here?" I asked, unable to hide the annoyance in my tone.

"Driving lessons." He answered while unbuckling his seatbelt before looking over his shoulder at his daughter, who'd gone from disappointed to excitement in a split second. "Come up here, T."

When they both exited the car, I hesitated before doing the same, climbing into the backseat so Lathan could ride shotgun.

My disappointment gave way to amusement when Tessa eagerly climbed behind the wheel of the massive truck, not showing an ounce of fear as she adjusted her mirrors and slid the seat forward several inches.

After listening to Lathan's instructions, she nodded, placed the truck in drive, then effortlessly maneuvered it with an ease that made me realize this wasn't her first time behind the wheel.

Last night, after stepping into my room after a long bath, I'd found her stretched across the foot of my bed again. I'd been tired and wanted to fall right asleep but I sat next to her, eagerly listening as she spoke about her upcoming birthday and the gifts she wanted.

A car.

Tickets to see R&B singer Gideon in concert.

And a spa day at Serenity for her and her friends.

That last one had been tossed out with a sly smile. She'd seen me wearing the customized robe I owned with their logo on it. Stripping down and letting someone rub their hands on my body had been a *hard no* for me but I visited the spa a few times a year for a basic mani-pedi when the woman I'd hired to do them at my home was unavailable.

"Damn, Tessa. *Slow down.*"

Instead of heeding his warning, she giggled, still weaving the big truck easily through the winding pathways he'd created with the large orange cones he'd pulled from the back of the jeep after she'd complained that driving around the empty parking lot was too easy.

I fought my laughter when he repeated it in a strained voice.

Until this point, Lathan had been patient in his instructions.

It was endearing to watch his calm parenting style, even though I still didn't understand why he'd invited me for what should've been a private lesson.

I leaned forward, watching as Tessa perfectly executed parallel parking between two cones before chuckling under my breath when she danced with her tongue out to the rap song playing on the radio.

"A'ight," Lathan scolded, smacking the button on the console to submerge us in silence. "You can cut that *hot girl* shit out."

Tessa giggled again and leaned over, pressing a kiss against his cheek. "Thanks, Daddy. I had fun."

Though he tried to hide it, I spotted the blush that stained Lathan's cheeks. My smile dropped when she unbuckled and got out while Lathan stayed put.

"Come up here, Rem."

I frowned, scooting over the seat and out the door that Tessa held open.

"Why?" He didn't say a word. Only nodded towards the open driver's door. "Oh *hell* no."

He remained unphased by my refusal. "If I remember correctly, Verse told me you don't know how to drive, right?"

I don't but that didn't mean I had a desire to learn.

So much time had passed since I'd got my learner's permit that I just resigned myself to never learning the skill and used driving services to get me around.

Like always, my dad had been too busy to teach me and he'd refused to pay for lessons, so he'd tasked his closest friends with the job.

The same friends who violated me each time he wasn't around. Obviously, I'd declined, throwing a fuss so big that he'd told them not to worry about it since I was being a spoiled brat.

That was a term he hurled at me often, usually when I made a big deal about him leaving me all the time.

"You're being selfish, Remedy. These kids don't have a parent who can provide whatever they want like you do. Nobody spoils them and buys them whatever the hell they want, whenever they want it. That's a luxury that you have and instead of being grateful, you're being selfish when I try to help other parents make their kids' lives better. I'm disappointed in you."

He'd made me feel guilty for wanting him around. He'd made me feel guilty for not caring about the material things he surrounded me with. I wasn't acting out or demanding his time out of *selfishness*.

I'd wanted my dad around to love and protect me at the same level he'd done for the kids who weren't related to him.

But I never gathered up the nerve to tell him my secret, so he never saw it that way.

I'd missed out on a lot of the things and experiences he gave to other kids. Though I was glad he was a positive influence in Uptown, did my happiness have to be the cost for the difference he made?

"Stop overthinking it and *get in*."

I huffed and climbed behind the wheel, tucking my hands between my thighs, refusing to touch anything. Though the urge to snap at being pushed from my comfort zone was strong, I held it back and looked into his calming eyes, feeling the tension seep from me. "All of that space back at the house and you brought us to a parking lot?" I asked in a strained, teasing voice.

"We're *starting* in the parking lot, Rem." He said with a chuckle, looking far too relaxed for a man who wanted to place his child's life in my hands. "Then we're getting on the road."

"Excuse me?" I shrilled, "You want me to drive on the road? *Today?*" My heart threatened to pound right out of my chest. "What if I hit something?"

"It's just a truck, Rem. If you ding it up, I'll get it fixed. No big deal."

If I *ding* it like he said, of course I'd foot the bill for repairs since

I'm the one that caused them. But the fear of doing any damage in the first place had me nervous and on edge.

"This is a mistake. You're crazy if you think I can do this."

I twisted to climb out of the open door but stopped when his hand wrapped around my elbow. When I looked back, he smiled, slipping his hand over my arm down to my wrist, tugging gently.

Reluctantly, I slid back into the car, facing forward with arms hanging limp by my side. Neither of them spoke, sensing I needed a moment to settle the surge of panic I'd felt a moment ago.

Lathan's hand remained on mine and the longer we sat there, the more I felt that familiar sense of calmness only he could invoke.

"Just relax." He urged, tapping his index finger against the skin covering my wild pulse. "You're not going to suddenly be a Nascar driver on your first try. Just ask Tessa."

I heard her suck her teeth from the backseat and my lips twitched with amusement. "Sure, go ahead and tell her." She said in a tone so sarcastic even Lathan had to smile. "You've only told *everybody*."

Now I *had* to know. Bouncing my gaze between the two of them, I asked. "What happened?"

"I took her to an empty parking lot near Gabbi's house." Lathan readjusted in his seat, slouching in that relaxed way I associated with him. "The parking lot was *huge*. Even bigger than this one. And we were the *only* car out there. Two light poles sat in the center of the parking lot and somehow she managed to hit not one but *both* of them. She only love tapped the first one. But she panicked, put it in reverse, then stomped the gas, flying backwards and hitting the only other object in the whole parking lot."

He broke off telling the story, loud laughter filling the cab of the truck as Tessa sulked in the backseat.

"Go ahead. Get your laughs out." She quipped before turning to me. "He's up there *he-he-he'ing* now but he was pissed that day."

"Only because you were doing the exact opposite of what I said. I know the truck can be fixed but *damn*. There's only two pedals and you kept hitting the *wrong one*."

"I panicked!" She defended herself. Tendrils of laughter now coated her tone and she tried to fight her smile. "Besides, who in their right mind takes a fifteen-year-old to practice driving in a monster truck?"

Enjoying their banter, I rested my back against the driver's seat, smiling when Tessa leaned between the two front seats, resting her elbow inches from my head.

"First, it's not a monster truck. I just had the Jeep lifted to match my size." He ignored her eye roll. "Second, it didn't take long to realize I should've started you a bit smaller, so I got over it. Right?"

"You don't think I should start smaller, too?"

His eyes swept over me after my question and though there wasn't a hint of seduction in his tone, I felt the suggestiveness when he said, "I think you can handle it."

"Was that a sex joke?"

Lathan broke our connection, whipping his head around so fast that even I had to join in with Tessa's loud laughter. "Con-"

"*Tessa Calloway.*" She finished for him in a tone that mocked his deep tenor. "I'm joking, Daddy, *gosh.*"

Lord, he had his hands full with her.

Too soon for me, their cute moment ended and identical brown eyes swung to mine.

"Ready, Ms. Remy?" Tessa asked before her father could. "I mean, you can't get worse than hitting two poles in an empty parking lot."

"That's true." I agreed before snorting when Tessa let out an offended squeak. As I tried to weigh the pros and cons, I squirmed under the intensity of their stares before sighing. "If I don't think I'm ready to get on the road, you promise not to force me?"

Lathan's expression gentled and his hands twitched as if he wanted to touch me but had decided to keep them to himself. Probably because Tessa watched the two of us like a hawk. "You know I won't push you for more than you're ready for. If getting on the road makes you uncomfortable, we'll save it for another day. There's no rush, babe."

I cut my eyes to Tessa, gauging her reaction to the endearment he'd let slip. But like every time he'd shown affection towards me, her eyes lit up with an unnamed emotion and a sly smile lifted her lips.

I think it was safe to say she was Team Remedy and Lathan.

"So, what do you say?" She asked. "You doing this or what?"

I licked my lips, switching my gaze over to the bright orange cones of the makeshift course before nodding. "Let's do it."

MY BODY ACHED DELICIOUSLY when I woke early the next morning.

Low groans expelled from my lips as I stretched tired limbs before turning away from the light peeking through the sheer panels leading to my second-floor patio and faced Lathan, who still hadn't woken up.

Yesterday's impromptu driving lesson had resulted in me having more fun than I'd had in years. I hadn't hit two light poles like Tessa but I'd flattened a couple of cones before finally getting the hang of it.

He'd taken both of us on the road and though Tessa was a *far* better driver, I'd enjoyed the time away from the house and looked forward to our next lesson.

Not wanting our time to end, we'd stayed out most of the day, letting Tessa dictate how we spent the day.

By the time we'd dropped her off at home to babysit, it was nearly dark outside. My mom had cooked, so we'd eaten an awkward dinner with her before retiring to my bedroom to indulge in my new favorite pastime.

Exploring.

Every chance I got, I was pushing Lathan's head between my thighs and from the enthusiasm he displayed each time, he was just as eager as I was.

I was quickly becoming addicted to the way his tongue slid through my folds.

The way he groaned, as if each taste of me was the best thing to pass his lips.

The way his eyes remained on mine, gauging my reaction to the lewd display he put on between my thighs.

He was turning me into a sexual fiend, one who craved him *constantly*.

Skating my gaze over his handsome visage, I drank him in, paying attention to every minute detail I'd either ignored before or had been too lost in my own thoughts to notice.

His lips were pouty and full, specifically the bottom, which protruded more when he was asleep. The thick beard he once sported had been trimmed, revealing more of the mouth I was becoming obsessed with. Reddish undertones contributed to the rich, copper-ish complexion that seemed to go on for miles.

Thick muscles, which had never impressed me before, bulged in some places while appearing sleek and chiseled in others.

Lathan was a naturally large man, probably an inch shy of six and a half feet, but the sculptured frame inches from me came from hard work and dedication.

Two qualities I admired in the man while also baffling me.

He didn't run or flee like many others when I pushed them away.

He didn't argue back, excluding the light jabs and retorts he'd tossed my way when teasing.

He respected my... *triggers* and accommodated them rather than ridiculing or embarrassing me.

He was gentle in a way that I wasn't familiar with, yet still strong enough to lead without becoming overbearing.

I respected him, which wasn't hard to do because he made it easy. But what surprised me was that I *liked* him. That was a feat because Remedy Sinclair didn't like hardly anybody.

I didn't like people, in general.

People were fickle, self-serving, and would disappoint you often, so I kept my distance, even from those I loved and had spent much of my youth with.

But with Lathan, I felt none of the usual things I did when someone got too close.

There was a comfort with him I'd only felt with Verse.

And this bond had quickly usurped that one since Verse was now in a committed relationship. I wasn't mad at him for it. Not at all. I was happy that he'd found *the one* and understood that our relationship would change because the rare moments of free time he'd once spent checking in on me were now dedicated to the woman he loved.

I'd also known that Verse was the glue keeping me connected to the rest of the crew. Most of them tolerated me more than anything. I knew they cared about my wellbeing but not enough to see past my hard exterior.

They didn't look past the mask I wore to see the *real* me. But I could understand why and expected it to happen. I'd prepared myself for it.

But what I hadn't been prepared for was Lathan.

The man had seamlessly wormed his way in without me realizing, somehow making the distance in my relationships with my friends feel less painful since I wasn't completely alone.

I wasn't sure if we'd be here if I hadn't had another Lanhol's episode but for the first time, I was grateful for my condition because it gave me these experiences with him.

And though I didn't expect them to last—let's be honest, a man like Lathan would never be fully satisfied being tied down to a woman like me—I would cherish them.

Shifting, I slipped my arm from under his, reaching out. My hand hovered over his face, waiting to see if he would stir from the movements I made. When he didn't, I pressed the pad of two fingers under the small double-Cs tatted under his eye.

After meeting his daughter, I now knew what it stood for. *Contessa Calloway.*

He'd confirmed it for me when I asked last night, revealing he'd gotten it done his first few weeks in jail after being sentenced to fifteen years with the possibility of parole.

"*I felt sick to my stomach when those bars first closed behind me.*" He'd said, fingers tracing up and down my spine with gentleness as we basked in the aftermath of another *exploration* session that left both of us spent. "*I'd fucked up and was told I'd be locked away from my daughter for fifteen years. A stupid mistake robbed me of the chance of being the father she deserved. So, a guy in there did tats and I got her initials on my face. Every time I thought about reacting to someone violently or doing something in there that would get more time added to my sentence, I would touch the letters.*" He'd done it then, eyes focused on something above my head, brushing his fingertips back and forth against the tiny font. "*It always grounded me. Helped remind me I needed to get home to her and make better choices. So I did.*"

With gentle strokes, I trailed my fingers from the inked skin down bearded cheeks and across full lips. His lids fluttered before they parted just enough for the swirls of brown in his gaze became visible.

His brows furrowed as he tried to focus before a tired smile lifted his cheeks. The hand at my waist tightened and he drew me closer, placing a soft kiss on my forehead before his lids fell closed again.

Not even a minute later, soft snores greeted my ears.

With a snort of amusement, I rolled from under his grip and showered in my bathroom before dressing in a simple navy blue dress.

After peeking at his sleeping form again, I slipped on a pair of sandals before sneaking out of the main house over to the guest house he hadn't slept in for what felt like forever.

I beelined for his workroom, pulling out my phone and snapping photos of every completed sculpture before sending them in an email to Miranda with detailed instructions. The man was gifted and though he claimed it was just a hobby, I saw his passion each time he stepped into this room and knew there was no way I could let the art go unseen.

"What are you doing?"

I jumped and whirled, eyes falling to admire the hard planes of his body. He'd pulled on basketball shorts and... that's it.

Even his big feet were bare.

I rolled my eyes away from his, wondering how much he'd seen. "What?"

"*What?*" He mocked my soft answer and I rolled my eyes.

"Nothing." I said in my normal tone. "Just looking."

He looked around the room and wondered if something was out of place.

I kept my face carefully blank, hoping this wasn't one of the moments where he saw right through me.

After a second scan of the room brought up nothing unusual, his gaze swung to mine and I fought the urge to take a tiny step back. Each time we locked eyes, it had the same effect of his fingers softly caressing between my thighs.

Walking right up to me, he brushed his thumb against my chin before dropping a kiss on my lips. I watched as he moved around the room, pulling out familiar items and setting up his workstation.

"Where do you go?"

He didn't turn to face me after my question but I spotted the hike of one of his brows. "What?"

"Where do you go?" I repeated, getting comfortable on my stool that was damn near plastered at his side. "Every few weeks, you used to disappear in the middle of my workday and have TJ come to RemEx until you returned. Where did you go?"

It had been bugging me for a while but I'd never asked because it wasn't my business. I'd kept the lines drawn in the sand and neither of us crossed them until recently. Since our relationship had.... *evolved*, now I felt comfortable asking.

When he didn't respond right away, I shifted on the stool, refusing to give up. "Were you visiting Tessa?" I prompted.

Finally, I got a head shake as he took out a glob of clay and smacked it on the table. "Nope." He said shortly. I was fully prepared to prod for more information but I didn't need to because he continued. "Therapy."

"*Therapy?*" My tone was high and incredulous. I had *not* been expecting that.

A soft laugh trickled from his lips as he smiled, still working on the clay, not looking up. "Don't knock it until you try it."

I scoffed.

As if I'd sit in front of someone and spill my deepest and darkest secrets for them to *judge* me.

"It's not what you think it is." He continued as if he could read my mind, this time gifting me his eyes. When I merely lifted a brow, he laughed again. "I swear, Rem." His lips stretched even more when my doubtful expression didn't ease. "You find the right one and you'll keep going back."

"Yeah, right."

His head tilted in contemplation before he nodded, as if coming to a decision. "You should come with me."

"*Excuse me?*"

"Not to talk." He rushed out before I could say a word. "Just to observe. To *listen*. That way, you can see what it's like without the pressure. You never know, it might change your mind."

"I'll pass." He was quiet for a moment. Reflective, before turning back to his sculpture without a word. Recognizing the shortness in my tone, I cleared my throat. "I appreciate the offer but I'm not sure if therapy is for me."

I breathed a sigh of relief when he glanced back at me. "The offer still stands if you change your mind."

Though I had zero intention of accepting, I nodded.

The minutes after we both fell silent seemed to fly by as he molded and scraped away at the glob of clay until a familiar shape took place.

"Is that a... flower?" I asked quietly, not wanting to offend him if it wasn't. There was a bud and petals, but the positioning and shape seemed off.

"Something like that." He muttered, still working. When he was like this, deep in the zone, his concentration level was at his highest and I didn't disturb him. Whenever he completed something or took a break, he always showed me his work and explained the thought process behind the idea, anyway. So instead of asking more questions, I fell silent and waited.

Like I'd expected, he finished about twenty minutes later. As he moved to stand, I twisted in my chair, giving him space to go to the bathroom and wash his hands.

When he returned, he walked right up to me. A squeak raised past my lips when he easily lifted me with his left arm and grabbed the finished project with his right.

He took three long steps, depositing me on the empty table where he placed his projects to air dry.

"What do you see?" he asked, holding the sculpture in my line of sight.

"A flower." I hoped he didn't expect me to know the exact kind. Thankfully, he didn't ask me to elaborate. Instead, he shifted the sculpture, turning it in his hands and angling it away so that I got another view of it.

"Now, what do you see?"

It took a few moments. Well, *minutes*.

I squinted and turned my head this way and that, trying to see what he wanted me to. He waited patiently, face blank and composed, as I observed his work.

But when I saw it, I couldn't *unsee* it and a gasp fell from my lips.

"Is that a... pussy?" I whispered, glancing around like a child who was afraid of getting caught.

His lips twitched in amusement. "Not *a* pussy. *Yours*."

I gasped so hard this time that I choked on it before grabbing his wrist, pulling it closer to my face, being sure not to make contact with the still soft clay.

Is that what it looked like?

I wasn't sure.

Granted, I'd never seen my... private area from any angle other than from above, so I wasn't an expert on what it looked like up close.

To me, it had always been just another body part. I cleaned it. I maintained it. I went to the doctor and had checkups, just like I did with my heart.

But I'd never thought of it any deeper than that. I'd never dwelled on it because it hadn't mattered. I didn't touch it in pleasure and I'd damn sure never expected to let anyone else do it, either.

But seeing it this way was... *something*.

Something Lathan's talent had brought to life, giving it its own purpose outside of being just another body part.

"Why?" I finally asked, after inspecting it from every angle.

"Because I'm obsessed with it." My eyes lifted to his, surprised at the growl in his tone. "I haven't even been inside it yet and I can't get it out of my mind. The smell of it. The *taste*. It's all I fuckin' think about now."

That dull throb between my thighs that had been present while I watched him sculpt had turned into a full ache.

One that I wanted the man standing in front of me to alleviate.

Until now, Lathan seemed content with our exploration phase but I had to admit that I was growing restless.

I wanted *more*.

"How's the heart?" He asked like always, sitting the sculpture down before cupping my hips.

"Fine." I muttered, unable to take my gaze from the bottom lip he kept running his tongue across. "Why?"

His thumb slipped down to toy with the ends of my dress. "Feel like exploring?"

"No." I blurted.

The way his expression fell was almost comical. "You don't?"

I shook my head, now mimicking him, biting my bottom lip. "I want to have sex."

The big man in front of me froze, eyes searing mine with an intensity I rarely got glimpses of. "You want to *what*?"

"I'm ready for more than just exploring. I'm comfortable with you and I want to have sex. *Now*."

I expected him to want to talk about it more. I expected him to ask more questions about whether I was sure.

Which I was.

I'd been thinking on this for the last few days but had chickened out before I could ask for it.

But Lathan surprised me when he lifted me again, cupping one hand under my ass and holding the small of my back with the other.

Excitement pooled in my gut when he turned towards the other bedroom in the guesthouse with lengthy and determined strides.

I guess we're about to do this.

THE SPEED with which Lathan carried me down the hall would've been comical if not for the vortex of emotions swirling in my gut.

His eyes remained locked on mine the entire time, studying me as if making sure I wasn't pulling his chain.

But I wasn't. Not at all. Twenty-plus years of fear, insecurity, and trauma had held me back from engaging in this act with any other person.

Trust was not something I gave easily but he'd earned it and I was more ready. Getting to the next level with Lathan felt more like a *need* than a want.

Normally, I would look around the room and observe the space he'd once spent so much time in but at this moment, all I saw was him. All I could focus on was the masculine, handsome face that was so perfect it looked like the sculptures he kept on the shelf down the hall.

With gentleness that I was quickly coming to associate with him, he lowered me to the bed and I instantly reclined, spreading my legs to make room for him between.

But he hesitated, hovering over me for only a second before attempting to roll next to me.

"You don't have to do that." That mind-numbing fear from the very first encounter we'd had was absent and I was grateful because I wanted nothing putting a damper on this experience.

I wanted this with him.

I wanted to give myself over to the experience and not worry about spiraling and ruining everything.

"You sure?" He asked. Though lust swirled in his gaze, concern overshadowed it. "You can still be on top if that makes you more comfortable."

As he spoke, his lips pressed against my forehead, resting there for a moment before trailing over the bridge of my nose, then finally meeting mine in a gentle kiss.

One so soft that it made me feel valued. *Cherished*.

"I'm sure." I whispered, groaning when he deepened the kiss, slowly adding more of his weight to me.

My heart thumped wildly as he undressed us.

I only moved when he requested, lifting my torso so he could my tug dress over my head, lifting my hips so the tiny panties I wore could easily slip over my legs. I enjoyed letting him take control, grateful that I could release the reins on something without fear of being let down.

A low, soft moan spilled from my lips when he settled between my thighs, completely nude this time.

Complete trust warmed my insides and I smiled at him after noticing his hesitation again.

It took a few more moments for him to relax once he realized I wasn't on the verge of a panic attack. But once he did, his sculpted arms caged me in and I basked in their protection, feeling safer at that moment than I had in a long time.

Immediately, my hands skated over his chest and broad shoulders, enjoying the heat of his skin under my fingertips. His skin was smooth and supple, despite the hard layer of muscles beneath the surface.

Fingers that I hadn't noticed moving down my side slipped over the curve of my hip to the place that throbbed for him.

"I thought I was gonna have to get you ready. Prepare you a bit more." He muttered against my mouth once his fingers found their way past my folds into my sopping slit. Just the idea of fucking him had me soaked and bucking against his hands. "But it feels like you're ready for me."

I nodded, widening my thighs and pulling him closer in a not-so-subtle gesture that hinted at what I wanted.

"Patience, babe." He reared back on his haunches, smiling when I slammed my fist on the bed in frustration. "I damn sure plan on taking my time and savoring this."

Before I could spit a venomous retort, two of his fingers slipped inside of me and instinctively, my hips lifted, practically begging for deeper penetration. My slickness eased his passage as he lazily withdrew them, locking his eyes with mine before sliding them between his full lips.

A spasm shot through me when his lids closed, tongue darting around the digits to savor the taste.

Overcome with impatience, I reached between us, grabbing the hard dick that was mere inches from where I wanted him.

Thank God one of us was still in our right mind because he brushed my hand aside, sliding on a condom before I could yank him towards me.

The Remedy who sat behind that white executive desk and kept everyone at arm's length would be embarrassed by my behavior. I imagined that version of me sitting prim and proper in the corner with crossed legs, an upturned nose, and pursed lips, reeking of disapproval.

But that judgmental bitch could kiss my ass because she'd never had this. She'd never experienced genuine passion before. She'd never wanted another human being's touch so badly that she felt *desperate* for it.

That was what Lathan made me feel and I would *not* be ashamed of it. At least not while in the moment.

Tomorrow was another day and I damn sure wasn't trying to rush into it.

Though I was desperate for him and eager as hell, I wanted to savor this too. I wanted it to last. I wanted the memories vivid and clear, readily available for me to replay in my mind like a highlight reel.

"How's the heart?"

I barely, just barely, resisted the urge to roll my eyes. "It's *fine*. Now fuck me."

A low rumbling chuckle had tufts of air brushing against my face but he didn't say anything else. Instead, his focus shifted, bouncing between my pinched face and the part of him that eased inside of me.

Despite having his tongue and fingers between my legs more times than I could count in the last few weeks, there was still a shocking twinge of pain.

I honestly hadn't known what to expect because my experience was limited and... *traumatic* at best.

But I knew this would be different. I knew *anything* I did with him would be.

He'd already shown me he would take care of my body. He knew when to push and when to pull back.

Hell, the man knew what I liked better than I did and used it to his advantage. *Often.*

Not that I was complaining. Anytime we were alone lately, my default position became spread eagle or straddling his face.

"*Umh.*"

My eyes bucked at what definitely sounded like a moan coming from his lips. I didn't get the opportunity to pull back and investigate further because his grip on me tightened as he moved at a slow, but steady pace.

I scooted closer to the languid strokes, arching my back, wanting every inch of the hardness he slowly fed me. I looked down and my heart skipped when the erotic visual of him slipping in and out of my most sacred place overwhelmed my senses.

A light tap on my chin had my gaze shooting back up to his, gasping once I met his smoldering gaze.

The gold chain he always wore hung loosely around his thick neck, swinging in my face each time he surged forward. I reached up, grabbing it and brushing my thumb against the cool gold, heat creeping into my cheeks when he winked at me.

The man was *inside* of me for Christ's sake but a wink had me blushing. I had officially lost my mind.

His lips were plump and swollen from our feverish kisses and I was sure mine looked the same.

As his fluid hips continued their pleasurable dance between my thighs, briefly, I wondered why I hadn't indulged in this act before. Or at the very least, attempted to please myself.

But as quickly as the thought appeared, I brushed it aside. If I had done any of that, the moments we've shared so far wouldn't have been this special.

I wouldn't have been able to share this with *him*.

"Lathan." I gasped, when his hands slipped from my pebbled nipple down to stroke my clit in tune with his increasing thrusts.

I yanked him down, pulling him into a kiss he eagerly reciprocated. His tongue swirled around mine as he continued his pointed thrusts, causing a wet smacking sound to join the chorus of our moans.

"*Oh, God.*"

The grip he had on my waist grew possessive, urgent. It was tight and he used it to yank my body towards him each time he thrust forward.

The sight of him above me, handsome face contorted, had pleasure flooding my body, overwhelming my senses.

I clawed at his back, wanting to pull him closer, needing him to soothe me through the panicked climax closing in.

This pleasure differed from the stimulation provided to my clit when he went down on me. Whatever this was, it was stronger, *deeper*.

My heart was about to pound right out of my chest.

As if he sensed the direction my thoughts traveled, his lips trailed against mine, tongue darting out to play as he asked his customary, "How's the heart?"

"About to go into overdrive." I said through gritted teeth, trying and failing to keep the guttural moans in my throat at bay.

To my surprise and dismay, he stopped moving completely, face twisting with concern. "You need me to stop?"

I smacked at his shoulder. "Not if your ass wants to live." When the tension in him didn't ease after my joke, I groaned. "I was *joking*. Yes, my heart rate is up, but that shouldn't be a surprise... considering what we're doing at the moment." Still no reaction. "I'm *fine*."

"You'll tell me if you're not, right?" I rolled my eyes at his demand and attempted to move my lower half up and down on his shaft. If he wouldn't fuck me, then I'd do it my damn self. He allowed me to get two measly pumps before his grip on me tightened, halting all movement. "You'll tell me if you're not." This time, the statement wasn't phrased as a question.

For the sake of resuming, I readily agreed with a nod before once again attempting to move against him.

This time, he allowed me, meeting my eager thrusts, feeding me inch after inch before slowly retreating and repeating the process all over again.

"Oh, no." I muttered not even a minute later.

My thighs clamped around his waist but he kept thrusting, lifting his face from its position in my neck to meet my gaze. "What's wrong?"

My eyes bucked as I frantically tapped at his shoulders, needing him to stop. *Now*. "Let me up, I have to pee."

His lids narrowed as his strokes slowed but didn't stop. "You what?"

Embarrassing heat consumed me and I wanted nothing more than to hide under the covers and stay there forever.

"I need to pee."

The urge had only gotten stronger since I first felt it and my walls clamped down around him, causing his lids to shutter closed as he groaned. "Don't fuckin' *do that*."

"Then let me up before I pee in this damn bed!" I snapped, no longer pushing against him because the swift strokes he'd resumed had my lower half quivering, distracting me from what I'd wanted.

His eyes opened again, meeting mine with that intensity I adored. "Trust me, babe. You're *not* about to pee on yourself."

I parted my lips to refute but the sudden urge to bear down came over me. "Oh, no. No, no, no, no, no." I muttered, trying and failing to not lose control because he obviously had zero intention of stopping.

"Don't fight it." His tawny gaze never left mine as he increased his pace, lips twitching with amusement.

Excuse me? Was he encouraging me to piss in this damn bed?

I was open to exploration with him but if he thought I was about to try that, he'd lost his damn mind.

"Stop fighting it."

I couldn't respond because my lips were tightly mashed together, struggling to hold back my cries as my eyes rolled back and I arched towards him.

The pleasurable agony I was in nearly rendered me immobile and I knew my body had reached the point of no return.

"That's it." He encouraged, slamming against me with precision. The humor was now gone and his mocha-hued eyes were glazed over, pupils blown from the lust easily flowing between us. "Let it happen."

So I did.

And what a glorious experience it was.

There wasn't a slow build up to my climax like it was when he used his tongue or fingers. This was an eruption and I detonated like a volcano that once lay dormant. Like someone had turned on the sprinkler system in their front yard, I exploded all over him and the bed.

"Oh, *fuck*." He groaned through clenched teeth, still slamming against me, shaking the entire bed from the force of the thrusts.

Not long after, he fell over the edge right behind me, gripping my hips as his became sporadic in their technique. That handsome face I enjoyed looking at *way* too much contorted as if in pain before a long, low groan greeted my ears. His entire body stiffened and the warmth of his release filled the condom.

All I could do was shiver and bask in the aftermath, enjoying the feeling of being under him without an ounce of panic in sight.

I pulled him closer and held his big body tight, not wanting to let go.

Once the tremors in his shoulders stopped, he moved to roll off me, and I started to protest before relaxing when he discarded the condom in the lined wastebasket near the bed before falling onto his back on the plush covers. Immediately, his arm shot out, wrapping around my shoulders and pulling me halfway on top of him.

That feeling of safety heightened, and I sighed, perfectly content in this position without either of us saying a word.

I hummed, snuggling closer when he wrapped one of my curls around his finger. He toyed with the strand, twirling it around, stretching it to its max near the middle of my back, before releasing, eyes widening with fascination at the way it sprang up and around before settling back in place.

"We should do that more often." I said through a yawn, burying my face in his neck, grinning to myself when his cheeks lifted with a smile.

"More often?" He parroted, grabbing another coil to play with.

"Yep." I said. "Like every day, several times a day if you're up for it."

His reaction wasn't limited to a smile. This time, he laughed and my body bounced up and down each time the manly sound rumbled from his chest.

"*I think I can handle that.*"

I CAN'T BELIEVE I let him talk me into this.

I felt out-of-place watching the comfort and ease that flowed from Lathan as he spoke with the beautiful woman he'd introduced as Dr. Tori.

There wasn't hesitation or discomfort when they spoke with one another. Rather than the invasion of privacy I'd imagined it to be, the session felt like a conversation between old friends.

I had to admit, my interest was piqued.

It made me wonder if this was everyone's experience with therapy or whether it was unique simply because of the woman sitting across from us with a demure smile and crossed legs.

"Obviously my relationship with my *employer* has changed."

My eyes bucked at Lathan's words and I tuned back into the discussion.

Dr. Tori's lips lifted in a smile as her gaze swung between the two of us. "And how do you feel about that change, Lathan?"

He glanced at me, eyes practically glowing with passion before looking back towards her. "I like it. I like *her*." He emphasized, giving me his gaze again as he spoke the next words like they were the easiest thing in the world. "When I first got out of prison, all I kept telling myself was to stay out of trouble. Not make any waves. Fly under the radar. And it worked... for a while." A soft laugh rushed past his lips as he shrugged. "But that way of living isn't satisfying for me anymore. If I'm being honest, it never was. But especially now. After watching her and all she's accomplished? Watching the way she works harder than any person in her company? It made me want to be better. She'd done that and changed my mindset without even trying. She'd done it just by being herself and doing what she did best."

My breath stalled, eyes going wide and mouth slackening at the sheer vulnerability this man was exposing me to. He not only spoke on his innermost thoughts, but he gave me a front row seat while he did so.

He allowed me to witness an experience I'd refused to consider for so long because I was afraid of not being taken seriously.

I was afraid of being called *crazy*. And even though some days I felt like I was indeed losing my mind, I'd still been too embarrassed to take the next step in getting help.

But that judgment I feared was nowhere to be found. From the beginning, the only thing I'd witnessed in this session was open, healthy dialogue.

I was nervous but excited. Not only was he being vulnerable, but he said he'd *admired* me. He cared enough to make me a topic with his therapist.

I turned in my seat and leaned forward, eager to hear more. But I tensed when conversation halted and they both swung their eyes to me.

"You wanted to say something, babe?"

Still unused to the endearment and the accompanying pleasure it caused each time he said it, my cheeks flushed.

"No," I said softly, hating how probing Dr. Tori's gaze felt. "Just getting comfortable." I made a show of settling back in my seat before producing a polite smile.

Seconds later, they resumed their conversation, moving the subject to his daughter.

"Sometimes with Tessa," Lathan began, "I feel like I'm making progress and elevating our relationship to the next level." He sighed, rubbing a hand down the side of his face.

I frowned, watching his profile as his expression pinched. The skin between his brows wrinkled as if in frustration.

I felt the sudden urge to reach over and brush my fingers there to smooth it out, not wanting to see him in distress. If we were alone, I might've. But since we weren't, I didn't want to draw attention to myself again, so I curled my fingers into a fist, pressing it into my thighs.

"Then other times, it's like I just got out of prison all over again. Like I'm trying to figure out where I fit into her life because she's shutting me out. She's shutting *everyone* out. And when she gets like that, I don't know what to do with her. Or what to say. What can I do to make this shit, *right?*"

"Take your cues from her." Dr. Tori suggested. "You were gone for ten years. Ten very important developmental years. There is no quick remedy or solution to make things smooth between the two of you." Her tone changed and she leaned forward. "Give yourself some grace and be patient. It's a marathon, not a sprint. Undoing the trauma and unresolved feelings for both of you might take just as long as it did for them to appear. When she doesn't know how to express her emotions in healthy ways, your job is to stay the course and *show* her. Show her how it should be done by opening yourself up to her."

Lathan seemed to stew on her words, shifting in seat, drumming the tips of his fingers against his thigh.

And through it all, I felt in tune with him and his emotions. Even when his attention remained on Dr. Tori, there was still a distinct awareness I had of him and each move he made.

It both freaked me out and comforted me.

I could say I'd had friendships and bonds with people in my life but this... this *connection* was one I'd never experienced before.

"Stop thinking that you have to have it all together *right now*. No one leaves prison unscarred. Some of those scars may heal completely while others simply scab over. They're still there. They're still visible and sometimes show up in your life when you least expect it, even though they are no longer the open, gaping wounds they once were."

Lathan rubbed a thumb back and forth across his bottom lip, processing her words. But Dr. Tori clearly wasn't done.

"Because prison is a place for *criminals*, we don't properly acknowledge the trauma experienced by those who go in and come out forever changed. PTSD in released inmates is just as real as it is for military personnel. The actions taken that led to the PTSD might be different but the trauma is still the same."

Though none of the words were directed at me, I still felt them resonate.

I'd made comments about Lathan's time in jail to get under his skin, especially when he first started working for me. Not once had he seemed to take my words seriously but hearing Dr. Tori verbalize the aftermath of what going to prison could do, I felt terrible for some of the things I'd said.

This entire time, he could've been suffering, battling his own demons after an experience like that but he'd never said a word.

"Well," Dr. Tori said with a smile. "It's been a while since we've had a session like this." Her eyes flashed to the digital clock on the corner of her desk. "We only have a few more minutes. Do you have anything else you would like to discuss, Lathan?"

With a presence more muted than when we'd first arrived, he shook his head then turned in my direction. I tensed in anticipation of the question. "You want to say anything, Rem?"

I did. So much. But forced myself not to, choosing instead to hold on to my demons a bit longer.

My responding smile was tight and forced as I turned down the offer. Lathan seemed too distracted by his own thoughts to notice my reaction but not Dr. Tori. A knowing look crossed her face. but she didn't call me out on my cowardice, *thankfully*.

Lathan's hand joined with mine as we walked towards the door. While him and Dr. Tori made idle talk, I couldn't take my eyes away from our connection, still in disbelief how simple things with Lathan felt.

Mere weeks ago, prolonged skin to skin contact made my anxiety spike.

But with him, I *craved* it. I needed his touch more than my next breath.

It balanced and settled me in a way that my hectic work schedule or the millions in my account never could.

"It was nice to finally meet you, Remedy." Dr. Tori said with a smile that spoke volumes. "I look forward to seeing you again."

For a moment, our eyes locked and a feeling came over me.

And I just *knew*.

I knew that as sure as my name was Remedy, one day, I'd wind up on this woman's couch.

It might not be this month.

It might not be this year.

But I'd be back and I hoped both of us would be prepared for the long-kept secrets and unresolved feelings that would spill from my lips.

"STOP."

I giggled, fighting off the attack of Lathan's lips across the side of my neck as we stepped inside my home. His beard scraped the sensitive skin, sending chills racing up and down my spine.

After Lathan's appointment with Dr. Tori, we'd made our way over to Harmony Medical Center for my checkup with Dr. Huang.

He'd been surprised and pleased that I'd complied with his instructions. Of course, Lathan deserved all the credit for that because without him, I would've done what I always did. Take a few days of working from home before returning to the office for my normal ten- and twelve-hour workdays without a care for my health.

According to Dr. Huang, if the results from today's scan came back positive, he'll clear me to return to work soon.

Instead of the elation I'd expected, mixed feelings sprang to life in my chest. Though I missed RemEx, I'd enjoyed the uninterrupted time at home without the stress of running a company.

The time spent with Lathan, even when we'd been at one another's throats, had shown me that there was more to life than the little bubble I'd created for myself and I wasn't ready for this reprieve to end.

Maybe I could adjust my schedule when I returned and allow myself more free time, especially if this *relationship* we'd developed continues.

"Is Tessa here?" I asked Lathan, stopping near the island in my kitchen after noticing the glass door that led to my backyard was unlocked.

Last week, I'd given her a key in case she popped up again and no one was home. The last thing I wanted was for her to be stuck outside, unable to get in.

His brows furrowed. "She's not supposed to come until tomorrow." His gaze remained on the glass door as he slid me behind him. I rolled my eyes when he reached for the hidden gun he kept tucked behind his back but didn't fight it, staying right on his heels as we crossed the room.

As soon as we stepped onto the concrete under the veranda, a familiar girlish giggle met our ears and I smiled, grateful that the lovely sound was coming from the sometimes-broody teen who'd wormed her way into my heart as easily as her father had. Both of us breathed a sigh of relief as we ventured further into the backyard, spotting Tessa sitting on the side of the pool near the rock waterfall.

She wore a cute, tie dye two-piece swimsuit. Her feet dangled in the shallow end while another girl who appeared to be around her age waded in the middle of the pool where the depth reached nine feet. The teen I'd never seen before had her head tossed back, still laughing at whatever conversation we'd interrupted.

To my surprise, Isabel sat on one of the plush patio chairs. Her feet were bare and tucked beneath her as she read one of the romantic suspense novels I'd noticed she had an affinity for.

Over the last few weeks, her and Tessa bonded and I couldn't help but to feel a twinge of envy at how easily they'd taken to one another.

Though I was glad there was another person Tessa had grown

close to, it was hard seeing my mother appear nurturing and open to a child when she hadn't been there for me.

Tessa's gaze brightened when she looked up and spotted us. I held up a hand over my eyes to block the sun, returning a smile that would've felt forced not many weeks ago.

"Hey, girls." I greeted, surprising myself and everyone out here that I'd spoken first. Deciding to shock everyone even further, I turned to my mom. "Hey, Isabel."

Her eyes ballooned in shock before stuttering out a "H-h-hey, Rem." Her gaze was intense as she watched me, probably wondering if I'd bumped my head or something.

I hadn't.

I was just tired of tiptoeing around my house, avoiding and ignoring her.

I mean, for Christ's sake, the woman washed, folded, and put away my clothes. Not to mention cleaning up around the house and fixing enough food for Lathan, Tessa, and I to last an entire week.

"Did you ask Rem if Tiana could come over?" Lathan's tone was firm but not harsh, like it always was whenever he disciplined or scolded Tessa. I admired his ability to express his frustration or tell her about something she'd done wrong without belittling or guilt tripping her.

It was a parenting style that I wish my father had adapted. If he had, I might've felt more comfortable confessing and trusting him with my secrets.

I'd been afraid that opening up to Big Tim would've been met with indifference. If he would've dismissed my claims against his friends, I don't know what I would've done, so rather than chancing it, I kept it to myself.

Tessa and her friend's shoulder sagged with disappointment and my stomach knotted in response, realizing I didn't like seeing her upset.

"I didn't." Tessa responded quietly as Tiana waded towards the edge of the pool. "I'm sorry, Ms. Remy. I should've asked first."

I ignored my mother's hiked eyebrows in response to the nickname I refused to let her call me. "It's fine. I don't mind."

Lathan's lips parted as if to refute but I latched onto his arm, squeezing it to silence him. His eyes slanted to mine, narrowed but he got the hint and turned back to face the girls. "Do you need a ride home later, Tiana?"

"No." Tessa answered quickly, earning a curious look from all the adults outside. "Mama's picking us up later when she gets off. Tiana's staying with me at my other house."

Lathan tensed but I smirked, finding it funny how she always easily referred to the home she lived in with Gabbi as her *other house*. It was cute.

"Alright." Lathan finally conceded. "I'll be inside if you need me."

Tessa sent me a grateful smile when he turned towards the house and I winked in response before following her father.

As soon as the glass door was closed, he sighed, raking his hands down his face. "I'm sorry, Rem. I know this shit was supposed to be temporary but now she's calling it her other house and inviting her cousin over and shit." I walked up, pressing myself flush against him, relaxing in his arms when he draped them around me. "She's even got Clarence wrapped around her finger. He notifies me of everybody who comes within fifty feet of this property but now he conveniently forgot to tell me she'd invited someone over?"

"I really don't mind." I repeated, resting my hand on the powerful chest mere inches in front of my face. "It's *fine*."

"No, it's *not*. She should've asked, Rem. I'm glad she's comfortable and happier when over here but... it's *not* her home and I don't want her taking liberties and overstepping her bounds. She still needs to respect that it's *your* home. Not ours."

One of my brows shot up. "You're right, it *is* my home. And if I say it's fine, then it is. If I say it's okay for Tessa to call it *her* home, then it is. If I say I'm fine with you calling it your home, *then it is*."

A battle of wills ensued as neither of us wanted to blink first. We were locked in a battle where neither of the strong-minded people involved wanted to bend or break.

What finally snapped me out of it was the loud smack and accompanying pain of his hand colliding with my ass.

"Lathan, *what the fu—*"

"Don't use your CEO voice on me." Though his tone was low and serious, the light in his eyes and slight lift of his lips let me know he was teasing. "Even if that shit gets my dick hard."

I burst into laughter, dropping my forehead against his shoulder. The hand that hit me moments earlier now caressed the slight curve, gripping and releasing as if there was an abundance of it rather than just a handful.

Lifting my gaze to his, my bottom lip slipped between my teeth as I looked at him in indecision.

"What is it?" He asked, immediately spotting the change in my demeanor.

I hesitated, relishing the way his eyes lingered on my face, a small smile still lifting the corner of his lips.

I couldn't get over the way he looked at me sometimes.

Like I was valuable. Like *I mattered.*

I couldn't accurately describe the way it made me feel but what I did know was that I never wanted it to end.

"Talk to me, Rem." He urged when I remained silent.

"Um..." I began, still uncomfortable with asking people for what I wanted, even with this. "Since Tessa's occupied and my mom's outside with them..." My words trailed until the end of the sentence was completely inaudible.

But it didn't matter because even though he hadn't heard the words, Lathan read my body language loud and clear.

"You asking me to fuck, Rem?" He asked, full lips curving up in a smile.

My cheeks heated and my eyes ballooned at the crudeness. "Closed mouths don't get fed, baby. Tell me what you want and I'll make it happen." Again, I chewed on the inside of my lip, unsure if I had it in me to do as he asked.

The F-Word didn't offend or make me uncomfortable. Far from it actually. I used it more often than I cared to admit, so delicate sensibilities wasn't the issue. It was the *way* he wanted me to use it. The *phrasing*.

Seconds later, while I was still indecisive, he bent, leaning down until his lips brushed against mine. "Tell me you want me to fuck you and I'll do it." He said against my mouth. "I'll make it so good for you, baby. All you have to do is ask."

There was another moment where I hesitated before I whispered a response so low, I wasn't sure he'd heard me. "Fuck me."

"What was that?" He urged, showing me a side of him that clearly he'd kept under wraps.

The Lathan I encountered every day was easygoing. But the intensity currently radiating off him, the strong vibes that seemed to pour from his skin had me wanting to see more of it.

"I want..." My tone softened as I completed the sentence. "I... I want you to fuck me."

His lips curved and he swiped his thumb against my chin before lifting me in his arms. A startled squeak escaped my lips as he easily carried me across the room and up the sweeping stairs that led to my suite.

"We'll work on the volume later but that'll do for now."

"You're a giant asshole, you know that." I retorted in my normal volume, hating the embarrassment still heating my cheeks from the words I'd spoken.

"I might be, but I'm *your* asshole."

As he carried me up the stairs, I buried my face in the crook of his neck, cheeks heating for an entirely different reason this time.

Mine.

24

LATHAN

I think I created a fiend.

A sex fiend, to be specific.

"*Shit, Remedy.*" Was all I could utter as I held onto her waist for dear life. The woman in question rode me like her life depended on it, completely absent of the shyness and insecurity I'd spotted in the hotel that now felt like ages ago rather than mere weeks.

That inexperienced woman now bounced on my dick like an expert, rotating her hips with a sensual swirl that got the job done for both of us, dragging her clit back and forth against my pelvis each time she sank fully onto me.

My balls tightened and I knew she'd better get to the end fast because I was moments away from blowing my load without her.

I liked to consider myself a gentleman in and out of the bedroom which meant Remedy always, *always* got hers first.

But the way she'd hopped on me the second I crossed her carpeted bedroom floor had caught me off guard. I hadn't had time to prepare or steel myself against her attack.

She'd started with a hand job that had pleasurable heat shooting through my dick.

Then, when she'd nearly driven me to the brink of insanity, she'd pushed me flat on the bed, swung her legs over me like an experienced cowgirl and took me for the ride of my life.

"Shit. Rem, *get up*." I huffed, knowing her window for escaping without getting filled was quickly dwindling.

Instead of hopping off at my warning, she moved faster, head tossed back and eyes closed as she rode me feverishly. What she lacked in technique, she more than made up for with passion.

Unbridled, *wild* passion.

Instead of trying to fight her off, I gripped her waist and lifted my hips, meeting her stroke for stroke. Her keening cries and spasming walls triggered my release and I held her tight, jerking her up and down on me in a rhythm that was just as chaotic as hers. The feeling of her hot, wetness coating my dick had me damn near trembling as the powerful orgasm had me huffing out harsh breaths.

We'd slipped up the other day.

Both of us had been too caught up in the moment and I'd gone in bare. Thankfully, I'd had enough discipline to pull out, expecting the scolding of lifetime when it was over for making such a careless mistake.

Instead, that one time had turned into a *preference* and now since getting our clean test results back, she refused to let me wear one, citing that the difference in how it felt was too steep to overlook.

Though the words hadn't been spoken, we were obviously exclusive so I agreed with zero hesitation.

The implant in her arm that she'd gotten a few years back to regulate her period also would protect us from surprise pregnancies, so it was a win-win in my book.

So I made myself available each time she requested sex, which was *often*. I enjoyed every minute and would never tell her no because... well, why the hell would I?

But I'd be lying if I said I wasn't *exhausted*.

Remedy, who now stretched out across my chest, snuggling

against me and looking extremely satiated, was the horniest woman I'd ever been with.

She wanted it all... the... time.

At this point, I wasn't sure if there was a drop of seed left in me. The woman was draining me dry.

I understood she was making up for lost time and I damn sure didn't mind being her test dummy. She could use me any way she wanted.

Besides, watching her discover her passion was a hell of an incentive. When she let down her walls and fully submerged herself in the pleasure, there was almost a curious innocence about her that called to me.

Glancing down, a familiar jolt shot through me like it did each time my eyes met hers. A soft, serene smile stretched across her lips and I brushed the damp curls that framed her face behind her ear before she lifted and eased her face towards mine. I licked my lips in preparation of the kiss, pausing when she stopped far enough to trace her tongue over the curve of my mouth instead.

I waited until she'd finished, watching her thorough heavy lids before saying, "You're just doing shit now."

She burst into laughter, a light tinkling sound that hit me right in the center of my chest before she resumed her favorite position, legs and arms entangled with mine with her face buried in my neck.

Springy coils of wine-colored hair tickled my nose, now frizzed and sprouting in all directions from the sweat she'd worked up.

That always polished, never-have-a-hair-out-of-place version of Remedy seemed to have faded right along with the woman who gave me hell at every turn.

That emerald gaze of hers still flashed with ire but most of the time, she was like *this*.

Soft and sweet.

When she wriggled, trying to find a comfortable position, I couldn't help but to notice the way my rough, calloused fingers looked out of place against the soft, supple expanse of her honey-hued skin.

We were opposites in so many ways, yet... I never felt more connected with anyone than at this moment.

While I tossed that realization around in my mind, she started rambling, speaking more comfortably than I'd ever seen from her.

At first, she spoke about an email she'd received from Miranda that outlined the new social media company that was onboarding with RemEx.

My data analytics knowledge was limited at best and forty-five percent of what she was saying went over my head but I still grunted and made affirmative responses at the appropriate times because I wanted her to keep talking.

I enjoyed the sound of it, especially when it spilled from her lips so freely and unfiltered.

Before I'd realized, she somehow seamlessly transitioned to discussing the tv series Tessa had convinced her to watch.

When the woman put her mind to something, she saw it through fully because after watching the first episode with Tessa, she'd stayed up nearly twenty-fours, binging two full seasons before the new one launches next week.

She'd wanted to catch up so her and Tessa could watch it each Sunday night and discuss the crazy plot lines. I'd tried to watch it with them but it was too much drama and felt soap opera-y so I planned to spend that hour in my workshop, either sketching out upcoming projects or diving back into some unfinished ones I'd set aside.

Twisting so we now faced one another, as she continued rambling, I admired her beauty with renewed appreciation.

The woman was drop dead gorgeous and each time I looked at her, I experienced that feeling in my gut like when the ride was about to drop off the edge of a rollercoaster.

I remembered the way my gut would roll and tighten with

nervousness but adrenaline and excitement still coursed through me in anticipation of what was to come.

That's how I felt with her.

An uncontrollable cataclysm of emotions that I was struggling to keep up with or understand.

But I knew that what I felt for her went past the simple realm of like and lust.

There was awareness and a connection that felt surreal.

Her emotions she tried so hard to hide were now as easily visible to me as the curls on her head.

I felt in tune with her. Like we were two halves of a whole working together rather than separate parts moving independently.

The discovery of those emotions was both thrilling and scary.

That curiosity I'd claimed was the only reason for my initial interest had morphed into something... *big*.

Something that consumed me and my thoughts.

"You're not listening." She stopped mid-sentence, dipping her brows in a frown that caused a cute wrinkle right between her brows.

"Simon's sister is actually his mom." I said, meeting her gaze. "She had him at thirteen and let her parents raise him as their own. Someone close to the family—*who they still haven't figured out is Lisa*—leaked it to the tabloids and their PR team is scrambling trying to make the story disappear because it's only a few weeks from an election. Ginny is sleeping with the son of the rival politician and plans on eloping. Meanwhile, he was sent there on a mission to get family secrets but now that he'd fallen in love with Ginny, he's conflicted on what he should do. Stay loyal to his family or protect the woman he loves?" I hiked a brow. "Did I miss anything?"

"You're an arrogant motherfucker, you know that?"

I laughed, stretching my arms wide before rolling to my back. She followed, plastering herself against my side so eagerly that I couldn't resist a chuckle.

"Shut up," she muttered, once again intertwining our limbs so thoroughly that I struggled to decipher where she began and I ended. "You're just... *warm*."

"That's what blankets are for, babe."

After smacking my chest, she rolled on top of me, caging me in with her arms. Her thighs straddled my waist and her lips were mere inches from mine.

That familiar stirring in my groin flared to life and my fingers twitched against her hips with the urge to trace her face. Though I'd already damn near committed each dip and slope to memory, it still wasn't enough time for me to fully comprehend the perfection to recreate it in my art.

I could only hope to replicate the flawlessness of her canvas.

"I like you, Lathan." She suddenly whispered against my mouth. So soft that I barely caught the words.

My lids were still parted, so I saw the uncertainty flashing across her face.

Immediately, her vulnerability humbled me. I knew that seeing her this way was exclusively mine and reserved for moments where it was just the two of us. And I cherished it.

I always would.

"I like you too." I mumbled back, knowing I was severely underselling what I felt.

But I'd go with *like* for now, not wanting to scare her off with too much too soon.

"Can you make me a promise?"

I didn't like making promises because I always felt like utter shit if I couldn't keep them.

I'd promised Tessa at her birth that I'd always be there for her. I'd promised my mom I'd always try to make good decisions. I'd promised my dad that I would always be a man and think for myself, not letting any outside influences sway or pressure me into making dumb choices.

And I'd let down all three of them with the same act, breaking their hearts and mine in the process. Since then, I'd steered clear of *promises*.

But for her, I'd try. I'd make her every promise in the world if she kept looking at me like that. If she kept speaking to me in that soft, vulnerable tone, I'd be willing to walk through hot coals barefoot to ensure any promises I made to her were kept.

Remedy had me *gone* and I don't think she was even aware of it.

"Can you promise that even if this doesn't continue..." she licked her lips nervously. "If we go back to a professional relationship..." *Not happening.* "I just need you to promise that you won't stop seeing me."

At first, confusion caused a frown to crease my forehead. Incorrectly, I'd assumed that she didn't want me to stop coming around or working with her if things didn't turn out the way I wanted them to between us.

But the expectant expression on her face had the lightbulb in my brain switching on. She didn't want me to stop *seeing* her. The real her.

The one I'd always suspected lived behind the mask but hadn't gotten glimpses of until recently.

Tightness reappeared in my chest and I squeezed my arms around her waist, unable to imagine how lonely it must've felt to have so many people in your life yet not fully being seen by *any* of them.

God, this woman tugged at my heartstrings.

"My eyes are wide open with you, Rem." I muttered against her lips. "I don't know how I missed it before but I see you. *All of you.* And there's no way in hell I can go back to the way it was before."

I meant every word.

There was no going back now.

How could I?

For weeks, I got to witness this complex woman go through the stages of discovering her sexuality and *taking* her pleasure when she wanted without shame or fear.

I'd gotten to watch her interact with my family for the first time.

She'd let down her guards and had fun, accepting every one of their loud, outspoken, country asses without judgment.

Somehow, she'd charmed my daughter, earning the stubborn teen's respect and admiration with nothing more than being herself.

She had a chokehold on my emotions, holding them hostage in the palm of her tiny hand. I was unequivocally hers at this point and didn't feel an ounce of panic or worry because of it.

I was right where I wanted to be.

Remedy might have a lot of things to worry about but me not *seeing* her again wasn't one of them.

And it never will be if I had anything to say about it.

"Being unseen around me is no longer an option. But if you need the words, I'll give them to you." I cupped her chin between my thumb and forefingers, pressing upwards until her fallen gaze met mine again. "I promise I'll always see you, babe. Even if you're mad, sad, terrified, or unsure... I won't lose sight of who you are. No matter what."

25

REMEDY

After three weeks away, I was finally back at work.

Lathan wasn't happy about it but after my last checkup with Dr. Huang, I'd made tremendous progress so I was cleared to return as long as I kept my stress levels low and took the anti-inflammatories regularly.

After readily agreeing to his terms at my Friday afternoon appointment, I returned to work on Monday.

But now that I had... Now that I sat behind the desk that I loved so much, it felt... *weird*.

I'd have killed to be back here weeks ago but now, all I wanted was to log off and go home. Honestly, I'd rather sit on my favorite stool in the guesthouse, watching Lathan work on his latest sculpture.

Or stretched out on a sofa in the theater room, barely paying attention to the movie on the screen as I listened to Tessa give hilarious commentary. I'd learned that the girl was one of those people who talked throughout the whole movie and couldn't resist making remarks about the actions of the characters and the decisions they made.

Once upon a time, that would've annoyed the shit out of me but now, I looked forward to the nights that Tessa stayed over, eager to spend time with the expressive young woman.

But what did those feelings mean?

What did it mean that the numbers, spreadsheets, and formulas that once soothed me now felt like a hindrance to what I actually wanted to do?

Why did I find my gaze darting to the corner of the room every few minutes, ogling Lathan who looked more than pleased in the new *adult-sized* desk and chair I had set up for him before we returned?

"Remedy?"

At Miranda's questioning tone, I swung my gaze from Lathan back to the extensive report Jaxon and Miranda put together in my absence.

"This looks good. The execution was flawless and it shows in the numbers."

Months ago, Jaxon had suggested we use our new machine learning technology to aid sports teams with their player performance analysis. I hadn't thought the payout would be worth it but I respected the extensive research he and Miranda had done so I gave them a chance, starting small and using a local university as a guinea pig to see if it was worth mass implementation.

I knew enough about most sports to not feel lost if I attended a game but other than that, my knowledge was limited so I hadn't understood how what we did would be beneficial to them.

But from what I was seeing, it was more than worth it and would open the door into a whole new field I hadn't considered before.

"Using the recruitment angle and the benefits of being able to tailor player's trainings, improve performance, and have an analysis on competitors is perfect. I don't think it would be a hard sell if we were to market this to larger universities and even professional teams. Great job."

His eyes bucked before he slanted a confused glance at Miranda, who returned it.

"You okay?"

I flushed at Jaxon's question, hating that me being nice was out of character.

But it was my fault. I'd been the one to perpetuate that image for so long.

"I'm fine." I said, now avoiding looking in Lathan's direction because I sensed his eyes on me. "I didn't get a chance to say it before but congratulations on your baby." His fiancée, Sinn, had given birth to their baby boy a week ago. "How is he? And Sinn?"

Again, he looked perplexed at my sudden interest in his personal affairs. But the mention of his family had his smile growing as he settled in his chair. "They're good. I mean, of course, it's an adjustment but... that's *expected*. But both are healthy."

"You didn't take paternity leave?"

He nodded. "I did. Three days."

A surprised frown marred my features. "You didn't want to take more time?"

He mirrored my frown, tilting his head. "Of course, I would *like* more time at home with them but I couldn't. You were out and Chauncey had already worked out his two weeks' notice so I had to come in."

Guilt assuaged me.

His wife had given birth to their first child and this man only allowed himself three days at home with them because of the job.

Not long ago, I would've been happy that he'd put the company first over any personal matters, but I realized now how unacceptable that was.

"Take as much time as you need."

His frown deepened. "Excuse me?"

"Did I stutter?" I pursed my lips as soon as the words were out, not wanting to be nasty with him. "I apologize." I ignored the way his eyes ballooned at the apology and continued. "What I meant was if you need to take three weeks to stay home with your fiancée and your son, take it. Send me an email detailing how long you'll be out and I'll take care of it with HR."

"Jaxon?" All our gazes lifted towards the door when his assistant, Finn, stuck her head inside. "Mr. Torro is on line one for your noon conference call."

I could tell Jaxon wanted to say more about what I'd just said but previous obligations prevented it. Instead, he stood, looking at me curiously. "Thanks, Rem. I really appreciate it."

I smiled politely, averting my gaze, watching Miranda twiddle her fingers nervously together once he closed the door behind him.

"Miranda, what's your educational background?" I ignored Lathan's curious frown from across the room, keeping my gaze on her.

Her brows peaked and she licked her lips nervously. "Um... I have a Bachelor's in Data Science and a Master's in Applied Data Science." She pressed her lips together, tightening her grip around the iPad she always kept close. "Do you want to know about my certifications, too?"

I shook my head and opened the manila folder in front of me, removing the paper. Scanning over the information I'd had HR put together, I confirmed that all my requests had been included before sliding it across the table for her to view.

"That is a job offer."

Her eyes widened but she didn't look at the paper. "You... you don't want me to be your assistant anymore?"

I shook my head, ignoring the pang in my chest when tears sprouted above her lids. "Your talent is being wasted by fetching me coffee, ordering lunch, and keeping my schedule together. I've seen the way your brain works. I've heard your suggestions in our meetings and have implemented *most* of them. You have just as much education and experience as I do in this industry, and it's time we put that experience to good use." I nodded towards the paper she still hadn't looked at. "Read it."

She nodded and glanced down, scanning across the paper, eyes widening as she got closer to the end.

"You want me to be the Lead Strategy Analyst? That means I'll..."

"Be in a position where you'll play a pivotal role in planning and implementing long and short-term strategic company goals." I got up from behind my desk, rounding it and sitting on the corner, looking down at her with what I hoped was kindness. "That position is parallel to the role that Jaxon has now and you'll have a dedicated team assigned to you."

"This position had a *fifty thousand dollar* pay increase. Six weeks of paid vacation. A company car..." Her words trailed as more tears threatened to spill over. "But... why?"

"You love REA just as much as I do and I think it's time you work in a position where you can display it. You've earned all of that and more, Miranda. You've put up with me and still been the oil that kept this machine running. This is my thanks to you for your many years of hard work and dedication."

The last sentence was barely out before she'd jumped to her feet and tossed her arms around me. My eyes widened and I flashed my gaze to Lathan who watched me with familiar heat smoldering in his gaze.

Was he serious?

He was thinking about fucking. *Now?*

When I didn't immediately return the hug, she tensed and attempted to pull away but I wrapped my arms around her back, reciprocating the gesture that didn't make me completely uncomfortable.

When I did, she finally let go of the tears she'd been holding and burst into sobs. "Thank you. *Thank you.*" Her voice was heavy, brimming with emotion.

I swallowed around the thickness in my throat. "You're welcome." When she pulled away and wiped at her face, I continued. "Whenever you're ready, you can go to HR and fill out the paperwork. Once you do, you can start immediately."

"But... what about... who's going to be your assistant?"

"With the systems you've put in place, I'll be fine for a couple weeks until I can hire someone else."

Another surprising hug brought her flush against me and again I returned it before nodding when she thanked me again and sped out of the office toward the elevators.

Lathan's heavy gaze remained on me as I pushed off my desk and walked across my office to peer out of the blackout windows that blocked anyone's view of seeing inside but gave me unobstructed access to seeing the outside.

Moments later, his presence was at my back and I relaxed, easing backwards, eager for his touch.

His arm came around my waist and my head fell back against his shoulder. He pressed a kiss against my forehead, mumbling against my skin. "You make my dick hard when you're being nice."

I burst into laughter, letting my lids fall closed before gasping when his fingers toyed with the bottom edge of my skirt. A quick glance towards my door revealed he'd closed it so my shoulders sagged in his embrace. My thighs parted, widening enough for his fingers to slip inside my panties, teasing me but not applying enough pressure to make contact with my aching clit.

"If this is my reward for being nice, I'll do it more often." I panted, spreading my legs further and grabbing his wrist to move his hand where I wanted it.

Right on top of my damp clit.

"That's where you want me to touch you?" he groaned, trapping the nub between two fingers and squeezing lightly.

This link between us was something I hadn't expected.

It was swift and felt like it happened overnight but at the same time, it was... *right*.

I was comfortable with him. I could be myself around him and it pleased me knowing that he'd seen my good, my bad, and my ugly. Though he didn't have the full details of my horrible past, he knew enough to surmise what had occurred and he was still here.

That meant more to me than he'd ever know.

"If being nice makes you hard, what happens when I'm mean?"

His fingers coasted through my wetness before he shoved two digits inside of me, curling them upwards. "My dick gets hard."

Another tuft of laughter rushed past my lips and I tilted my head back, relaxing into the kiss he pressed against my lips. His fingers increased in speed, repeatedly brushing the inside of my sensitive walls while his thumb strummed my clit like the strings on a guitar.

The pleasure was rising quickly and I tensed in preparation of falling over the edge. But just before I did, he stiffened behind me, stopping all movement.

Before I could ask what was wrong, a deep voice drawled from behind us.

"When I said *protect* her, I'm not sure *that's* what I meant."

I flinched at Verse's voice, hating that I'd been caught off guard. I briefly wondered why Miranda hadn't warned of their arrival before remembering she'd taken off to HR minutes earlier to accept her new position.

Guess I'd better start locking the door.

With minimal movements, Lathan discreetly slipped his fingers from inside of me, leaving an unsatisfied ache in their wake. His big frame effectively blocked me as I adjusted my clothing before we turned together, facing Verse and Hakeem.

Though I felt like a teen whose dad caught her sneaking a boy in her room, Lathan looked completely unruffled and cooler than a cucumber as his head remained lifted, refusing to break the eye contact.

The hand he'd just pleased me with had disappeared in his pocket, while his other linked with mine.

"This is a big change from *get rid of him immediately.*" Verse continued with a hiked brow, swinging his disapproving gaze between us.

Hakeem stood there, as unaffected as always, wearing his customary all black ensemble and dark shades that hid his penetrating gaze.

"What are you doing here?" I asked, hating the breathless quality to my tone.

"I can't come visit you no more?" The lazy drawl revealed that right now, I was talking to VP and not Verse Presley, the media mogul. This was the man who'd donned himself my protector after my father died.

"You usually call... or text... or *something* before popping up."

"I was in the area and wanted to check on you, that's it. It's been a while." His gaze moved from me back to Lathan, hardening. "But from the looks of it, you're *more* than fine." I parted my lips to defend myself but stopped when Lathan squeezed my hand. Of course, Verse noticed because he frowned at the connection before leveling that same glare at Lathan. "Let me holla at you for a second, Lath."

I tensed and so did Lathan before his eyes slid over to me.

"She'll be a'ight." Verse added, moving towards the door. "Keem'll stay with her."

Lathan released my hand and leaned over, placing a kiss against my lips without caring that both men in the room probably weren't happy with him at the moment. When he pulled back, he winked at me confidently before sauntering out.

My heart stuttered with nervousness when the door closed behind them.

"He's a big boy, Rem." Hakeem said, startling me. The man could rival a monk with his ability to remain silent in every situation, even when words were necessary. So having him saying something unprovoked had caught me off guard. "He can handle the heat coming his way."

Though the words were probably true, they did nothing to quell the nervousness coursing through me. I finally had something *good* and I was happy.

If Verse said or did something to run Lathan off, the old Remedy would return with a vengeance.

26

LATHAN

"I believe the contract you signed was for protecting her, not fucking her. Or am I mistaken?"

Sunlight streamed in through the office windows on the left side of us. From this vantage, there was an impressive view of the river and the park on the other side of it.

I enjoyed when Rem conducted meetings here because when the technical terms and jargon went over my head, I zoned out, fingers twitching against the stubborn wood with the urge to sketch out the breathtaking view.

But today, my eyes didn't drift in that direction. Instead, they were too busy being locked in a staring contest with a man whose stubbornness could rival my own.

Though Verse was a few inches shorter than my six-and-a-half-foot frame, it didn't matter because his power and presence filled the conference room down the hall from Remedy's office more efficiently than his physicality ever could.

I respected the man in front of me because of what he's done for his friends and family and how his generosity extended to everyone around him.

I respected this man for taking a chance on a convict who'd reached the end of his rope and exhausted all his options on finding gainful employment.

That respect I had for him was the only thing that kept me from reacting to his harsh tone.

I could understand that him walking in on me and Rem in that position might've been a shock, considering that one stipulation when I signed the contract to be her bodyguard had been to keep my dick in my pants.

I'd done exactly that for two years but my eyes had truly opened and seen Rem as she truly was and *not* what she presented to the world.

Once I saw past that, resisting my pull and attraction towards her became difficult.

Now, I wanted that woman every hour of the day and I damn sure wasn't going to let this man scare me off, no matter how much I *respected* him.

"I can understand you feeling caught off guard." I placated, refusing to look away from the challenging stare he'd locked me in.

"Then you'll have no problem with terminating whatever this is, right?" The chair he sat in squeaked as he subtly swung it from side to side, keeping his eyes on me.

I knew it was meant to be intimidating but that wouldn't work. *Especially* with this.

Remedy was worth whatever heat was about to come my way, even if that meant losing my job.

"No offense, VP, but that's not a call for you to make. If she wants me gone, then I'm gone. But unless those words come from *her* mouth, it ain't happening."

The pad of his thumb and forefinger rotated in tightly circles against one another. "So that's that, huh?" His tone was low, now filled with curiosity rather than the simmering anger from moments earlier.

"Look," I began, wanting this conversation to be over already. "I understand you might not like what's happened and how it's happened between me and Rem but I'm not about to apologize for how I feel about her. Nor am I going to tuck my tail and run because you don't like it. You want to fire me for violating the contract, then that's what you'll have to do. But I'm still not leaving *her*."

Respect gleamed in her eyes as he sat back in his chair. He scanned my face, probably searching for deception or weakness.

Whichever one it was, he'd find neither. I'd meant every word I said.

Remedy could be a pain in the ass but she was *my* pain and until *we* ended things, I was staying right by her side, being exactly what she needed.

His head tilted. "You're willing to lose your job over this... *relationship?*"

I nodded. I'd already made myself clear so there was no need to repeat it.

Verse humphed again, mimicking my cross-armed position and meeting my gaze before looking away with a nod. "Garryn's throwing me a surprise party for my birthday next weekend. I snagged Remedy's invitation before she could give it to Krystal to deliver. I wanted to bring it by myself and check on her."

The sudden subject change caught me off guard but not enough that I didn't comprehend his words. "If it's a surprise, then how do you know about it?" When Verse merely lifted a brow, I couldn't resist a chuckle. "Say less." The man was resourceful and had his fiancée wrapped around his finger, just like he was around hers. It probably hadn't taken much bribing on his end to get her to spill the beans.

While my laugh subsided, he slid a red and gold envelope across the table. I didn't immediately reach for it, still not understanding what the hell had just happened.

"So, what does this mean?"

"What does *what* mean?" He asked, pushing up from the table.

I remained seated, keeping my gaze on him. "*This.* You dropped the subject of me and Rem and invited us to the party like its nothing. We good?"

There was no hesitation in the nod he gave me. "I remember when you first came to HB Corp. You were at the end of your rope and so damn frustrated. You needed this job. *Bad.*"

Tension coiled in my muscles at the reminder of how desolate and desperate I'd been but I sensed no malice in his words, so I waited while he continued.

"You're a good dude, Lathan. And I respect you. I respect the way you looked out for your family, even when you were down and out. They always came first, no matter what." He paused at the end of the table, adjusting the lapels on his jacket, moving closer to me. "If you're willing to sacrifice your job... your *stability* for her, then I know your feelings are real. I have no choice but to respect that bond and accept it."

Still shocked at the swift turnaround, I watched silently as he took another step closer, unable to resist throwing out one last warning. "My job is always to look out for and protect those I love. It's what I do best. She was the most important thing to the man that damn near taught me everything I know which means the responsibility of her well-being then fell to me, which I take seriously."

I turned my chair to face him fully, not shying away from another intense battle of wills we'd been locked in since stepping in the room.

"The last thing I want is for her to get taken advantage of or hurt but if you continue to show that your intentions towards her remain pure, I'm cool." His lids narrowed, tone dipping with malice. Seeing him like this, I understood why the reputation of VP remained solid in the streets of his hometown many years after his departure. Just like Remedy's father, Verse's fingerprints were all over Uptown.

But that still didn't strike fear in my heart. My father had raised me to fear no man besides the one in the mirror. The only man that deserved my fear was *me* because I was the only one truly capable of causing irreparable damage in my own life.

"But the second that changes?" He continued, "The second you do anything to make me doubt your intentions towards her, my permittance of your relationship will disappear just as fast as your position at HB Corp."

I'd maintained my cool until then. But that comment raised my hackles.

For Remedy, I understood not wanting to cause any tension between them because of their relationship but I didn't need his acceptance or permission for *shit*.

I know the woman probably pacing nervously down the hall would've wanted me to let this go but I couldn't.

Not when his tone dripped with arrogance and condescension.

I mean, I get it. I understand.

I got a dick too and sometimes, we like to puff out our chest in attempts to assert our dominance over other males in the vicinity when we want our way.

But I wasn't deferential by nature.

And I damn sure couldn't continue to idly sit by in silence while this man thought his *permission* was the only thing keeping me and Rem together.

Though I seethed internally, my breathing remained even and calm as I tilted my head, spewing words I knew would gut him.

"Do you know her mom is here? That she's been living with us for nearly a month?"

"What?" His brows hiked with incredulousness, but I wasn't finished. Remedy might hate me for this later but that veil he had over his eyes when it came to her and his so-called protection needed to be ripped off.

Somebody needed to let him and everyone else who cared about her know just how *protected* and cared for she truly was.

"Do you know she has a heart condition? Do you know what she went through in her childhood? Before her dad died? Do you know *anything* about her besides surface bullshit?"

A humorless chuckle rushed from his lips. "You've been around, what? Two years? And you're telling me, someone who's known Rem her whole life, that you know more about her than I do?"

"What I'm trying to tell you is that as much as you like to tout about how much you've protected her and looked out for her, you've done a *shit* job so far."

His neck reared back, face contorted. "Excuse me?"

"She's been over there *drowning*." I pushed to my feet, feeling my anger roll over me. Not because of what he'd said and not because of the way he'd try to punk me moments earlier. This all-consuming anger that I'd worked years on overcoming was solely on her behalf. She deserved better from every person who claimed to love her. She'd *always* deserved better. "That woman has been over there fighting so many fuckin' battles alone and not one of you saw it. For years, she suffered and you got the nerve to have your shit puffed out, bragging about how you've protected her. *Fuck outta here.*"

I knew I was toeing a thin line and was likely speaking the exact words that would cost me my job but I didn't care.

Remedy deserved to have someone in her corner, fighting alongside her rather than against her.

Verse's brows remained furrowed as he glared hard at the table in front of him. Despite the contorted expression, he appeared subdued or deflated, as if in disbelief that he'd failed at protecting her.

"What battles is she fighting? Why is she drowning? What the fuck happened to her?"

The questions were spat in rapid succession, but I knew they wouldn't be getting an answer. At least not from me. Making him aware of the cracks in what he thought was bulletproof protection was as much as I was willing to do.

The details surrounding her trauma would have to come from Rem.

"It's not my story to tell. Just know that I'm not walking away from that woman until *she* tells me to go. Too many people have walked away from her, disappointed her, overlooked her, brushed her aside or held her at arm's length. Too many people have failed her in unimaginable ways and I won't be added to that list, even if it means going back and working the drive thru at a burger joint."

I saw that my words had their intended impact because he dropped in the chair he'd just vacated, reclining as his thumb working back and forth across his bottom lip.

Like I'd done with Tessa, he needed to shed his ego with Rem.

He needed to shed everything he *thought* he knew so he could see her for who she really was.

She deserved that, especially from such an important figure in her life.

And if I could make that happen without hurting her further, I'd help in whatever way I could.

27

REMEDY

"You good?"

Keeping my gaze on the high-profile occupants of Verse's lavish birthday party, I nodded at Lathan's question, waiting for the second half of it. Moments later, he didn't disappoint when he asked. "How's the heart?"

"Fine." He sighed with exasperation at my use of the word. He *hated* it. "Better than fine." I added, flashing a half smile.

He sucked his teeth. "I'll accept that."

His arm stretched across the back of my chair, lightly brushing his fingertips against the exposed skin on my left arm and I leaned into it, always eager for his touch.

I'd purposely picked this inconspicuous corner of the ballroom to stay out of the spotlight.

Though Garryn ensured it would be a media and paparazzi free event, that hadn't stopped everyone in attendance from snapping photos on their phones, using the moment to boost their social following.

Laughter, conversation, and loud music filled the space, and if I'd been alone, I might've been upset by how removed I felt from all of it.

But the man sitting on my right side, the one warming me with the heat emanating from his big frame, made it a lot less lonely.

A flash of red in my peripheral had me turning in that direction, watching as Garryn strolled towards us in her customary skyscraper heels. I could walk in heels but the woman wore hers so effortlessly, it was like they were an extension of her.

Amidst playing hostess while wearing the hell out of an ankle length, fitted, and bold blood red dress, she'd ventured over to our table multiple times to check on us.

Neither of us had moved, except the onetime Lathan fetched us drinks from the open bar.

"It's me again." She announced her approach. Rather than hovering behind our chairs like she'd done before, she sat in the empty seat on my other side, letting out a sigh.

Immediately, she reclined, lifting a foot and rotating it in the air with her pretty face contorted.

Well, I guess she was human, after all.

"I think I just saw Deacon." I lifted my head as Lathan scanned the room for his cousin. "He said he'd be here but I hadn't spotted him yet." His eyes fell to me. "I'm gonna go holla at him real quick, okay?"

I nodded, waving him away. I wasn't a child. I didn't need his constant supervision.

Like always, he seemed to know exactly what I was thinking because he narrowed his lids and I fought my laughter.

"Tell Deacon I said hi."

After standing, he pressed a kiss against my forehead before striding across the room with a confidence that never failed to get me hot and bothered.

"I'm thinking about hosting a brunch for my bridesmaids before shopping for my wedding dress." Garryn said, pulling my attention from the man I couldn't stop thinking about. "Would you be interested in coming?"

Just last week, she'd invited me for lunch but I'd had a previous engagement. She'd taken my refusal in stride, promising we'd get together another time.

I didn't understand why she was putting so much effort into getting to know me. I'd expected to show up to the fitting, get measured, and then be at the rehearsal and wedding.

I hadn't expected so much determination on her part and I wanted to know the reason for it.

"Why are you trying so hard?" I asked. She planted her elbow on the table, resting her chin on her fist as she waited for me to elaborate. "Verse already loves you. He's *marrying* you soon. You don't have to try to win him over anymore by being nice to me."

The answering smile she gave me had held a twinge of sadness. "You and I are more alike than you realize, Rem."

I highly doubted that.

Seeing the doubt on my face, she chuckled. "The Garryn sitting here right now is not the same Garryn before Verse came into my life. *Trust me*."

"Facts." Both of our heads lifted to see Verse approaching behind her, teasing smile in place. "She was mean as hell."

"Oh, *shut up*. You loved my mean ass."

"I did. Still do. And always will." His words caused a blush to stain her cheeks and I wondered if that's how I looked each time Lathan was around.

I wasn't sure if it showed on the outside but it damn sure was present on the inside.

"So damn charming," she muttered under her breath as an insult that made him laugh. She pushed from the table, smoothing down the material of her dress before pressing a kiss against his lips. "I'm going to go check on Onyx." Before walking off, her eyes swung to me. "We'll get together later about that brunch, okay?"

I nodded and she smiled before striding off in those heels, not revealing an ounce of the discomfort she'd been feeling moments earlier.

Occupying the seat she'd just evacuated, Verse kept his gaze on her, unashamedly staring until she disappeared from view.

When his gaze swung back to mine, I tensed, hating this weird divide that seemed to exist between us now.

Before leaving my office last week, he'd said a hasty goodbye after his talk with Lathan and it'd been radio silence since.

Tonight, when I'd arrived, each time I found him in the crowd, his eyes had been on me. I wasn't sure what they said between them last week but something had definitely shifted and my stomach tightened with the anticipation of it.

Before Verse could say a word, I searched the room, finding Lathan immediately. It was hard not to, considering how much taller he was than the average person. He stood with Deacon, laughing hard at something his cousin said.

As if sensing when my eyes were on him, his flashed to meet mine and that infamous smirk quirked up his lips.

I flushed, unable to stop it. Anytime Lathan's eyes met mine, I thought about us in bed. Limbs tangled, skin slick with sweat.

I felt like something was wrong with me because I thought about sex *all* the time.

Thankfully, each time I did, he indulged me.

Deacon frowned at his distracted cousin, then followed the direction of his gaze, meeting mine before giving me a sly grin and wave that had me chuckling and returning it.

When Deacon resumed whatever he'd been saying, Lathan held my gaze a few moments more before turning back to his cousin, who'd nudged him to get his attention.

"You really like him, huh?"

"I do." I answered Verse, meeting his gaze head on.

"He and I had a talk last week."

Oh. I guess we were diving right in then.

"I'm aware."

"Do you know what about?" When I shook my head, he reclined in the seat, thumbing back and forth across his bottom lip. The silence between us became thick but I waited, not wanting to speak first. "He told me some things. Things about you. And things about myself that opened my eyes a bit."

Oh hell, Lathan.

When I remained silent, he continued. "He told me I did a *shit* job of protecting you. My ego had me wanting to deny it immediately but then, I thought, what if I had?"

"What did he tell you?"

He snorted an unamused laugh. "Not a damn thing, unfortunately. He told me it's not his story to tell. That I would have to hear it from you." More frustration laced his tone. "Somehow, some way... I've failed you and it's eating me up that I can't pinpoint when. Help me understand where I went wrong, Rem."

I sighed, knowing I wasn't ready to tell him about *that*, especially here, of all places.

I'd need more time to gather my thoughts and prepare myself for the crippling emotions I was sure would be dredged up.

My discomfort must've been obvious because he sighed. "We can table it for now. But I want to talk about this eventually, Rem. If there was something I did or didn't do that directly or indirectly caused you harm, please let me know. It's killing me to think that I've been sitting back all these years, constantly talking shit about how I protect everybody I love and the whole time, you were suffering under my watch."

I didn't want him to believe that whatever trauma was inflicted had occurred recently or directly as a result of something he'd done. It happened when we were kids. There was nothing he could've done to stop it.

Do I wish he would've seen or recognized the damaging lasting effects it had on me? Yes, I do. But he still shouldn't feel at fault for what happened and I needed to make him understand that.

The only one who could've done anything about it had died before I made him aware of what was going on.

"You are not responsible for what happened to me." I said, hating the way his shoulders collapsed at my words. His lids blinked rapidly and his entire frame seemed to diminish in front of my eyes. I knew he'd been expecting, *hoping* that I'd refute Lathan's claims and say that nothing *had* happened and I was fine.

But I wasn't. And I hadn't been in a long, long time.

"It was years ago." I continued. Bile threatened to rush up my throat and I tightened my grip around my clutch. "But I'm still not ready to talk about it. I just wanted you to know that it had nothing to do with you or something you did."

I should've known that vague answer wouldn't satisfy him.

"But *something* happened. And the effects of it still bother you? Still... *hurts* you?" At my reluctant nod, he released a weary sigh. "And I should've recognized that."

Again, I didn't want him shouldering the blame for something he couldn't control.

But I didn't get a chance to say anything because he sighed. "You said you weren't ready to talk about it, so I won't push you. I was just making that observation." He suddenly looked as if the weight of the world was on his shoulders and I felt guilty for being the one to put it there. "I guess I should go make my rounds." His tone revealed that he'd rather be doing anything but that.

"I mean, it *is* your party." I joked, hoping to lighten the mood. "You can't stay ducked off in the corner with me all night."

He smiled, thumping the back of my hand like he'd always done when we were kids whenever I had a smart comeback. Back when our biggest worry had been how long we could stay at the arcade after school before our parents came looking for us.

He stood, barely making it three feet before being stopped.

"*Christian?*" Verse exclaimed, causing my stomach to drop. "Yo, I haven't seen you in years, unc. How you been?"

"*Life's been good, VP.*" The voice of my nightmares said. "*I live in Dallas now, you know. Got my own business out there, thanks to you.*"

My breath quickened and without turning to face the man who responded in a low voice, I *knew*.

Low, shallow gasps rushed out as I tried to catch my breath. I needed *air*.

"*It's good seeing you, too.*" He said as Verse walked away.

Though the words hadn't been directed towards me, I felt the chill they caused down to my marrow. I needed to move, to get *away* before he noticed me or before I laid eyes on him.

But I couldn't. I was frozen in place, crippled by the same fear that kept me silent for so many years.

"*Remedy?*"

I flinched when he addressed me, refusing to turn in my seat. My eyes slid to Lathan who still spoke to Deacon, then Verse's retreating back before finally swinging to Hakeem who stood close to them, eyes trailing Garryn, making sure no harm came to her.

Silently, I prayed that someone, *anyone* would look in my direction and see the fear crippling me.

But they never did. All of them were engrossed in something else, not paying me the least bit of attention.

It hurt.

Just like back then, I was so close to people who cared about me, so close to people who declared themselves as my protectors but I was terrified and they didn't see it.

"Remedy? Is that you?"

My heart pounded wildly in my chest and the hairs on my arm rose as he came around to stand in front of me. Though he'd aged, he still looked the same and it paralyzed me.

I couldn't move. I couldn't blink. I couldn't speak.

That blank slate that I'd become notorious for abandoned me as I felt my face collapse, contorting with terror.

I couldn't catch my breath and my chest tightened to the point that I feared I was on the verge of having another episode.

Why was he here? Why *now*?

All these years, I'd never run into him or any of the other men who'd hurt me. None of them had ever attended my dad's birthday celebrations or events Verse hosted. For years, I'd prayed they were six feet under or locked behind bars. Even if the charges that kept them there had nothing to do with me, I would've been glad that *someone* had received justice.

But clearly my prayers had gone unanswered because he slipped in the seat Verse had just vacated, looking as if life hadn't chewed him up and spit him out. He didn't look like he'd suffered one bit. He didn't look like a man who had restless nights, fucked up relationships or a fear of intimacy like I had.

The bastard looked at *peace*.

Meanwhile, I felt like I'd been tossed back in time and he was above me again, mumbling *sweet nothings* in my ear as if what he'd done to me was a consensual encounter rather than what it truly was.

A *violation*.

"I'm not going to waste your time." He said and my stomach balled in knots. "I only came because I wanted to tell you this, then get out of your hair so you never have to see me again."

I felt anger at his audacity but fear overshadowed it.

I'd vowed to myself to never feel this way again, but here I was, helpless to the way it crippled me.

I wanted to move past this.

I wanted to be over it and be normal.

But I couldn't.

When his hand reached out, I swiftly retreated, ignoring the stinging pain of my back meeting the chair I sat in.

I can't believe he'd had the audacity to try and *touch me*.

He sighed as if disappointed. "I've had to live with what I did... what *we* did to you for a long time and I know it was wrong. I apologize for it, Remy." He paused when I flinched before continuing. "*Sincerely*." He flicked his gaze around my face as if waiting for me to accept it but I remained silent. "Big Tim had done too much for us to betray him that way. He didn't deserve that." He seemed to recognize how fucking ridiculous that statement was because he corrected himself. "I mean, *neither* of you deserved that, especially you."

If I wasn't so paralyzed by fear, I might've sputtered out a disbelieving laugh.

The man who'd violated an innocent child was apologizing because my *father* hadn't deserved the betrayal. Not because of the effect it had on me... not because his ass had done it for years with nobody knowing... not because he'd moved on to live his life while I was left with the residual effects.

My father's generosity towards him was the only thing that made him feel guilty for what he'd done.

Ain't *that* some bullshit?

28

LATHAN

Something was wrong.

Despite being across the room, my eyes trailed in Remedy's direction more times than I could count. She'd been wearing her mask tonight, face carefully blank, not making much of an effort to make those who greeted her welcome.

But now that I'd seen her without it, I didn't understand how everyone else didn't recognize it.

Like I'd taken a course on Remedy Sinclair, I recognized her mood changes despite her expression remaining the same.

I could tell when she'd been annoyed by a woman who'd come to the table earlier to chat with her about business. And I could tell when she'd grown uncomfortable after one too many people approached her when we first arrived, engulfing her in hug after hug before she could refute them. I'd offered to step in but she refused, saying she was *fine*.

She'd patted their back awkwardly, not giving herself completely to the hug before taking a step back, sliding her gaze in my direction.

Just like I couldn't keep my gaze off her, she couldn't keep hers off of me.

Which was why I realized that the discomfort she'd tried to mask all night had morphed into an expression I'd never seen flash across her beautiful face.

Terror.

She looked like she'd seen a ghost as a tall, muscular man sat in front of her wearing an expression of guilt.

Not bothering to excuse myself from the conversation with Deacon and Verse, who apparently had known each other for years, I slipped past Hakeem's wide shoulders.

I ignored the way Verse's eyes trailed behind me. I was too focused on crossing the room to get to the woman who held the glass in her hand so tight, I was afraid she'd shatter it.

"There aren't enough words I can say to apologize for what I did." I heard him say to her once I was within earshot. "It was wrong. It was sick. And there was no excuse for it. And I'll live with that regret until the day I di..."

Despite being on the receiving end of an apology, Remedy paled at each word he spoke, so I interrupted, knowing I needed to end whatever the fuck this was. "Aye." The man's eyes swung to mine, filled with remorse, but Rem's remained on him as if she couldn't make herself look away. "Who are you?" I asked, squatting next to her and wrapping an arm around her waist, becoming more concerned when even that didn't break her stare.

The man flashed a quick glance at her struck expression before smiling sadly. His shoulders were slouched, demeanor subdued, causing him to give off the aura of a man much smaller, despite his height nearly matching mine. "Just an old family friend." This time when his gaze swung back to her, he gave her a small nod. "Y'all have a good night."

I wanted to keep my gaze on him as he turned to walk off but the slight tremors I felt against my side were all that mattered. "Talk to me, Rem." I urged, sensing that despite her not saying a word, she was spiraling, plummeting into a place of darkness where I couldn't reach her.

"Can we leave?" The brokenness in her tone ripped at my core and I fought down the rising anger I felt. The urge to chase down the man who'd caused that reaction in this beautiful woman was strong, but she was all that mattered.

Ensuring that she was okay was all that mattered.

One lone tear trailed over her cheek and my chest tightened as she slipped her hand in mine.

"We can leave, babe."

29

REMEDY

If I could stay in bed forever, I would.

With my head buried beneath a mountain of comforters, I was content with wallowing all weekend until I went back to work on Monday.

The television played quietly in the background, serving no other purpose than to break up the silence I'd been submerged in since last night.

Since getting home after Verse's party, I'd been cooped up in my room, refusing to come out even to eat. Lathan had ventured to my door multiple times but I kept shooing him away, not ready to face him or answer the questions about my bizarre behavior last night.

I knew he'd be able to see right through me and being read was not high on my current list of things to do.

I pulled back the cover to get some air, peeking around my stark white clinical room.

I'd never noticed before but it was sterile, boring, and lacked any personality. *Like me.*

At one time, neutrality calmed me but now that same monotony felt stifling and restrictive.

There was a knock at the door.

I ignored it like I'd done to the others, expecting whoever it was to leave me alone. But this time, it opened. I lifted my head just enough to watch Isabel breeze in. A pleasant smile stretched her lips and I couldn't place when the hell she'd gotten comfortable enough to just walk in freely.

Through narrowed lids, I continued to trail her, watching as she parted my blinds, slamming me with unwanted sunlight. Bright green eyes that matched mine flashed in my direction.

"Get *out*." I grumbled after tossing the covers over my head. Moments later, the side of my bed dipped and I flung the covers off me again to glare at the woman who'd sat. "What part of *get out* was hard to understand?"

Again, she ignored my request. Now that she was closer, I saw that the smile I'd thought was pleasant appeared strained around the edges, tight with the tension that I now realized filled her.

"Talk to me, Rem."

"Excuse me?" My neck reared. "Why would I want to do that?"

"Because I sense you need it." Her smile was sad as her head tilted, surveying me with tenderness. I could only imagine what she saw on my face as she sighed. "Ask me anything. Talk to me. Yell at me. Scream, cry... do something." For once, exasperation crossed her features as she tossed her hands in the air. "I've been here a month and we've barely exchanged more than two sentences at a time."

"There's a reason for that."

She ignored my mumbled comment, tilting her head. "Then last night, you came in visibly upset before locking yourself in here. Whatever it is, let me help. I *want* to help. Even if only a little."

Her request was met with silence.

"Was it Lathan? Did he upset you?"

More silence.

"Verse? Hakeem? Someone you work with? Someone at the part-"

"Can you not?!" I snapped, scooting up in the bed until my back rested against the headboard. The reopened wound from last night still felt raw. *Exposed.*

"Baby, I *know* you're angry with me. And likely disappointed. And I'm noy asking for forgiveness. What I'm offering is a chance for you to release that anger you've been holding on to." She reached out, placing a hand on top of the blankets covering my lap. "Whatever it is, I can help. Let me help fix what I broke."

Her words caused a red haze to come over me.

"You think you can help me? You think you can fix me?" A humorless chuckle rushed out and I pushed from the bed, pacing across the floor, keeping my gaze averted. I felt a loss of control approaching and I tried to stamp it down. I tried to fight it but I couldn't. I was so damn full of emotions that keeping them at bay was impossible. "You want to talk, huh?" I asked, finally lifting my gaze to hers. "Okay, let's do it."

She seemed to recognize the deterioration of my state and she stood and moved towards me but I held out a hand, stopping her.

"No, you want to talk. Let's talk. Just don't be surprised when this confession isn't what you thought it would be."

I licked my lips, then raked my nails through my disheveled hair before giving up when the curls kept popping back to their original position.

"Where do you want to start, *mom*?" I asked sarcastically. "With you walking out on me like I meant nothing? Or do you want to talk about the shit I went through after you left?" She parted her lips to answer but I waved away the words before she could. "You know, let's not beat around the bush. Let's jump right into the molestation." The word was sour on my tongue, filled with bitterness.

Her eyes widened and she stumbled back, sinking onto the bed, looking shell shocked.

She wanted me to talk?

So I did.

I told her about everything that was done to me.

I told her about the sexual acts I'd been forced to perform.

I told her about the culprits being the same men that my father called his brothers and my friends called uncle.

"These were the same men he looked out for." I mumbled, hugging myself as I continued to pace. Now, I was purging my feelings, letting everything up and out without sparing her a glance. This was no longer for her. It was for *me*.

"Those men's kids benefited from my father's kindness and generosity and they still did that to me!" I scoffed. "My dad was arrogant, thinking he and I were untouchable because of his reputation. He believed his street cred was enough to protect us."

Before I could stop it, my hand shot out, knocking over a dull white vase that I just realized I *hated*. "Where was that respect for him when those men violated me and touched me while I was under his roof? How did that street cred protect me when I was upstairs going through hell while he was downstairs, entertaining the guests that were always in and out of the house? Those men knew he never saw me and they took advantage of it."

She looked horrified. Her face was contorted, soaked with tears as she sat there, cupping her hand over her mouth. "Oh, no. baby. *No*."

"You left me there! You packed up and left me there with them." I paced, muscles tightening with the agitation flowing through me.

This reaction was what I feared.

The calm, and composed veneer I'd perfected over the years was now shattered. All the ugliness and pain that lay beneath had been uncovered.

And right now, when I needed that composure I coveted, I couldn't find it because my defenses had already been breached.

A six-and-a-half-foot man who made me feel alive and his sixteen-year-old daughter had snuck their way in, giving me joy I hadn't expected while also leaving me defenseless against the onslaught of emotions I'd held at bay for far too long.

And I couldn't control them.

I felt them *all* and I wanted to keel over or fall to my knees from the weight of it.

"I needed you. I needed him. And neither of you were there for me. Neither of you protected me when I needed it most. It's not fair that everyone's life kept moving forward while I felt trapped for so many years. I didn't care about the nice clothes or shoes Daddy bought me. I didn't care about the birthday cards you sent every year. I didn't care about any of it then, just like I don't care about it now." My hand waved around the room wildly and I felt like I was cracking at the seams, about to become unhinged in a way that I never had before. "All I wanted was for someone to love me enough to save me! And nobody ever did."

A soft gasp at the door drew both of our attention, snapping me out of the haze I'd been in.

I'd been so focused on purging my secrets that it wasn't until my words trailed and my vision cleared that I noticed the tears streaking my mom's cheeks and the two people who stood in the doorway, looking shell shocked.

My heart sank.

I hadn't wanted him to overhear that. I'd wanted to shield that part of me from him.

Now he would see me for what I truly was.

Tainted. *Broken.*

My eyes swung from his concerned ones, turning back to my mom. Isabel lowered her hands from her mouth, lips opening and closing like a fish out of water.

After begging me to talk for so long, when I finally did, she was speechless.

Figures.

"Rem."

I was so distraught that I couldn't tell which one of them had called my name. It sounded like it was coming from the other end of a long tunnel, distorted and muffled.

"*Get out.*"

"Babe?"

"*Get out!*" I yelled it this time. I felt myself crashing and I needed to be alone when it happened. Hollowness was settling into my chest and I just felt tired. Exhausted in a way I hadn't felt in a long time.

My nose burned and I knew from the stinging behind my lids that tears would soon follow.

They weren't moving fast enough for me to hide it from them so I whirled, racing across the floor towards my bathroom and slamming the door before any of them could follow me.

With my movements on autopilot, I climbed up the three steps that led to my bath, sitting in the empty tub fully clothed. Like I'd done each time my emotions and circumstances overwhelmed me as a child, I drew my knees up to my chest. My shoulders sank and my teeth buried into the flesh of my forearm, holding my guttural sobs at bay as tears rolled over my cheeks.

Before long, even my forearm wasn't enough to muffle the cries.

I cried so loud and so hard that I hadn't noticed I wasn't alone anymore until the sound of his shoe dropping to the floor startled me. When I glanced up, he was right there, climbing the steps. I met his gaze before cringing at the pity I saw there before dropping my head, knowing I looked a mess.

But my disheveled appearance didn't deter him.

If anything, his movements became surer and more determined as he swung his legs over the edge of the deep tub before sliding in across from me, still fully clothed in the sweats and hoodie he wore earlier.

I kept my gaze averted, too embarrassed to meet his again, hoping he'd get the hint and leave. But as the minutes passed and he stayed there, I sighed wearily, wanting him to go away so I could revert to crying and falling apart in private.

"I don't want to talk." I said shortly.

He didn't move a muscle or take his eyes off me as he spoke. "I won't make you." He finally shrugged. "I just want to hold you."

"Why?" I croaked, voice thick and strained from all the stress I'd put it through. "Why bother?"

"Because seeing you hurt hurts me and if I can make what's going on just the tiniest bit better by sitting here in silence and holding you until you've cried every tear, I'll do it."

Why did he have to be so... *him?*

Why did he always know what to say or do?

Hell, I didn't even know what to do with *myself* most of the time. Yet he seemed to be perfectly in tune with me and my emotions because, like it did every time I thought something was going to come between us, his kindness undid me and made me crave him and his embrace even more.

My lips trembled and my shoulders sagged.

"Rem, baby, ju-" He didn't have time to finish his sentence because I launched myself at him, plastering my front against his, wrapping my arms tight around his neck as if I was afraid to let go.

Knowing exactly what I needed, he reciprocated the hug, squeezing me and murmuring calming words in my ear that caused the tears to start up again.

"What do you need from me?" He asked, brushing up and down my spine in a soothing motion. "What do you need me to do to make this better?"

I sniffed, brushing at my falling tears with my fingers before burying my face in his neck. *"This.* Just keep doing this."

Time became a nonfactor as he held me.

We could've been there for ten minutes or ten hours for all I cared. The point was, it didn't matter because I knew his arms were the safest place to be.

I had no doubt that the man holding me would look out for my well-being, regardless of the situation. Even though we would be more comfortable in the bed, I didn't want to leave the sanctuary we'd temporarily created.

Once my sobs subsided, I shifted in his lap, now sitting sideways rather than straddling him.

The new position was much more comfortable and able to accommodate the sleep I felt coming over me.

"Can I ask one question? There's just one burning in my mind right now and I have to ask." I stiffened but kept my eyes closed as he kept talking. "If you don't want to answer, just tell me to mind my fucking business and I will. You know I will, babe."

"What is it?" I asked through a loud yawn.

When he didn't immediately ask, I looked up, finding his gaze locked on me. My throat felt scratchy and eyes swollen with tears. My lips felt cracked and dry, desperate for hydration.

Long story short, I probably looked like a hot ass mess but still, the softness in his gaze, the unwavering stare that lit me from the inside out made me feel like I was the most beautiful woman in the world.

"Was that him last night?" He finally asked, brushing a thumb under my eye to catch a stray tear. I wanted to play stupid or pretend like I didn't know what he was asking. But I was so tired of pretending. So tired of deflecting. So tired of putting up a front everywhere I went, so I answered him honestly.

"One of them."

He stilled underneath me, jaw clenching.

Other than the tension in his body that hadn't been there moments earlier and the slight tightening around his eyes, he outwardly didn't have much of a reaction to my words.

"Okay." He whispered. "*Okay.*" I didn't know what that meant and really didn't care to ask because he squeezed me tight, pulling me close against his chest. I snuggled in like a child, allowing the safety of his arms and strength in his presence to soothe me until I fell asleep.

30

LATHAN

I'd lost count of the hours I'd spent in this tub with Remedy, who was still sprawled across my lap, knocked out.

I was afraid to move because the first attempts had woken her and she'd wrapped her arms around me each time, squeezing like my embrace was enough to keep her safe from her demons.

I'd just returned from picking Tessa up from Gabbi's house when we overheard her.

At first, because the home was so big, we hadn't noticed what was going on. But as we climbed the stairs, following the noise that escalated from a muffle to yelling, both of us exchanged curious glances.

I'd told Tessa to go to her room but of course she didn't listen. Instead, she followed right behind me and matched my quick pace.

My intention was to go in and break up whatever was going on between Isabel and Remedy.

But then I started processing her words. Started actually *listening* to what she was saying. Each word spoken revealed the depth of trauma this woman had suffered and I'd been wholly unprepared for it.

One of them.

Three simple words had fucking gutted me.

I'd felt *less* turmoil when the judge sentenced me to fifteen years. But those words from her tonight outweighed that, feeling like a Mike Tyson punch to the gut.

One of them.

God.

How many people had hurt her? And for how long?

When I'd first come in and spotted her huddled in the corner of the tub, I'd decided that I wouldn't force her to give me any details she didn't want to share. But that hadn't stopped the questions from burning the edge of my tongue with the urge to ask.

For the last few hours, I'd sat here, numbly, wondering how the fuck I could get away with murder.

Because that was the only fitting end for men like the monster who'd not only violated a child but had the nerve to approach her as an adult and ask for forgiveness.

I'd do another bid in a *heartbeat* if it meant slaying the demons that had haunted this woman for years.

Jesus.

Each time I thought I knew her, more was revealed.

The puzzle I'd compared Remedy to weeks ago was more complex than I could've imagined. The journey to peeling back every layer was arduous. The path to penetrating this woman's defenses was like a battlefield, lined with mines and obstacles to deter anyone from venturing too close.

But I'd take that chance.

For her, I'd be willing to go to the ends of the earth. I'd slay every dragon and defeat every demon. Whatever she needed me to do, I would because she was worth it.

She was *more* than worth it.

I just hoped I was worthy of *her* when it was all said and done.

31

REMEDY

I DIDN'T DRINK because my abusers always came to me after they'd indulged.

As if they needed the liquid courage to build up their nerves.

I'd been the one in need of a numbing agent to get me through the bullshit they'd done, not the other way around.

But each night, they reeked of it and the smell threatened to suffocate me when they crept in my room. And because of that, not a drop of it had passed my lips. Ever.

But after *seeing* one of them then blurting out all my secrets earlier, I gave in.

I indulged.

Okay... I *overindulged*.

I'd gone right for the bottle of vodka, ignoring the brown liquor because it reminded me too much of them.

I'd planned on one drink, mixing it with orange juice and sipping the bitter concoction, realizing I'd added way more liquor than mixer.

But I'd forced it down with a grimace, gulping the entire cup in three big swallows to get it over with.

The liquor wasn't hitting fast enough, so I started drinking directly from the bottle. An hour in, I stood in the center of the theater room, humming the new Gideon tune I'd overheard Tessa listening to the other day. My eyes were closed and the clear bottle was hugged tight against my chest.

"Rem?"

I continued humming, turning to look over my shoulder at Lathan. He stood in the doorway of my theater room, frowning at me swaying before turning his gaze towards the mess I'd made on the bar when I got into a fight with a pile of napkins trying to clean up spilled orange juice.

"You okay, babe?"

There was a delay in my brain as I processed his words before I responded with, "It's not fair."

His expression morphed into... something that made my chest tight but I was too drunk to figure out what the fuck it meant so I started humming again, swaying lightly.

"What's not fair?"

"Nothing," I muttered, then frowned, "Everything. *Everything.*"

"You want to talk about it?"

"I don't want to talk about anything."

That blissful place of ignorance and detachment I'd drunk myself into started fading and feelings I was trying to numb threatened to creep back in.

No.

Nope.

Not to-*fuckin'*-day.

I deserved a break so I took another swig. Then another.

"Then you don't have to talk about anything," he said, approaching me with measured steps and hands held up like I was an uncaged animal.

I frowned, tightening my grip on the bottle, daring him with my narrowed lids to take it.

"I thought you didn't drink."

"I don't."

One of his brows hiked on his forehead. "I think that *don't* is now *didn't*."

"Semantics." I took another swig.

"You willing to share?"

"Not if you're going to take it and keep it."

His lips twisted up in a half smile before he grabbed the bottle, taking a big gulp. While he drank, I stumbled to sit on the oversized theater couch, watching him from the corner of my eye.

Of course, he followed, sitting on the opposite end. He took another swig before passing it back to me and I readily accepted.

Back and forth we passed the bottle until nearly none remained. While I seemed to get drunker with each sip, he was still annoyingly sober, not taking his eyes off me once. When the last drop made its way down my throat, I sat the empty bottle on the floor next to my feet.

I sighed and reclined, mind flip-flopping between whether getting drunk lived up to the hype or whether it was overrated.

I wasn't sure if making that call was fair at the moment. Maybe I'd have a more accurate assessment in the morning if I wasn't puking up my guts.

Turning sideways, I lifted my feet from the ground, swinging them in his direction. Immediately, he caught them, resting them in his lap, absentmindedly rubbing and squeezing while keeping his eyes on me.

"You're really just going to sit there, staring at me?" I mumbled, taking a loose curl and twirling it around my finger.

"Um hmm." He mumbled, releasing my feet and tossing his arm over the back of the plush sofa.

"Why?"

"Have you seen you?" He scooted closer until the back of my thighs rested on top of his. "I can't think of a better way to spend my time."

Despite feeling flattered at his words, I rolled my eyes and he laughed. Hoping to make him uncomfortable, I adjusted my position, twisting to my side to return his probing stare. His lips twitched when he realized what I was doing but he kept watching me, scanning my face as if committing it to memory then roaming over my body before returning to his gaze to mine.

It was heavy and... *intense*.

I couldn't seem to sit still as I tried my hardest to appear as cool and aloof as he did. But after not even a full minute, I realized I was in over my head.

I should've known this was nothing to him because he'd always met my gaze boldly even back when I claimed to hate him.

The longer he stared, the more I felt the urge to talk. Normally, I'd be grateful for the silence but the liquor had loosened my tongue. Unspoken words and thoughts threatened to spill over, so I gave in, blurting the first thing that came to my mind. "It's not fair."

One brow cocked. "Am I allowed to ask or are you still not talking about it?" Glad that he was still teasing me after everything he'd heard, I kicked him in the side, feigning annoyance. "I'm joking, babe. You know you can talk to me." When my lips pursed, he laughed again. "I'm all ears."

With liquid courage courtesy of the empty bottle resting on the floor, I spoke. "I have all of this. I built all of this." I waved my hand in the air, gesturing to the home surrounding us. "From the outside looking in, I have a life that many people would kill for... more wealth at my fingertips than I can spend in an entire lifetime... yet..."

After a few moments where I didn't immediately pick up where I left off, he rubbed a soothing thumb across the top of my foot. "Yet?" he prompted.

"Yet," I continued. "I hurt every day. I'm *miserable*. I have so much baggage and not a clue what to do with any of it."

"Unpack it." He said simply. This time, my eyebrow was the one lifting. "You've carried it long enough, Rem. I think it's time."

I huffed, hating that he'd made it sound so simple because to me, it wasn't. "And where am I supposed to start? How do I unpack?"

"One bag at a time." His tone revealed he was speaking from

experience. "You take one bag, inspect the contents, and sort it. Decide what lessons you're going to keep that'll help you down the line. Purge things that don't serve you or improve your life. Some of them will be easier to deal with than others. Some will take minutes, some will take years. The good thing is that the bags are yours. So you don't have to be on anyone else's timeline as you unpack."

His words made sense.

But would I be successful in implementing them?

Only time would tell.

But for now, while I felt comfortable enough to speak openly, I took his advice. "Can I unpack one right now?"

His thumb stilled its soothing circles. His eyes scanned my face, searching before he nodded. "You already know the answer to that."

I licked my lips, releasing the grip I had on my curls. "It was hard growing up, even aside from... *that*." I attempted to pull my feet from his lap but he stopped me. I took that as a sign to keep going. "So many people needed, depended on, looked up to, and idolized my dad that it felt like when he shared so much of himself with Uptown, there wasn't much left for me." This time, I successfully snatched my feet from him. Before he could protest, I crawled across the space separating us, sidling up against his side, speaking freely. "Nearly all my memories of my dad involve someone else. People were always in and out of our house and he was always being called on. Attending my tennis matches and track meets became a distraction because so many people required his attention. He'd been there for seventeen years of my life and I still felt like he missed so much."

With my cheek resting on his arm, I lifted my head to meet his gaze. "I just wanted him to see me. I just wanted *anyone* to see me."

Still do.

He must've recognized the unspoken addition to my sentence because he leaned down until his forehead met mine. "Like I told you before, I see you." Instantly, my lids filled with tears and I tried to turn away but he stopped me with a single finger against my cheek. "And for as long as I have breath, I always will."

Pushing up to my knees, I swung my leg over his hips, straddling him. His russet gaze never wavered and neither did mine as I leaned forward, pressing a kiss against his lips.

"I miss you." I mumbled, tracing the outer edge of his full lips with my tongue.

He smiled against my mouth, planting a hand on each side of my waist. "I'm right here, babe."

I shook my head, rocking my hips back and forth in a sensual grind. "No, I *miss* you."

The humor he'd just displayed disappeared and he gripped my hips, stilling my movements.

"What's wrong?"

"C'mon, babe. We don't have to do that. Not tonight."

My neck jerked back and I looked at him incredulously. "*What?*" I shifted in his lap, attempting to reach between us before huffing when his hands blocked mine. "Why the hell not?"

"Because..." he said, blocking my wandering hands again. "I'm not trying to go there with you tonight." When I continued looking at him with a lifted brow, he sighed. "After what I learned today, sex is the further thing from my mind right now, Rem." My cheeks flooded with heat, embarrassment rolling over me in a vicious wave. "Hold up." He chided, shackling my wrists with his hands when I tried to climb off him. "I can see your mind racing and coming up with some *bullshit* about why I'm turning you down. So before you fall too deep in that rabbit hole, let me tell you, whatever you're thinking is probably *wrong*."

"You don't know what I'm thinking." When I yanked my wrists this time, he released me, sighing when I pushed to my feet.

Sitting for so long had fooled me into thinking I was sober or, at the very least, on my way there. But the second I took a few steps, my body reminded me just how much I'd imbibed tonight. I swayed, gripping the back of the sofa for support.

Lathan was on his feet not a second later, steadying me with sure hands. "Your ass can barely stand up straight and you're trying to fuck?"

I sucked my teeth. "Last time I checked, standing up straight isn't a prerequisite."

"But being sober is."

"Not when it's us." Reaching up, I raked my nails through his beard, smiling to myself when he leaned over, pressing further into my hand. "I trust you with my body, no matter what state I'm in. Drunk, high, sober... it doesn't matter."

My declaration caused his nostrils to flare and I tilted my head, spying something in him through my drunken haze. Simmering just below the surface, I caught a glimpse of something that piqued my interest.

Sober Remedy might've backed off but clearly intoxicated Remedy was a glutton for punishment because I decided to push his buttons.

I'd heard his mention of taking anger management classes after prison and the work he'd done on changing the way he reacted when angered or provoked.

I didn't want the man to lose complete control but the way he wanted me to be with him—free, uninhibited, and without filter—I wanted the same from him.

Until now, I'd thought the gentle giant side was who he was all the time.

But that one glimpse moments ago... the quick flash in his gaze revealed that he still held parts of himself back and that just wouldn't do.

I appreciated his protection and his looking out for my well-being. But I didn't need him to do that here. Not with us.

The trust I'd built with him in the bedroom hadn't faded just because I'd run into a former abuser. Though that bag still had a lot of unpacking left to do, I felt relief knowing that the secret was finally out. I'd feared him losing his desire for me. I'd feared him walking away from me.

And he'd done neither.

So I wanted to do this with him, my way. But first I had to get him out of *his* head.

With my gaze locked on his, I recalled the sensuality Envy embodied at *Greed* weeks ago. The fluidity of her movements looked nothing like mine but the lust that sprang to life in his gaze revealed it didn't matter.

What I was doing was enough.

Allowing my curls to fall over one shoulder, I unbuttoned the oversized shirt of his I wore, biting on my bottom lip teasingly before letting it drop. "Sure you don't want to fuck me, baby?" He blew out a harsh breath. That had been my first time using an endearment and the effect on him was immediate. Now, with my gaze locked on the bulge slowly tenting the front of his sweats, I continued my strip tease, giggling when he had to catch me after I tripped on... *nothing*.

His firm eye contact finally broke, dropping to my hands when I gripped the waist of my panties, easing them down my thighs until the only articles of clothing remaining were a pair of thick, fuzzy socks, and my bra.

He focused on the apex of my thighs and I parted them, giving him a lewd view of just how ready I was.

Flashing his gaze up towards the ceiling, he laughed humorlessly. When he started strolling towards the door, my heart stuttered in my chest and I opened my mouth to ask him not to leave. But the words didn't have time to pass my lips because instead of leaving, he twisted the lock in place then moved back towards me.

"You want to get fucked, hmm?" I could practically see the anger rolling off him as he strode over, stripping out of his hoodie by pulling it from the back of his neck. The t-shirt he wore was removed the same way, discarded carelessly on one of the bar stools.

When he stood in front of me, my tongue swiped against my lower lip, unable to stop admiring just how damn *fine* he was.

When I reached up to touch his bare chest, his hand caught mine midair. "You trying to push my buttons?" When I let my silence serve as my response, he shook his head, releasing then turning me around. Stepping up behind me, both hands circled my waist, resting there momentarily before gliding up my torso, lingering around my stiff nipples, causing a low moan to rush past my lips. "Okay," he said, using his bulk to bump against my backside, guiding us towards the couch we'd just vacated moments earlier. "Let me show you what happens when you poke the beast."

CLEARLY I WASN'T the only one who'd been holding back in this relationship.

I wasn't sure if the liquor had finally hit Lathan or if my words pushed him over the edge but what he showed me after was a side of him I was *not* expecting.

Lathan had a rough side. A *wild* side.

And I don't know what the hell was wrong with me, but I loved every bit of it.

"*Ohhhh*." I moaned, rising on my tiptoes, trying not to fly over the sofa from the vicious lunges coming from behind.

"This what you wanted?"

The walls of the theater room were padded and soundproof, so I allowed the full effect of my pleasure to ring out.

"This what you wanted to see? To bring out of me?" His knees dipped, hips snapping back and forth at a quick pace, hitting the right spot each and every time.

I tried to ease myself off the fullness I felt, leaning further over the back of the couch. But he recognized what I was doing and gripped my waist with one hand while grabbing a fistful of my curls with the other, yanking me back towards him.

"Oh, shit." I cried out when a spasm shot through my core, enjoying the rough treatment only because it came from *him*. His hips slowed momentarily, giving me a moment to catch my breath. I could feel his curious gaze so I twisted my head to look over my shoulder, knees nearly buckling when I glimpsed his body.

He'd been angry when he pushed me over the back of the couch, choosing to lower the waistband of his sweats just enough to free his dick and balls. Now they were pooled around his ankles and I caught glimpses of the thick, powerfully corded thighs each time he retreated before slamming back into me.

When my gaze locked on his, he twisted more of my hair in his hand, tightening the grip until no slack remained. With intense scrutiny, he watched my face as he tugged on it, brows lifting slowly when I cried out, gushing around him.

"You like that shit," he mused in a quiet tone. "You like when I'm rough with you, Rem?" When I bit my lip, he tugged on it again and my body betrayed me, clenching around the dick still fully lodged inside.

I felt wrong admitting that I liked it. Especially considering my past.

But that experience and what Lathan and I did together was miles apart. This was on *my* terms. And I trusted him to know and understand my limits. I trusted him to respect my request to stop if things went too far.

"What have you been doing in your spare time, babe?" He asked, keeping his gaze on mine as I watched him over my shoulder. "You been doing research?"

Dammit, how did he know?

Since people just barged in my room unannounced nowadays—Tessa and her dad included—each night, I spent my time in the bath doing... *research* as he'd called it, trying to learn as much as I could about sex since I'd missed out for so long.

And by doing that, I discovered something about myself.

The scenes where couples engaged in rough sex drew my attention the most.

Full blown BDSM or degradation was a bit out there for me, but to each its own. But the rough sex that I enjoyed was when the man pulled the woman's hair, smacked her ass a few times, or was just more *aggressive* with her in the bedroom.

"What did you find?" His tone was impossibly patient, lacking the anger threading through it not long ago. Now, his curiosity peaked. His hips had paused, giving me a brief respite while his hands continued stroking over my flesh. "Tell me what you learned. What you liked."

Having this conversation with him should've felt weird since my upper half was bent over the sofa and he was still fully submerged in my warmth. But it didn't.

"Spanking." I whispered. "Hair pulling."

I'd also stumbled upon *praise kink* and had a love/hate relationship with it.

Though the phrase *good girl* did nothing for me, hearing the woman's partner praise her in other ways or verbalize his adoration for her and her body or what she was doing to him seemed to get me going.

"Praise." I added just as quietly.

"Hmm." He mused. "Go on."

I bit my bottom lip, swinging my gaze from his. "That's it." *For now.* I still needed to do a bit more *research* on certain things before I could accurately assess whether I liked them being done to me.

"So... if I heard you correctly, spanking is a turn on?"

I parted my lips to say yes but all that emerged was a squeak when his palm landed soundly on the outside curve of my ass. Immediately, I pressed further into his pelvis, moaning when he sank fully inside again.

"You want to be spanked there?" He asked before slipping the same hand around my waist, brushing his fingers against me before placing a quick slap against my damp folds. Electricity ebbed through me, awakening each inch of flesh as it traveled all over. "Or here?"

Oh *shit*.

I hadn't seen *that* done during my research but I damn sure wanted more of it.

"I'll take the way you're squeezing my shit as the answer being *yes* to both."

Liquid heat raced to my core when he started moving again. Random smacks against my ass and clit paired with the hair pulling had me feeling like I was floating in a sea of ecstasy.

Low mumbled words of praise passed his lips soon after as he gave me exactly what I wanted.

"Show me how good you can cum for me."

My body seized at his words before my thighs trembled. "*Awh, Lathan.*" The most powerful orgasm I'd ever experienced hit me like a speeding train. I was glad my face was buried in the soft cushions because I feared that if it wasn't, drool would seep from the corners of my mouth.

The pleasure was so intense that it left me in a stupor. Inch by inch, the tension released from my frame until I resembled a rag doll, limp and lifeless.

The only thing keeping me upright was his firm body pinning me against the back of the sofa.

While I went through that life changing experience, Lathan thrust back and forth, though much gentler than the pistoning he'd been doing before I fell over the edge.

"Rem?" He asked when my body remained limp. "*Rem.*"

Without lifting my head, I waved a hand in the air, hoping he could understand my muffled words. "Don't mind me. I'm just going into cardiac arrest." His hips instantly stilled and I cursed under my breath, forgetting how he did *not* play when it came to my heart condition. "It was a joke." I rushed out before he could get upset. "Just playing. The heart's *fine.*"

Without saying a word, he retreated and my walls clamped down around nothing, missing his intrusion already.

Before I could complain, he whipped me around, lifted me in his arms, then carried me over to the bar, planting my ass on the edge.

Through heavy lids, I watched him pull up a stool, positioning it between my spread thighs then sitting on it. It lined his face up perfectly between my spread thighs.

"You didn't..." My words trailed when he shook his head.

"You owe me a couple more before I get mine." When my mouth dropped open, he smiled. "You said you *missed* me, right?"

Without warning, he leaned forward, dragging his tongue up through my folds before his lids fell and he sighed as if I was the best thing he'd ever tasted.

"Let me show you how much I missed *you*."

32

REMEDY

SOMEONE WAS WATCHING ME.

Even in sleep, that eerie feeling of having eyes on you was unmistakable.

I didn't make it known that I was awake.

No, I was still in too much pain for that.

Clearly, I'd overindulged the night before and the pounding headache and rolling nausea was payment for my recklessness. After Lathan and I used each other's body like we'd never done before, we collapsed in the theater room, sleeping for hours before he woke in the middle of the night and carried me upstairs.

I'd insisted on a shower, refusing to get in my bed before rinsing off the nasty things we'd done to one another. Though he was as annoyed as I was, he obliged.

The hangover hadn't started yet because I'd honestly still been drunk when we woke up. Becoming irritated with how long I was taking, he snatched my loofah from me, gliding it all over my body in circular motions just like I did. After pulling all my hair up into a makeshift bun and covering it with a shower cap, he'd pushed me under the waterfall showerhead.

Once the last bit of soap rinsed down the drain, he'd carried me back to the bedroom, stomping the entire way. His movements had been jerky and impatient as he'd dried both of us off before we climbed under the covers. As if the mini tantrum he'd been throwing moments earlier never happened, his arms curled around me, pulling me in close against his chest.

"*You better not move a minute before ten.*"

I'd snickered then broke off into a yelp when his hand swatted my ass. With as much as we drank, it hadn't taken long for both of us to drift off and we'd slept.

Hard.

At least until the feeling of being watched woke me.

The heat I normally felt against my back when waking up was absent, so I figured it was Lathan standing in the room, being a creep. Snuggling deeper under the cover, I planned to ignore him before my lids popped up at the whispered, feminine tone.

"Ms. Remy."

Instead of the man who caused the lingering soreness in my thighs, his offspring squatted next to the bed, brows lifted expectantly.

My head pounded and my mouth felt like it was stuffed full of cotton. I knew I'd overdone it last night but underestimated how bad the aftermath would be.

Before making any sudden movements, I took inventory of my body, realizing I still didn't have a stitch of clothing on.

"Tessa." I whispered back, matching her tone.

Her lips twitched in amusement before she started speaking in that rapid-fire way I adored. "I had to sneak in because this is the only time I could get you alone. My dad is *always* with you."

My expression fell, wondering if she resented how much time her father spent with me. I didn't want her to feel neglected the way I had. She must've recognized what was going through my mind because she scoffed and waved her hand in the air.

"Don't feel bad about it. I'm *glad*. If he's always with you, then that means he's not on my case. I appreciate your sacrifice so I can have peace."

A surprised snort of laughter rushed from my lips before I cupped my forehead, groaning at the persistent dull ache.

Tessa didn't seem to notice because she continued with her purpose for disrupting my sleep. "My birthday's coming up soon."

I rolled my eyes and she smiled. "How could I forget?" She'd only reminded everyone she encountered *every* single day.

"Then you know why I'm here."

"Actually, I don't."

After flashing a glance towards my closed bathroom door where the shower was still running, she sighed. "Okay, I want a car for my birthday."

Slowly, in a move I'd witness her father do more times than I could count, one of my brows rose slowly. "Are you *asking* me to buy you a car?"

Which honestly wasn't an issue because I could afford to buy her any car she wanted without causing a dent in my account. The reason for my reaction was the ongoing debate with her parents that she was losing miserably about getting one for her birthday.

Lathan and Gabbi both had firmly been in opposition and I'd stayed out of it.

"No." She said as if offended before a thoughtful expression crossed her face. "Unless you *want* to."

"Tessa."

"I'm joking." She said with a smile. "I'm not asking you to buy me a car. But I'm recruiting you to help convince my dad that I *deserve* a car. My mom is now neutral, saying she's staying out of it so it's up to me, you, and Ms. Isabel to convince him."

"How am I supposed to convince him that buying *you* a car is a good idea?"

There was a pause before she spoke again. "Ms. Remy, I'm not sure I like your tone."

Another snort of amusement rushed out. "I'll see what I can do,

Tessa. But don't be mad at me if it doesn't work. You know how stubborn your dad can be."

"I *know*." She complained, tossing her hands up. "It's like talking to a brick wall." She stood from her squatted position without a groan and I envied her youthful knees. I would've been hurting if I'd stay down there that long. "So, we have thirteen days to complete this operation. I'm counting on you."

The urge to laugh was strong but the seriousness on her face had me pressing my lips together, nodding my head in agreement. She moved as if preparing to leave the room before stopping, flashing one last glance at the door where water was still running.

"What?" I asked, wondering what was on her mind now. When she worried her bottom lip between her teeth and still didn't say a word, I pressed the comfort against my bare breast and propped on my elbow. "Tess?"

"I thought I heard you out here." Lathan greeted before she could respond. He walked out of the bathroom with a towel around his waist.

Trailing behind him was the tantalizing sandalwood scent that he wore so well.

"Daddy, nobody wants to see that." Tessa pretended to gag, turning and leaving the room.

Once the door closed behind her, Lathan moved around the room, comfortable in his nudity as he got dressed.

"Sure you don't want to come?"

Since Deacon was still in town until tomorrow, he'd invited Lathan out. He'd tried to turn him down, not wanting to leave me but I'd convinced him I was fine. All I wanted was to stay in bed and nurse this hangover, so I'd be a functioning human again when it was time to work on Monday.

"Getting up to pee sounds like a feat right now. I'm sure going to a loud ass club or bar might *actually* take me out."

He chuckled at my sarcasm, coming over to the bed to kiss my forehead. "Sure you don't need me to stay?"

"The only thing I need protecting from is this headache. As long as TJ or Clarence don't bring their ass up those stairs to bother me, I'll be fine." My lids had already closed by the end of the sentence.

When I felt Lathan tugging on the cover, I groaned. God, I just wanted to *sleep*.

"Here." I peeked my lids to see two white pills in his hand. Without questioning it, I snagged them and popped them in my mouth, washing them down with the bottle of water he passed me next.

"Guess you can't hang with the big dogs, huh?"

"At *all*." I muttered, pulling the covers back over my head. "Now go away."

Again, he laughed while his hand patted the curve of my hip. "Feel better, babe."

Lord knows I was going to try.

A PHONE RINGING woke me hours later. Peeking one eye open, the first thing I noticed was how dark it was outside. The sun had been on its way to setting when Lathan left earlier so that meant I'd been out for at least a few hours.

Who was I now?

Sleeping in the middle of the day? Taking random naps? Preferring to stay home over going into the office?

I'd been away for only a few weeks, not *months*. Yet, the routine I'd developed during that brief time seemed to have bled over into my new normal.

I wasn't even sure if I could go back to the insane schedule I'd forced myself to work for so many years.

There were people waiting for me at home now.

People I was eager to see and who were eager to see me. It made clocking out at a decent hour much easier than I expected.

"Hello?" I answered once I snagged the phone from the charger.

"Ms. Remy?" There was a tremor in Tessa's voice that had me sitting up in bed. The raging hangover had ebbed and a dull throb behind my eyes felt a hell of a lot more manageable than the crippling headache from earlier.

Though getting drunk was an experience I could now check off my bucket list, it was not one I planned on repeating.

"Yeah?"

"Um..." Her pause had me instantly alert.

"What is it?" My tone was short and sharp, but her hesitation had me worried.

"Can you come get me?"

My eyes ballooned. "You want *me* to come get you?" There was no hiding the surprise in my voice.

Despite her shaky tone, a low snicker greeted my ears. "I know. I *know*. But my grandma jumped on me." Immediately, I was swinging my legs over the edge of the bed moving towards my closet to pull on something to wear. "She wouldn't stop hitting me so I left. I walked to my friend's house." She paused a second then the words started spilling out so fast I could barely keep up with them. "My friend said I can stay here until my mom gets off but her brother and his friends are having a house party. And it's a lot of people here. A lot of *older* guys. I came outside when they wouldn't leave me alone. I called Dad too but he didn't answer. Mom's at work and I know she can't answer when she's on the floor. Uber doesn't come to this neighborhood after ten and I..."

Any fears I had about driving alone, especially at night, dissipated the more she rambled. I pulled on the hoodie had Lathan tossed over the back of the vanity chair before grabbing my wallet.

"Take a deep breath, honey." I soothed, recognizing the panic threatening to take over her. "Send me your location. I'm on my way."

I HADN'T BEEN this deep in Uptown in years.

Tessa's mom lived more on the outskirts like I had growing up, which was still bad but nowhere near as rough as the apartment complex her friend lived in on the intersection of 54th and Lennox.

Hakeem and Verse had grown up here and from the appearance, not much had changed.

On my second trip circling the block, I noticed Tessa standing outside the complex like I'd told her *not* to.

Her arms were folded, face uncomfortable as a group of guys stood in her face. Immediately, my foot stomped the brakes, causing the car to jerk.

I'd barely put it in park before I was out of the driver's seat, not caring that I'd completely botched the parallel parking I'd just done.

Common sense would've had me thinking this through but that fled the second I spotted the discomfort she wore.

With long strides, I closed the distance. Sparing none of the men a glance, I pushed past them, reaching for her arm and pulling her towards me.

"*Whoa*, lady." One of them muttered angrily, trying to stop me.

A second one reached out to grab my arm and I tensed. My stomach threatened to roll with my normal discomfort but it quickly dissipated and I yanked her behind me, out of their reach, squaring my shoulders.

The fourth one who appeared older and closer to my age didn't say a word, eyes squinted as he stared at me. He stood further to the side, shrouded in shadows so I was unable to make out his features.

"Who the fuck are you?" The second one spat, face contorted.

"None of your *fucking* business."

Immediately, he stepped forward, as if to get in my face but his approach was stopped by the fourth one finally stepping up, holding up a hand before the guy could get too close.

"You know who that is, P?" He asked in a quiet mutter.

The mouthy one sucked his teeth. "Do it matter?"

"Yeah." Number Four snapped back, stepping further into the

glow of the streetlight, revealing a face that felt familiar. Deep in my mind, brain cells were working overtime to place his face.

"It fucking matters when she's *VP's* people." He sized up his friend before swinging his gaze to me. "Big Tim's daughter, right?"

I squinted, still digging through the files at the back of my mind, trying to conjure up his face from my past. "Leonard?" I finally whispered, unsure. When he nodded, I breathed a sigh of relief. Though two years younger, he and his siblings had also been benefactors of my father's work in the community, so he'd been a regular fixture in my home.

Though I never was close with people around my age, Leonard had always been nice and treated me with respect despite his circumstances.

I was surprised he'd recognized me. Though we'd attended school together, I'd steered clear of Uptown probably longer than Tess has been alive.

"Yeah, that's me." I whispered.

"Told you." He taunted the younger man who looked irritated. "Now fall back. You're asking for hell to rain down on all of us if anything happens to her. Especially while *here*." He swung his gaze over to Tessa. "This your kid?"

I nodded, understanding the underlying reason for the question.

"She's protected." He declared before cutting his eyes at the one he'd called P. "*Both* of them are."

I didn't miss the irony of the statement but showed no outward reaction. My father's name was protecting me from the grave when it hadn't been enough to spare me while he'd been alive.

Hmph. Maybe this was his way of making amends from the other side.

All I did was nod gratefully, eyeing all four of them before easing back towards the car, keeping Tessa behind me.

Leonard smirked at what I was doing and hefted his chin in my direction. "Go ahead. Ain't nobody gonna touch y'all out here. You're good."

Not wanting to question him or test the theory, I whipped around, hightailing it to the car, dragging Tessa along.

The silence between us was thick and heavy as I concentrated on maneuvering us out of Uptown. Once we crossed that familiar bridge over into Sienna Falls, we both sighed with relief. Though glad she was okay, my stomach twisted in knots with the realization that anything could've happened.

When we pulled up to a red light, my hands rotated nervously against the leather steering wheel of the car and she slanted a look in my direction.

"We might make it home alive if I drive."

Her joke broke the tension that filled the car and we both chuckled softly.

"You're probably right." Though I knew enough not to kill anyone on the road, my skills were nothing to brag about. *At all.*

Tessa, on the other hand, belonged on a racetrack with the way she never became rattled and easily maneuvered in traffic, high speeds or bad weather.

Whatever obstacle Lathan tossed her into while driving, she excelled at it.

Twisting towards her, my stomach clenched when I finally got a good look at her face under the streetlights illuminating her side of the car.

Her bottom lip was obviously busted, swollen and split with dried blood resting in the seams.

Long, claw-like marks stretched across her bare neck and jawline. My gaze traveled the line upward, clenching my fist when I realized they started just under her eye.

If I could get my hands on Ms. Gloria...

When I lifted my gaze, I noticed her eyes were glued on me. "What is it, Tessa?"

Her brows furrowed as she asked in a quiet tone. "Are you okay?"

I frowned. "I'm *fine.*" When her troubled expression didn't smooth, I eased through the green light, then flicked my gaze briefly back in her direction. "I'm more concerned about you being okay."

"What I mean..." She hesitated again and whatever she was about to say seemed heavy so I steeled myself in preparation. "About what we heard the other day... are you okay?"

I'd almost forgotten that she'd been in that doorway with Lathan as I'd spilled all my secrets to Isabel. God, I wish she hadn't overheard that.

"It was a long time ago." I muttered and averted my gaze, hoping that was the end of it.

"It happened to my grandma too. A long time ago when my mom was a kid." My head whipped back in her direction, surprised at the ease with which Tessa spoke about such a heavy topic. "My mom told me when I asked why Grandma was the way she was. My mom said she'd gone through something traumatizing and never got the proper healing afterwards, so it soured her towards life until she became like... *that*."

The strings around my heart that I was getting more acquainted with tugged when Tessa pushed out a heavy sigh. "She'd told me that's why she keeps extending grace to my grandma because she understands that she'd been through something tough." She shrugged, glancing out the window, looking much older than her sixteen years. "I can appreciate trying to sympathize and be understanding but when she's that hurtful, when do you protect yourself and your children from it instead of putting up with it?"

I held back a shocked gasp, wondering if that's how everyone felt about me.

Though they believed my change was because of my dad's death, I wondered if everyone kept their distance to protect themselves from me and my... coldness.

Had I been so wrapped up in my trauma that I'd ignored their attempts to sympathize with me? Had I been so dead set on being a certain way that I'd snubbed their attempts at giving me grace and understanding, much like Ms. Gloria did to her daughter?

But we weren't the same. Right?

I might rely on my coldness and distance to get me through tough situations and to keep myself mentally strong when memories threatened to make me weak... but I never—and I mean *never*—wanted anyone to view me through the same lens as Ms. Gloria.

I hadn't known of her trauma when we'd met and I'd judged her harshly for the way she came off, similarly to the way I hated when people did it to me.

It both hurt and humbled me. And the realization I'd come to yesterday washed over me before I could stop it.

I didn't want to be this angry anymore.

I didn't want people to walk on eggshells when I stepped in the room.

I didn't want the people I cared about to invite me places out of obligation. I wanted them to *want* me there and I wasn't sure if that was the case anymore.

"You're not like her, Ms. Remy." My eyes widened slightly when she spoke my exact thoughts aloud. "Just because you went through the same thing doesn't mean you're the same person. She hurts others to make herself feel better. You just keep your distance. You're not mean, or violent, or nasty with every person you meet. Not like her. I tried to understand for a while but... after meeting you and finding out what happened to you, I realized she was *choosing* to be that way and I can't do it anymore. That's why I always want to be at your house. I'm happier there."

I couldn't explain that going through what Ms. Gloria and I had could change you in ways you never thought possible.

I couldn't make excuses for her behavior, just like I wouldn't make any for mine over the last two decades, but I knew that we'd both been dealt a shitty hand and didn't deserve what had happened to us.

But like Tessa said, though I could be called many things, an abuser wasn't one of them.

People could say I was blunt, lacked tact, or was intimidating...

I'd accept all that. But purposely hurting others after knowing what it felt like to be at someone else's mercy was never something I wanted to do.

But still, I had to fix the relationships I'd damaged.

To fix me.

I didn't want to be the sixty-something year old woman that everybody steered clear of.

I didn't want to be the woman who died all alone in her home, remaining there for days, weeks, or months before someone notices.

I didn't want that to be the end of my story.

I wanted a happy ending.

I wanted an ending that made me smile the way the woman always did at the end of those sappy romance movies Tessa liked to watch.

I deserved a happy ending and I felt like I was finally ready to take the first step towards it.

I FALTERED as I exited my bathroom.

My bed was empty, missing the man who'd been stretched across it earlier when I stepped in the shower.

After toweling off and slipping on shorts and a matching cami, I padded barefoot across the floor and down the hall in search of him.

When Tessa and I made it back to the house, Lathan had been waiting in the foyer when we walked in, livid when he'd thought we'd gone *joyriding* of all things.

But one glimpse at the bruises on Tessa's face and the concern on mine drained his anger as quickly as it had appeared.

He'd quickly ushered her upstairs to the bathroom to get a better look at the damage before coming into my room to give her privacy while she showered away the stressful night she'd had.

I found him exactly where I thought he'd be, sitting next to Tessa's sleeping form in the bedroom down the hall.

His chin was dipped, shoulders slumped as he stared down at her. He looked defeated.

Like the wind had been sapped out of his sails and he was floating aimlessly in the middle of the ocean, unable to steer in either direction.

It was a look I was more than familiar with. I'd witnessed it in the mirror more times than I could count. But seeing it on him, this big powerful man who I felt could conquer anything, it felt *wrong*.

Taking a few minutes to observe him, I crossed my arms, watching unashamedly before he could notice. He was unnaturally still and quiet, resembling one of his perfectly curated sculptures that rested on the shelves in my guesthouse.

My gaze skated over to Tessa, stomach tightening at the darkening bruises on her face. Sympathy roared in my gut for this beautiful duo. They'd become my family in such a short time and witnessing them hurt affected me.

Finally, he moved, taking a deep breath before resting his head against the back of the chair, closing his eyes. I walked in sliding my arms around him from behind, relishing the firmness of wide-set, compact shoulders underneath my fingertips. I leaned over, resting my cheek against the top of his head, grateful my clumsy efforts to offer comfort seemed to soothe him.

We remained like that for several minutes before I reached for his hand, pulling him up and out of the chair. He followed, quietly trailing me down the hall to my bedroom.

Leaving the door cracked open, I guided him over to the bed before gesturing that he sit, glad when he did. His eyes remained on mine as I stripped off his shirt and shoes before pressing him back until he lay flat against the mattress.

I climbed in next to him, head resting on his shoulder, legs tossed across his. Each inch of him was roped with muscle, yet he seemed soft underneath me, tender in a way that sent my pulse racing.

"I wasn't there." He broke the silence first. "Just like I wasn't there for ten years. Every time she needs me, I'm not there."

My stomach flip-flopped and I cupped his chin until his gaze met mine. "That's not true. *At all.* You made a mistake ten years ago and you've been taking the steps to rectify it since. She knows that if you would've seen the call, you would've answered and been there for her in a heartbeat. You didn't *ignore* her, Lathan. You forgot your phone in the car. It happens." When he didn't look convinced, I brushed my fingers through his beard, smiling when his lids drooped. "Parenting is hard enough without you taking the blame for something you can't control. Gloria did this to her. Not you. The only person who deserves your anger is her."

He pressed his face further into my palms and pleasure coursed through me, but not in a sexual way.

This feeling was strictly emotional. Just being this close to him, being able to hold him similarly to how he'd done for me during a rough time and reciprocate that tenderness pleased me in a way I once thought impossible.

We fell into a comfortable silence for several minutes before he suddenly swung his gaze to mine, looking at me with an emotion I couldn't accurately describe. His lips were parted, expression soft and open in a way I hadn't seen before. The eye contact he'd locked me in was strong and intimidating, saying so much that his unmoving lips had yet to reveal.

"What?" I asked, pulse fluttering just as wildly as the butterflies in my stomach. Instead of answering, he licked his lips so slowly I could almost feel the caress between my thighs.

He shook his head. "Nothing. Just realized something."

When he didn't say more, I sucked my teeth. "Okay. Annnd?"

He chuckled, kissing my forehead. "*Annnd* I'm not going to tell you yet. If I do, you'll probably go running for the hills."

Immediately, I tried to figure out what the hell he could be referring to but of course he recognized what I was doing.

"Stop trying to figure it out, Rem."

Rolling my eyes, I snuggled deeper in his embrace, shoulders relaxing as his deep voice rumbled his chest as he spoke.

"Thank you." He whispered. "For being there for her tonight. You didn't have to but you did and I appreciate it."

"You don't have to thank me." I countered. "I love that girl just like I love y-" My voice trailed and my eyes bucked as I realized what I almost revealed. What I didn't recognize I'd felt until that very moment.

When silence continued after my words trailed, my gaze traveled up his torso and neck before lifting to his eyes. His gaze was firmly planted upwards, looking towards the ceiling with a half-smile in place.

"Yeah, me too."

33

REMEDY

LIKE I'D DONE ALL each time over the last three days, I walked into my office and glanced toward the empty desk and chair in the corner.

Lathan had stayed home with Tessa after speaking with her school. To avoid comments or rumors about her bruises, they agreed to let her do virtual learning for the next two weeks.

God knows I missed the man in the corner but I understood he was where he needed to be.

The replacement bodyguard he'd sent in his stead did nothing but sleep down the hall in my conference room but I damn sure wouldn't tell Lathan that.

It would ruin the bit of freedom I'd discovered and enjoyed.

My head lifted from the manila envelope I'd been flipping through, watching my new temp Monica walk past my door, towards the elevators.

Though not as efficient as Miranda, she was still good at her job and I appreciated that.

I also was making more strides in not scaring the hell out of her.

I was being *nice* and though it felt like I could accomplish shit quicker without the niceties, I still tried.

Seconds later, Monica knocked on my open door. "Ms. Gabrielle is here to see you."

I flashed her a tight smile before nodding. I rose behind my desk, watching as Gabbi walked in looking *nothing* like the put together woman who'd been a force in her living room that day she and Lathan tag team parented Tessa.

Now she looked weary and worn down as she sat on the opposite side of my desk.

"How are you?"

She scoffed and I didn't take offense, knowing her frustration was aimed at her current situation despite her words being directed at me. "I don't even know how to answer that."

She sighed, slouching in the chair as she rubbed the tip of her nose wearily.

"Do you know she asked to move out permanently and live with you and Lathan?" She scoffed. Well, I guess we were diving right in. "Do you know how that feels? As a parent, as a *mother*? To know that your child feels so unsafe in an environment that *you* put her in that she'd rather live with someone else?"

I thought the question was asked rhetorically but when she tilted her head as if expecting a response, I spoke up. "I don't. I'm not a parent. So, I can't understand how that feels."

Not wanting to drag this out, I leaned forward, getting to the reason I'd ask her to be here today. "But what I *can* relate to is being a child in a similar situation. I can tell you I wished my dad cared enough to notice what was going on and change it. I wished my dad stopped what happened to me and protected me. That's all a child wants when someone hurts them. They just want their parents' love and their ability to protect them or prevent it from happening again. They just want to know that you care and that you're there."

Her eyes fell to the hands wringing in her lap. I cleared my throat, still not fully comfortable dealing with others emotions but forged on.

"I've gathered that you staying with your mom because of financial limitations."

She nodded. "After my divorce, I didn't have much left. So I moved in with her. But I'm paying most of the bills since she retired so I can't save enough to get out."

I licked my lips, hoping my next words didn't offend her. "Are you willing to do whatever it takes to get out of your current situation? To change you and your kids' lives for the better?" When she gave a slow nod, I slid a pen and blank piece of paper across the table. "Every bill or debt you owe? Write it down. Loans, credit cards, student loans, car payments... whatever it is, write down who you owe and the amount."

Her neck jerked back. "What?" She laughed incredulously. "Why? So you can *pay* them?" Despite the sarcasm in her tone, I remained stoic, simply nodding my head in response. "No. *No.* That's too much. My daughter has already been practically *living* with you. You don't know me like that, Remedy. I can't ask you to do something like that."

"You're not asking me to do anything, I'm *offering.*" When she started shaking her head again, I leaned forward, planting my elbows on top of the desk. "Are you willing to do anything for your child? Your children?" Surprise at my question had her hesitating before a reluctant nod lifted and lowered her head. "Then put aside your pride to do this for them. Don't let pride be the reason your kids grow up in an environment that I'm offering to help you out of. It's not fair to them." When she continued glaring at me in indecision, I barely resisted the urge to suck my teeth. "If people finding out is what you're worried about, then don't. No one outside of this room has to know. If anybody questions it, you can tell them you got a raise at work." I tilted my head. "Or you can do what I would and tell them to mind their nosy ass business."

A startled laugh broke free from her chest and eased the tension.

I expected her to argue more or make me work harder to wear her down. But she didn't. Instead, her eyes welled with tears as she picked up the pen. I felt myself getting choked up watching the raw emotion on her face.

Once she finished and slid it across the desk, I expected anger but she looked relieved. Once I had that piece of paper, I slid a manila folder across the desk to her that was about an inch thick.

"Each of those stapled packets is the information for the savings accounts I've opened for each of your kids, including Tessa. Funds can be accessed by you after they turn fifteen or by them at eighteen. There's also the name of a realtor in there that I've heard great things about. Call her, find a home, let me know the price and it'll be yours." Gabbi looked shell shocked at my words but I wasn't done. "I'll buy the home outright and you won't owe me anything."

When her lips parted to argue, I forged on. "But, *if you insist*, we can work out a monthly amount that you're comfortable with. The repayment terms will be totally up to you. And if at any point it gets to be too much, let me know and we can adjust the amount or call it off. Like I said, the home will be paid for and in *your* name. Now as far as your mom..."

Before I could finish my sentence, she scoffed. "You don't have to worry about her. I should've known she wouldn't change after she did the same thing to me growing up. I'd hoped her motherly instincts would kick in and she'd be more loving towards them but wishful thinking on my part." She sighed, shaking her head. "Moving in with her and giving her access to my kids was a mistake. One that I'll never make again."

"You're a great mom, Gabbi. And you've been a great daughter too because you gave your mom chances, even after she no longer deserved them." I tapped the tip of my nail against the folder sitting in front of her. "All you have to do is sign those packets and change you and your children's lives forever."

Relief flooded me when she picked up the pen once more, signing the papers in front of her. By the end of next week, she'd have confirmations of every debt she owed being cleared.

Once done, her lips parted and I already knew what question was coming next.

"Why? Why are you doing this? For me? For *us*?"

I pressed my lips together, feeling my skin prickle with the normal discomfort from talking about things from my past. "Like I said, I wish there had been someone there to help me when I was in a bad situation as a child. Your options are limited by not having the funds while mine was just having no one there to truly see me. I wish someone would have stepped in to fix it or make my life better. So I'm hoping to do that for you and your children, the way I prayed somebody would for me. Every child deserves peace and a healthy environment to grow up in. I love your daughter and if I can help provide that for her and your other kids. Then I will."

To my surprise, her lips curved up in a smile. "*And* because you love Lathan." My face flushed and her smile grew. "You don't have to say it because it's written all over you." Her smile dropped and her expression returned to the serious expression she'd worn when walking in. "You're good for him. He didn't think anyone noticed but he'd just been *going through the motions* since getting out of jail. Since working for you, I've seen more life and passion in him than I have in the last few years. Even when he used to bitch about you." We both laughed when she paused. I couldn't blame him. I'd been *awful*, especially those first few weeks.

"Thank you for what you've done for him. Thank you for what you've done for Tessa, thank you for what you're doing for me. Thank you for what you're doing for my whole family. And I know the amount of money that you're dropping means nothing to you. But I want you to know that it means *everything* to me."

In the grand scheme of things, the amount of money I'd spend on getting them out of their situation was but a drop in the large pool of wealth I'd accumulated over the last decade. But that had nothing to do with my decision and I wanted her to know that.

"Knowing that I can help you and your children into a safer environment means everything *to me*. Since being a teen, my dad hustled and did whatever he could to make money so by the time I was born, we were able to live comfortably. I can't recall a time in my life where I was *without* money, but I can recall being without love for a *long time*. And that's a terrible feeling. But your family is filled with it. I see it in Tessa. I see it in the way you care for her. The way you sacrifice for her. It's *that* type of love that I would've gladly sacrificed every dollar for."

SINCE THAT FIRST SESSION, I'd gone with Lathan two more times to therapy.

Each visit went the same, they talked with that comfortable familiarity that came with time and I sat there, purposely avoiding Dr. Tori's probing gaze.

But her manner of speaking was so calm and inviting that I sat up, leaning forward and wanting to speak.

Each time, she'd noticed and opened the invitation but I chickened out.

Spilling my guts to a man I now knew intimately was completely different from revealing my secrets to someone I'd only seen a handful of times.

But the urge was there.

And it had only strengthened in intensity after that talk with Tessa when I'd picked her up from Uptown.

Maybe that was why I stood outside of the familiar glass door, knocking on it gently despite the rolling tension in my gut.

I'd saw an opportunity to sneak away and I'd taken it.

Lathan had stayed at home with Tessa again and the guard he'd assigned in his absence was fast asleep in the break room at RemEx, like always, unaware that I'd left in a company car.

I'd nearly had a heart attack driving downtown but I was getting better at it. Doing so in the middle of the night when traffic was sparse was a *lot* different from in the middle of rush hour traffic.

Miranda and I agreed that if the guard woke up before I returned, she'd tell him I was in an important meeting in the private conference room.

Because of client privacy, no one besides me, Lathan, Miranda, and Jaxon were typically allowed behind those closed doors so it was a believable lie that would buy me time.

My plan was to be gone less than an hour.

Instead of the pretty receptionist from the last time Lathan and I was here, Dr. Tori opened the glass door, smiling in that friendly manner that both eased and made me nervous.

"Ms. Sinclair-"

"Remedy," I interrupted.

She briefly looked startled before nodding. "Okay, Remedy. What can I do for you?"

I hesitated, unsure how to answer that. I knew *why* I was here but the courage I'd had on the drive over seemed to have dissipated. Vanishing mere moments before I'd lifted my hand to knock.

My indecision and discomfort must've been obvious because she smiled. "I have a few minutes to spare before my noon appointment arrives. Come in."

I flushed, realizing I probably should've called and made an appointment. Just showing up unannounced to a therapist office, one you'd never had a session with, was presumptuous but I'd acted without thought.

I apologized for my unexpected appearance then followed her in. This time, I ignored the warm tones in the room, unable to focus on anything but calming the building anxiety at my core.

I wanted to be here. I needed to be here but I doubted my ability to do the next step.

Talking.

Minutes passed where I sat silently and she waited, not pushing or rushing me into a saying a word.

That should've eased me but all it did was make me even more nervous so I sighed, tightening my grip almost painfully around the purse strap I'd yet to release. "I'm sorry I wasted your time." That same purse strap was tossed over my shoulders and I scooted to the edge of the seat, prepared to get up and leave but her voice stopped me.

"I had a client once." She began with a gentle smile. "A young woman with a... *chip* on her shoulders."

"Should you be telling me this?" I interrupted, "You know, to not violate client privacy and all that."

She laughed, flashing white teeth and deep dimples. "I promise... no names will be shared."

She waited until I relaxed in my seat once more before pulling me into a tale about her client who'd grown up in a horrible environment. She'd been moved from foster home to foster home, barely having time to settle before being relocated again.

Her head tilted, eyes softening with an unnamed emotion that made me squirm. "The people entrusted with her care took advantage of that vulnerability and... hurt her. Beat her. Molested her." I flinched at the word. The one I'd refused to associate with my experience until I'd blown up at my mom. I hadn't wanted to use it before then because it would've been too... *real*. "When she turned thirteen, she ran away, figuring she'd have better luck on the streets."

My eyes widened at the parallels between this story and my own.

I ran away once.

When I was twelve, my dad had been in Virginia, visiting potential colleges with high school athletes who were graduating soon. My abusers had taken advantage of his absence and I'd fled as soon as they finished, packing nothing but a hoodie, a few pairs of shirts, jeans, sneakers, and the stuffed tiger Verse won at the school carnival weeks earlier.

For three days, I attended the private school across town like normal but when the bell rang each afternoon, I hid in the girls' locker room, staying in the broken bathroom stall for hours until the last janitor was gone for the day.

I'd eaten food from the cafeteria, showered in the locker room, and slept on the leather sofa in the teachers' lounge.

For most kids my age, that would've been a miserable existence. But not for me. Those three days had been the most *peaceful* I'd had in a long time.

I would've stayed there forever if I hadn't gotten caught by a janitor early the next morning.

He'd been from Uptown so instead of reporting it to the administrators, he called my dad who'd returned the day before but hadn't been home to notice that I wasn't there.

He'd come to get me and that was the only time I'd been on the verge of spilling my secret. I'd wanted him to know. I'd wanted him to save me.

But he never gave me the chance.

Instead, his scolding and lecturing dominated the entire car ride home, not letting me get a word in.

"*What the hell is wrong with you, Rem?*" He'd angrily snapped. "*Sneaking around and spending the night in your school like your ass doesn't have a home to go to. Be grateful that you have as much as you do because a lot of your classmates don't have the luxuries you live with. Stop being a spoiled brat. You have a life that so many kids dream of. Be grateful for it and quit acting out for attention.*"

I'd been devastated. Hurt.

Not once did he ask *why* I'd run away. Why I'd chosen to sleep on a couch in a teacher's lounge over the princess canopy bed I'd had since I was a little girl.

He never asked why I did *any* of the things I did.

Instead, he lectured and grounded me, then was gone again on a business trip less than a week later.

"Where did you go?"

I jumped, lifting my eyes from my wringing hands up to Dr. Tori's face, realizing I'd zoned out in the middle of her story.

"What?"

"Just now. Where did you go? You checked out on me."

"Nowhere," I answered quickly, averting my gaze. "I'm listening."

Seconds passed silently and I could tell she wanted to ask questions but she didn't. A slight nod was the only sign of her acquiesce before she picked up where she'd left off.

"After a year on the streets, she met an older woman who took her in and bought her nice things. She thought she'd hit the jackpot. Everything was good until the women started asking for favors." Her thick thighs crossed but her unwavering focus never faltered as she continued. "It started small. Slip this in your pocket. Take this duffle bag to the man waiting on the corner. Over time, those small favors turned into big ones. But the girl was just so happy to have a roof over her head that she did it. She slept with this man to help cover the rent. She slept with that man to get groceries. Before she realized, she had a rotating group of clients who came to see her regularly."

I hadn't expected that turn in the story but my eyes were wide and my attention rapt on her.

"She was 19 before she escaped that toxic cycle. After, she swore to never trust another person. And that mindset turned her mean. Violent. She hated the world and pushed away anyone who tried to get close. She eventually started attending college but even then, she kept every single person at arm's length. Too afraid to open herself up to being hurt or taken advantage of again."

A knock at the door startled me out of the trance since she'd had me in.

"Yes?" Dr. Tori called out.

Her secretary peeked her head in, smiling politely at me before turning to her boss. "Your noon appointment is here."

Dr. Tori smiled politely and thanked her before turning back to me with a regretful expression on her face.

"I'm sorry. I've taken up all your time," I apologized, eyes on my purse as I searched for my wallet. "How much do I owe you?"

"Not a dime."

When I tried to argue, she waved it off, walking just ahead of me towards the door that sat at the end of the hall that led to her waiting area.

Right before her hand touched the doorknob, I spoke up, unable to resist asking one last question. "What happened to that client?" I needed to know. I needed to know whether someone who had been through so much overcame it.

I needed to know if a second chance was truly possible.

Because if she'd gotten one, then maybe... just maybe I'd get one too.

"Where..." I cleared my throat. "Where does her story end?"

Tori smiled, propping her shoulder on the back of the door. "Her story's *still* ongoing. She has good days and bad days. Flashbacks that threaten to toss her back into the past. But she went to therapy. She healed. She forgave people who damn sure didn't deserve it." Her eyes flashed to a framed photo and I followed her gaze, ogling the image of her and another woman smiling brightly at the camera, flashing their wedding rings. "She met *someone*. Someone who made it easy to let her guards down. Someone who showed her what it really meant to be loved and what a special place it could be." Her smile wobbled a bit and I froze as realization washed over me. "Now *that* client owns her own practice where she works way too many hours a week, trying her best to help other people who look like her to heal from their own past. To overcome their demons. To break generational curses that have crippled us for far too long."

I felt... frozen. Unable to move.

I couldn't believe that the woman she spoke of and this whole, healthy human standing before me now were one and the same.

"It wasn't an easy journey," she continued. "It was ugly. Hard. *Triggering* and sometimes I wanted to give up. Sometimes I *gave* up, which is normal. Forcing yourself to do something or make a change before you're ready can be damaging and cause setbacks. Go at *your* pace. Take *your* time. Scream, cry, yell, fail, fall down, and get up, then do it all over again. It might not seem like it but each time you do, you learn something. Even the smallest lesson learned, even the tiniest step forward is progress, Remedy. Celebrate it, even if no one else does."

Like she hadn't just spoken words that would resonate with me for the rest of my life, she smiled that warm smile of hers and stepped back, giving me a clear path to the now open door.

"Take care of yourself, Remedy. My door is always open if you need it."

34

REMEDY

"Were you able to get that report updated and distributed, Miranda?"

"Yes." She responded and I could picture her in her new office, still smiling in excitement from the position she now held.

Every time I walked into her office, she was looking around as if in disbelief. I'd had to fight my grin each time I caught her.

"Thank you." I said, now not as uncomfortable using the words. "And did Mr. Horton ever get back with you about the adjustments to our offer?"

There was a pause and I heard the clicking of her mouse before she responded. "Yes, he asked for more time for his legal team to review. He said if they confirm that everything's okay, we should expect an answer by next week."

Sensing the end of the call, I got up from my seated position in the office I'd set up on the first floor. The room had once been a second sitting room that I never used so I had Lathan pull everything out and replace it with the office furniture I'd ordered online.

Since I planned to work from home more often, I needed a dedicated space to work that didn't have many distractions.

Since my bedroom had the space, I'd tried working in there but that damn television I'd had Lathan set up occupied more of my time than necessary.

Now, with only my desk, file cabinets, and bookshelves in this office, I could focus on my actual work rather than streaming one of the many shows Tessa had gotten me hooked on.

"Anyone have anything they'd like to add?" I asked as I stretched, moving down the hall in my socks.

When no one said a word, I was grateful because we'd already been on this call for over an hour.

"Alright, everyone, keep up the good work. I'll be back in the office on Friday. If anyone needs me between now and then, you know how to reach me. Enjoy your day."

The other five people on the call gave their own variations of the farewell before we disconnected. Right as I removed the earpiece, I slipped it in the leggings I wore that had *pockets*, pausing on the threshold of the kitchen.

My eyes landed on my mother's frame as she worked a damp towel across the counter, cleaning up whatever residue remained after the lunch she'd prepared.

Not long before my meeting started, she'd brought a bowl of chicken tortilla soup. It had been my favorite food she'd made as a child before she'd left. I used to ask for it so much that she would make huge batches and freeze it in smaller portions to make it easier to pull down and prepare whenever I craved it.

I'd attempted to make it like she did as a teen but mine never tasted quite like hers so I'd abandoned it, figuring I'd never get to taste it again.

When I realized what was in the bowl she'd brought me, I'd scarfed it down so quickly that she probably hadn't even made it back to the kitchen before I asked for a second serving.

Her eyes lifted and instead of anger, they warmed at the sight of me, crinkling at the edges as she smiled. "Hey, baby."

"Hey, mom." Though I'd pulled my gaze away, I felt the shock jolt through her at the greeting.

I felt guilt and remorse for how I'd treated her. I'd been unfairly holding her feet to the fire for what happened years ago without giving her the opportunity to make things right or even tell her side of the story.

She'd tried multiple times and I fought her at every turn, making shit difficult.

I'd understood Lathan's side of his story and his efforts in making amends with Tessa so why couldn't I extend that same grace to my mother?

She'd been here over a month and stayed despite how nasty I'd been towards her. Moving towards the island, I stood on the opposite side, watching as she set aside the towel she'd been using to clean the counter, giving me her full attention.

Before she could say a word, I blurted out. "I'm sorry."

A startled laugh rushed past her lips, causing my brows to raise at the unexpected response to my apology.

"You're *apologizing*? After everything you went through... you're apologizing to *me*?" A scoff rushed out as she shook her head. "I never want to hear those words come from your lips. Not if they're directed towards me. You have every right to be angry. I left and didn't come back. That was me, not you. And learning what you went through makes me realize why your anger was so deep, so severe." She paused, pressing her hands against her lips. "You deserved so much better. From everyone, including Tim."

My stomach tightened at the mention of my father.

I still had conflicted feelings towards him. Though he hadn't been the one to harm me, he'd been *there* and ignored the signs.

Maybe I was still being unreasonable with the blame I placed on him but I wasn't ready to absolve him of anything.

Not yet.

"Your dad loved you but he was blinded by his loyalty to his neighborhood. He tried so hard to fix everyone else's problems that he ignored the ones going on right under his roof. And I know that feeling all too well."

Her brows drew together and she crossed her arms protectively. "Do you remember the day I left?"

I shook my head. "No, not really. Just that you two argued the night before."

The only thing I recalled was my mom crying and my dad yelling. They'd argued for a long time, well into the night. It had gone on so long that I'd fallen asleep near the top of the stairs, wondering when they'd come tuck me in.

When I woke the next morning, my mom was gone.

"We argued about me going back to Puerto Rico." Her eyes lifted from the island, meeting mine. "I wanted to take you with me. He was still heavily involved in the streets. Living a dangerous life and... I was tired. So *tired*." She sniffed, tapping her nails against the countertop. "Of course, Tim wouldn't hear of it. He told me he'd kill me before he let me take you."

My eyes bucked, watching her face crumple as she recanted the last argument with my father.

"I don't think he meant it *literally*. But I knew he wasn't going to let me leave. Not with you." She sighed, now lost in the memories. "And I... I was *young* and in love. For a long time, I thought Tim could do no wrong but when the honeymoon phase passed, I realized that Tim just... Tim wasn't what I thought he was. The rose-tinted glasses were off and I realized I'd committed to a man who would never love me as much as he loved Uptown. I couldn't compete with his need to be everyone's savior." Her eyes closed, tears spilling over. "So for my sanity, I left. I lost sight of who I was in that relationship and the only way I could find it again was by leaving. But if I'd known I was leaving you behind to... *that*. If I'd thought one second that your father would ignored you the way he ignored me..." Her hand moved to cover her mouth. "I'm so sorry. I'm sorry Rem for failing you."

I didn't know how bad I needed to hear those words.

That was all I wanted. An apology.

I'd needed for someone to admit that they'd wronged me and feel actual *remorse* for it.

And because of it, I could give her the words I'm sure she needed to hear as well.

"*I forgive you.*"

BEING HERE after staying away so many years was sobering.

The gravestone for Timothy "Big Tim" Sinclair was as well-kept and neat as it'd been when we laid him to rest nearly twenty years ago.

Every year for his birthday, we'd had a huge party to honor him but this year, Verse sensed my emotions surrounding my father had changed and was finally spilling out of the vault of secrets I'd kept so he'd decided to skip the celebration. Instead, I'd asked him to meet me here on my dad's birthday.

He stood silently to my right, dressed in all black while my mom stood on my other side, looking just as conflicted as I did.

We'd been attempting to rebuild what had been lost over the last two decades.

I wished I could say that it was an easy journey but it wasn't. Long buried feelings still came up from time to time but rather than lashing out or ignoring it, I was talking through them. Acknowledging them and giving her the ability to explain her side.

The day after I'd shown up to Dr. Tori's office unannounced, I'd called back and scheduled an appointment for the very next day. Lathan had gone with me, waiting in the lobby while I'd spent an entire hour in the purge corner, letting out words I'd never dare utter to anyone about the atrocities done to me as a child.

Even my mom had gone to a couple with me and visited Dr. Tori for private sessions to deal with her own traumas.

I suspected there were other darker things between her and my father that she wanted to protect me from.

Though I'd asked, she refused to tell me, stating that exposing me to things that happened before I was born was pointless. I could only hope she received the healing she needed because over the last few weeks, I'd learned to lean on her.

We didn't have a traditional mother and daughter relationship... but we were *friends*. And that was a start.

"I heard you had a run-in in Uptown." Verse broke the silence after my mother walked back to the car, leaving us alone.

My brows shot up before relaxing, not surprised.

The man's tendrils still had a firm hold on our old neighborhood. Though illegal activities were a thing of his past, he kept his finger on the pulse of the city he and my father loved so much.

"Something like that." I finally responded.

He lifted a brow. "That was dangerous, Rem. And not very smart. You should've called me or Keem to go with you."

I rolled my eyes. "I didn't have time to sit down and think about my actions. She called because she needed me and I went. Was it stupid? *Yeah.* Of course it was. But thanks to you and *Big Tim*..." There was no mistaking the sarcasm in my voice "We were *protected*. We're fine."

He didn't respond right away, instead studying me in the way that always unnerved me. He now knew I had secrets so that cursory surface glance he used to cast my way now penetrated my guards, seeing deeper.

"We never got to have that talk." My face contorted at the abrupt subject change. "Now's a good time."

Normally, I would've hesitated but not this time. Not after all the work I'd done. I wasn't hiding anymore.

So, I turned to my father's grave and let the words fall from my lips with an ease that felt *good*. Each time I told this secret, it got easier.

Many times, I had the urge to stop because of the devastation contorting his features. But I didn't.

I forged on, letting the words flow.

I don't know how long it took. It could've been five minutes or thirty. All I knew was there was a weight that lifted once the last words I spoke were carried away by the wind whipping around us.

Several moments passed without him saying a word, so I looked over, finding his eyes red, wet, and focused on me.

When he swiped at his nose, I reached over, rubbing a comforting hand across his broad back.

A snort filled the air as he shook his head. "You're comforting *me*... after telling me you were going through *that*? For years?" He licked his lips, swinging his gaze back to my father's headstone with a glare. "How many was it?"

I tensed at that question because I knew where answering it could lead.

"Why?"

"You *know* why, Rem."

I'd be lying if I said the thought of getting revenge on those who hurt me hadn't crossed my mind. But I didn't want anyone I cared about to get caught up in the type of violence we'd left in the past.

I knew if Verse couldn't directly get his hands on the perpetrators, then he'd send Hakeem in his stead and I damn sure didn't want that. The big silent man had a past that was as traumatizing as mine though he'd never spoken a word about it.

The only reason I knew was because Gia had let it slip once after getting drunk. Being Verse's older sister and one of the few people Hakeem was close with, she'd known the full extent of the things they'd seen and done to survive.

"How many?" He stressed, clenching his fist and releasing it. I could practically see the energy coursing through him. Like Lathan, the man had a vicious temper in his youth that he'd learned to control with age.

But the quickest way for it to return was harming those he loved or cared about.

When that happened, Verse Presley reverted to VP, the man whose name still had the power of protection in a neighborhood with the highest crime rate in the entire state.

"Three."

He sucked in a breath, probably not expecting the number. Two had been onetime situations but the man I'd run into at Verse's party had been the main culprit. The abuse from him had gone undetected for years. It had gotten so bad that he'd grown cocky, no longer caring to wait until my father was gone.

At times, my father was in the house, distracted and occupied by all the things that took precedence over me.

"Who?" I should've known that question was coming next. "All I need is a name."

"It doesn't matter now."

"It will *always* matter." His voice rose, shaking with the anger I could practically see pouring from him. That protective streak he was known for was in full force. "You were supposed to be protected. And we *all* failed you." A weary hand wiped across his face. "Everybody thought you changed after Big Tim died but... *damn*, you were dealing with all that shit on *top* of his death." He scoffed again. "He had the nerve to walk around like a fucking God amongst men while his own daughter was suffering under his watch. How the fuck did that happen?"

I hated I was the one to snatch off the rose-tinted glasses he had for his mentor.

My goal had not been to tarnish my father's memory but I had to free myself from the burden of the secret and the only way to do that was speaking my truth.

I owed myself that much.

He stared out in the distance, jaw clenching. I let him have his moment, waiting until he turned to me. "I need their names, Rem." When I sighed and rolled my eyes, he shrugged. "You know I'm not going to let this go. I *can't*. I made a promise that I would look out for you and I failed at it. Let me try to fix it in my own way. Give me their names."

"And if I give them to you, then what?" I tossed my hands up before letting them smack against my thighs. "What are you going to do?"

His answering smile was deceptively soft. "That's not for you to worry about. Let your conscience stay clear. I'll handle it."

I whipped to face him, lids narrowed. "We don't live in Uptown and you're damn sure not VP from 54th anymore. You're *Verse Presley*. A multi-millionaire whose face is on the cover of at least three magazines in the lobby of REA. This vigilante shit isn't what you do and it isn't what Keem does anymore, either. Is what happened to me fucked up? *Yes*. Did I wish and pray for someone to retaliate on my behalf for years? *Yes, I did*. But not if it means ruining my friends' lives. You're about to get married. You really want to risk getting locked up for something that happened so long ago? I'm working on getting past it. I'm working on healing. Please don't add the stress of having to worry about you, Keem, or whoever you'll send after them. Just... *please* let it go."

His nostrils flared and he shoved his hands in the pocket of his coat, glaring at me.

If he thought that would work, then he really didn't know a damn thing about me. Intimidation tactics were my specialty and I wouldn't wilt under his. The only person who had that ability was Lathan.

"If I promise not to go after them or send anyone after them, will you tell me their names?"

I huffed in exasperation. "Verse, w-"

"If these are men I still associate with... men I've helped or *put on*? I need to rectify that shit, immediately. Nobody is eating off me if they've done that shit to you. You can ask me to not go after them but not this. I can't ignore this."

Verse was stubborn and always thought he knew what was best

for those around him. I appreciated the gesture but didn't want him to jeopardize everything he'd built.

The longer I watched him, the tight anger dropped from his expression, giving way to desperation. "Please. Just tell me, Rem."

So I did, knowing it would break his heart.

"Mark. Jamal. *Christian*."

I knew the first two would irritate him because they'd worked closely with my father but the last one would devastate him. And I witnessed it as his face crumpled and his shoulders slumped.

Christian was my father's right-hand man since they'd been kids. Verse had revered him with the same respect he had my father, even affectionately calling him uncle.

His gaze swung back and forth helplessly before he tensed and I recognized the calculated glint in his eyes. "He was at my party." I nodded. "I spoke to him, hugged him, then he went to..." His eyes flashed. "He came to *you*." Another nod. "After what he did, he had the nerve to come to my shit and speak to you? Approach you? What the fuck is *wrong* with him?" The last question was bellowed, drawing my mother's curious gaze.

Verse paid her no mind as he paced. Looking like a caged animal waiting to be unleashed.

"Verse..."

"What did he say? What did he want?"

I sighed, recalling the conversation that had crippled me. "To apologize." When his neck reared, I held up my hands. "Trust me, I *know*. But all he wanted was to apologize and assure that I'd never see him again."

Before I could react, he wrapped an arm around my shoulders, yanking me towards him, pressing his lips hard against my forehead. "I'm so sorry you went through that. I'm sorry nobody saw what you were going through. I'm sorry I didn't see it, Rem."

I returned the hug, grateful it didn't fill me with discomfort.

After holding me for a long while, he placed one last kiss against my forehead before stepping back. "You ready?"

I looked back towards my dad's headstone, pinching the material of my dress between my fingers before sighing. "Give me a minute."

He nodded, flashing one last look towards my dad's grave before walking off.

I watched until he stood next to my mother before turning back to the grave.

Timothy "Big Tim" Sinclair
Father. Brother. Mentor. Protector. Legend.

I sighed, dabbing at my eyes when tears welled above my lids.

I just stood there, reading the inscription over and over, letting it wash over me before I said words that I never thought I'd be able to. Words that freed me. Words that I knew did more for my healing than they could ever do for him.

"*I forgive you.*"

35

LATHAN

"What's this?"

Remedy's head turned my way from her lounged position on the sofa in the theater room. Tessa reclined next to her, head resting against the side of Remedy's thigh, gaze focused on another of those damn romantic comedies they'd developed an affinity for.

Rem's hair was loose, curls springing free in every direction. She wore one of my hoodies and a pair of her shorts the same deep gray as the thick socks on her feet.

She looked comfortable, relaxed, and absolutely adorable.

"What's what?"

Walking further into the room, I held up the cardstock in my hand before reading the inscription aloud.

I skimmed over the top of the paragraph, ignoring the filler words before dropping my gaze to the bottom paragraph. "After reviewing your application, the committee of the Springfield Art Gala would like to formally invite you to take part in our showcase where your artwork will be displayed and auctioned off."

After reading the last line, I looked up, finding her gaze on mine.

But the easiness she'd displayed moments ago was gone. In its place was nervousness, as if she'd gotten caught doing something she shouldn't have.

"What's this, Rem? I know I didn't fill out any application."

Her nails raked through her curls before she cleared her throat, straightening in her seat. "I took pictures of your work and had Miranda submit the application." When I said nothing, she stiffened even more and my lips twitched with the urge to smile when she adopted her *intimidating* pose that never worked on me. "I'd honestly forgotten about it until now."

Again, I remained silent and she shifted nervously. I could tell she was waiting for me to explode or rant about her doing this behind my back.

I rounded the couch before sitting next to her. Instantly her knees drew to her chest as if to protect her from the anger she thought would come.

But there wouldn't be any.

Not when time and time again, she kept displaying that kindness she extended with no thoughts of having the gestures reciprocated.

This morning, Gabbi had called me in tears, telling me about the things Remedy had done for her and the kids. She'd been grateful and more excited than I'd seen from her in years. She'd worked so hard for so long only to feel like she'd taken steps backwards rather than forward. When all she wanted was to provide for her kids and provide them with a life that she'd been deprived of.

And with one meeting, my baby had made it happen for her.

She'd changed not only Gabbi's life but all the kids, including Tessa and I'd always be grateful.

Ignoring the way Tessa's nose scrunched, I grabbed Rem's face and pulled her closer, pressing a kiss against her lips. "Thank you."

She pulled back enough to meet my gaze. "You're not mad? For overstepping?"

I shook my head. "You're so intricately involved in every aspect of my life now Rem that it's *impossible* for you to overstep."

"So... you're not mad?" She repeated.

Her tone had my brows raising. "No... why?"

"Good, cause there's more."

Curiosity filled me when she leaned forward and pulled out a neat stack of business cards from her purse.

"Daaamn, these are *cold*." I said, pulling one off the top, admiring the brown and gold hands logo I'd sketched on a piece of paper before discarding it on my desk. It had been a design I'd sketched over and over again before balling it up, knowing that the possibility of me turning my hobby into a living was slim to none.

"I had someone in our graphic design department work up some ideas. That's just a basic design so if you want it to be changed, let me know and I can put you in touch with them." Her gaze skated away from mine, looking blankly towards the screen. "You're good, Lathan. *Too good* for your art to stay in my guesthouse. It deserves to be shared."

I swallowed hard, feeling my throat tighten at the kind words from her. My gaze dropped to my hands, giving myself a minute to work through my thoughts.

When I felt like my throat wouldn't crack when I spoke, I met her gaze. "You know I love you, right?"

She froze, eyes bucking almost comically. "You... what?"

"Love you." I repeated just as confidently as I had the first time. "So much that it's impossible to measure." I swiped my thumb across her bottom lip, smirking at the shiver that went through her. "I see you and I love you for who you are, Remedy Sinclair. And I promise I always will."

"*Aww, daddy*! You been watching romance movies too?"

Remedy snorted, covering her mouth with her hands as leaned back, shoulders bouncing with laughter.

"I swear to God, Tessa..."

Before I could finish my scolding, Tessa tossed her arms around Remedy's shoulders. "I love you too, Ms. Remy." She pulled away, cupping Rem's jaw the same way I had before mocking my deep tone. "*And I always will.*"

She must've known I was about to launch at her because she leapt up from the sofa, running out of the room, leaving a trail of high-pitched cackles behind her.

Once she was gone, I turned back to Remedy, finding her gaze on me.

"Do you mean what you said?" Her tone was low, timid. "That you... *you know*."

"Have I ever lied to you?" When her head shook slowly, I smiled. "And I don't plan on starting now. I meant what I said. I love you. Have for a while now. *Known* for a while now... I just had to make sure you were ready before I told you."

I didn't expect her to blurt the words back to me and that was okay. I'd been patient with her thus far, so I'd continue being patient going forward.

She was worth the wait.

She always would be.

36

REMEDY

All I could focus on was the inches of skin pressed against mine. He was warm, acting as my personal furnace, heating me all over.

With his eyes locked on mine, Lathan's hand glided down the plane of my stomach until it rested just above the place that throbbed in need of him. When he continued hovering there, I raised my hips, hoping he'd catch the hint and touch me where I needed most.

I was instantly rewarded when his long fingers curled, spreading me to tease my clit.

I jolted, squeezing his brawny forearms, bucking my hips towards him. His fingers moved in tight circles against me, working at a pace that had me lifting on my tiptoes.

His eyes never left mine. His stare was firm and intense as he watched me, feeding on my reactions, mumbling those damn words of praise that had my knees buckling as pleasure crested.

His left arm captured my waist and held me up while his right slipped from between my thighs and lifted until two damp fingers disappeared between his lips.

My core throbbed at the sight, contracting in anticipation of what came next.

Before I could blink, I was flat on the bed, legs spread for him to stand between.

His big hands weren't gentle as he grabbed my hips, yanking me to the edge until our pelvises nearly aligned.

Then he did *that thing*.

The thing I'd seen guys do during my *research* and was curious about it.

The thing where he grabbed the hard shaft that jutted out from his pelvis. He glided it through my folds a few times before creating a lewd, wet smacking sound when he smacked it against my clit.

"*Uuugh*." I groaned, spreading my legs, hoping he'd do it again. I could see why the women in the videos yelled out when on the receiving end.

It felt so *good*.

"Eyes on me."

Not realizing I'd closed them, my lids sprang open, widening at the menacing look he wore.

Lathan, in the act of sex, was potent and I loved it. I appreciated him holding back for me when I'd been in my exploration phase. It'd been what I needed at the time until I grew comfortable.

But this?

This passion and intensity he radiated now was what I craved. What I *needed*.

His gaze seared me as he studied every one of my reactions to what he was doing. As if filing the knowledge away to put to good use at a later date.

My mouth hung open on a soundless moan that lodged in my throat as he entered me. Slowly at first, then slamming the last few inches home with a rough thrust.

Shit.

That alone had me on the verge of exploding.

His left hand tangled in my hair, tugging on the strands, smirking when I moaned in pleasure. His right remained on my hip, keeping me from fleeing and pulling down into his hard thrust each time he surged forward.

It was just enough and too much all at the same time.

Whoever uttered the words *never give yourself wholly to a man* had never experienced this. Never felt the bliss of having a man like Lathan between her thighs while completely at his mercy. Never knew what it was like to trust someone enough to give yourself over to the moment, knowing you were completely safe in your partner's hands.

It was a blissful feeling, one I chased as often as he'd allow me.

Underneath my fingertips, his body vibrated with intensity. With narrowed lids, his face contorted as he continued rocking against me.

My walls tightened and his rhythm stuttered, becoming rough and reckless as his forehead met mine while emitting low groans.

Our lips touched and his tongue joined the party, twirling sensually around mine, contrasting the violent way we clashed below.

The entire bed shook from the force of his strokes and my hips hung suspended in the air. Clutching his brawny forearms, I held on for dear life while he took me on a wild ride.

When the beginning stages of my orgasm crept up, he yanked away from my lips. At my disappointed groan, he smiled. "I want to see."

So he watched me with scrutiny that felt intimate rather than invasive.

He watched as the trembles started and my body writhed on the bed when the pleasure took over.

He kept his frantic pace going but his eyes never left mine as I flinched from the intensity of the mounting orgasm before giving myself over to it.

When the pleasure reached its peak, he shoved himself in to the hilt, holding onto my waist as he reached his peak right after me.

God, we were perfect together. Two halves of a whole that once floated through life aimlessly before flourishing once we came together.

His weight sagged on mine and he stayed buried in my warmth as if not wanting to leave me.

And I didn't want him to.

Like every part of him did, his weight comforted me and I wished we could stay there forever.

But after a few minutes, he rolled next to me, chest heaving with the intensity of what we'd just done, Turning to face him, I propped my cheek on my palm, planting my elbow in the soft mattress. It took a moment but he glanced down, meeting my gaze.

"I think I love you too." I finally responded to the words he'd revealed earlier.

His cheeks instantly stretched with a smile, leaning to kiss my neck. "What I gotta do to make that *think* into a fact?"

I returned his smile, loving that his eyes instantly fell to my lips, watching them like they were his favorite thing in the world.

"You know that thing you do with your fingers…" I began with a tease, wiggling my eyebrows.

A startled bark of laughter rushed from his throat before he playfully nipped at my ear, causing my own giggles to burst free.

"If that's all it takes, baby, then your ass is already head over heels. I do that thing with my fingers almost *every night*."

Another round of laughter filled surrounded us before we settled again, limbs tangled together.

His even breathing soothed me and I lifted my head to meet his low-lidded gaze, smiling at the exhaustion lining his features.

"Thank you."

My words were quiet but the stillness around us allowed them to reach his ears.

"For what?"

A humorless chuckle rushed out as I trailed my finger down his cheeks, following the line his beard made on his handsome face. "Where do I start?" Licking my lips, I rolled to my side so I could meet his gaze head-on as I spoke. "For *everything*. For seeing me. For loving me. For being there and not giving up when I *know* that was the easier option."

I'd hoped to get the words out before tears started but the tickle at the back of my throat let me know that I didn't have long.

But I didn't mind if he saw them. He'd already seen every face of mine and he was still here, staring at me with the same adoration I felt blossoming in my chest for him.

"Thank you for allowing me to love *you*... and your daughter." I blew out a shaky breath when the first tear spilled, then sighed when he smiled, using it to give me the courage I needed to continue. "You gave me a family while the one I had was fractured. You gave me the courage to love *myself*." My voice cracked on the last word. "I love you in a way that I thought impossible." Tightening my arms around him, I sighed in contentment, repeating his earlier words back to him. "I love you for who you are, Lathan Calloway. *And I always will.*"

EPILOGUE

"My favorite couple!" Dr. Tori exclaimed when Lathan and I walked in, hand in hand.

We'd become regular clients, coming in every two weeks.

Lathan and I did plenty of talking on our own but having an unbiased—despite her calling us her favorite couple—opinion sometimes was exactly what we needed.

Six blissful months of our relationship had passed and I was happier than I can ever remember being. Of course, I still had dark times, still had *moments*. But nowadays the good definitely outweighed the bad and I was *happy*, which was an emotion I once considered impossible for me a year ago.

Since getting together, Lathan built a workshop near the back of my property. It was long overdue because he'd outgrown the second bedroom in my guesthouse with the abundance of pieces he'd been commissioned for.

The vast space near the back of my property was unused and perfect for him to work on his craft. He'd begun selling his art online full time in between the larger gigs and was making a *killing*.

After cutting off Ms. Gloria and pressing charges for what she'd done to Tessa, Gabbi found a spacious five-bedroom home on the outskirts of Sienna Falls which placed her closer to her job. With the breathing room I'd given her by taking care of her debts, she'd been able to send the younger kids to childcare and enroll them in after-school programs while she worked.

Tessa still lived part time between both homes, helping her mom out when she could without the added pressure of feeling like their primary caregiver.

"How are you?" Dr. Tori asked me after we'd all been seated.

Instantly, I smiled, looking over at Lathan whose eyes were already on mine. "I still have good days and bad days. But therapy has helped. I'm learning to heal. And to forgive people who *damn* sure didn't deserve it."

When she smiled, I knew she recognized the words she'd spoken to me that first time I'd shown up, wide-eyed and completely at a loss on what to say. The session where she'd shared parts of her story that resonated with me.

I looked down at my engagement ring, continuing to repeat her own words back to her. "I met *someone*. Someone who made it easy to let my guards down. Someone who saw me despite my *many* flaws. Someone who showed me what it really meant *to be loved*."

"And are you happy, Remedy?" She asked. That was a big thing I'd cried about in many sessions. Before meeting Lathan, trying to find a time in my life where I was just *completely* happy had been more difficult than I realized.

So, my assignment was to do something for myself each week that made *me* happy. Even if I was already in a good mood or not feeling down, she'd said stealing those little moments would teach me how to find happiness within myself first. If I did that, then the way I felt about *me* would show up in my relationships with others.

And she'd been right.

I looked at Lathan, then thought about Tessa who was such an important part of my life. I thought about my mom who lived in the guesthouse full-time now. We also had a long road to go to achieve complete healing but we were well on the way to it and I now cherished her presence and considered her an important part of my tribe.

I thought about my relationships with my friends, the ones I'd pushed away over the years but now they visited me regularly and I did the same.

I thought about the sisterhood I'd developed with Garryn. She'd been right when saying how alike we were and once my guards were down, I was able to realize how much. Since then, we'd developed a bond that felt familial, and I looked forward to standing with her and Verse for their upcoming nuptials.

I thought about Gabbi who'd also become like a sister and was now in the very early stages of a relationship.

And finally, I thought about Lathan, the man who loved me in spite of it all. The man who'd loved me through my faults and stuck with me while I learned to love myself.

"I'm the happiest I've ever been. I'm healthier than I've ever been." Tightening my fingers around his, I rested my head against his shoulder, preening under his affection when he kissed my forehead. "And I wouldn't have it any other way."

She smiled before swinging her gaze to the man who could set my soul on fire with one look. "And you, Lathan?"

That familiar half-smile lifted his generous lips as he tightened his hand around mine. "I mean..." He began in a low tone that made me grin. "Both of you know exactly how I feel. I only sit in here and *ramble* about it every two weeks."

While she chuckled, I nudged him playfully. "That doesn't mean I don't want to hear it *again*."

He rolled his eyes. "Her ass is spoiled, bossy and demanding as hell. And it's starting to rub off on Tessa. I want a *refund*."

"Lathan!" Dr. Tori and I exclaimed at the same time, making him laugh.

"*Jokes*." He stressed, "Just jokes, babe." The humor from moments earlier faded, giving way to that intensity that he reserved for me. "You know the way I feel about you can't be described with mere words. You complete Tessa and I... you complete *me* in the best way."

His stare didn't waver from mine and I couldn't look away, even after Dr. Tori reclined in her seat, pressing a hand to the center of her chest.

"You're the blessing I never saw coming. You're the other half of me and I love you, Remedy soon-to-be Sinclair-Calloway."

My lips quivered in anticipation of the four words that had becoming the signature we always stamped at the end of our *I love you's*. The words that brought me joy like I'd never known before.

"*And I always will.*"

The End

KEEP READING

There's a small bonus chapter at the end from Hakeem's POV.

If you've read In This Moment (which I hope you have), then you're aware that Hakeem is a mysterious fan favorite.

To preserve my sanity, I'm not going to announce a release date for his project yet but I will say I'm shooting for a late summer/early fall release.

Don't forget to join my mailing list and follow me on all the socials to be the first to know about any upcoming releases.

BONUS CHAPTER - HAKEEM

It's been a while since I'd done a job like this one.

Now, following behind Garryn while simultaneously avoiding her probing questions was how I spent my days.

Before I'd made the long drive to Dallas, Verse asked if I was sure about going through with it. He'd made it clear that he wasn't *sending* me there because he'd made a promise to Remedy. And though Lathan was aware of my plans, he'd also stressed that he wasn't asking me to do this, also not wanting to break the promise he'd made.

But after hearing what they'd done to her, neither of them had to send or ask me to go *anywhere*.

I volunteered.

Nothing would please me more than making sure the man who hurt one of *us* was taught a lesson.

Despite the cold air surrounding me, I was warm from the adrenaline that had me rushing through my veins since I arrived hours earlier. I felt restless from it, eager to do something besides sitting in this darkened area, waiting for my prey to arrive.

No matter how many suits I wore, no matter how many meetings

I'd taken with politicians and wealthy socialites... at my core, I was still the same man I'd been in Uptown.

For so long, since being a child, violence had been my existence.

From the household I'd grown up in to the employment I'd gained under one of the most powerful men in the southern United States as an enforcer. All my life, I'd used my size and ability to intimidate others to make money.

But this trip today? This was *personal* and I'd gladly do it without needing a penny of repayment.

Seconds later, the distinct sound of tires rolling over gravel met my ears and I straightened from the dark tree line surrounding the site, watching a man get out and walk towards the half completed building he'd commissioned.

Lighting was limited, considering it was the middle of the night, which was perfect for what I had in mind.

Christian Gavin, a now known child molester, had sanctioned the construction of a youth center, of all things, in Dallas.

The fuckin' *audacity*.

There couldn't be a conscious housed in his mind if he thought this was a good idea after what he'd done.

When he stopped mere feet from the structure, my eyes flicked to the cement truck I'd checked for keys earlier before purposely making my footfalls audible so Christian could hear my approach.

I'd only taken three steps before Christian whirled, gun in hand. But I kept walking towards him, expression blank as I approached.

I could tell the moment he recognized me because he relaxed, slipping his finger from the trigger to rest on the side of the gun.

Big mistake.

"You always were a sneaky muthafucker, weren't you?" He joked, sizing me up.

Ignoring him, I surveyed our surroundings, making sure there were no witnesses around for what would happen next.

My reputation for being a paranoid, silent asshole benefited me because the true reasoning behind my actions escaped him.

"Shifty as hell, too." He continued before shrugging. "But I guess with a past like yours, it's understandable."

Nodding towards the half-finished project, I asked. "This is it?"

He nodded. "Yep. Without your help, this project will never get completed."

I was here under the guise of helping him find who'd been sabotaging his work. The construction company he'd been contracted with suddenly pulled out. The permits and grants he'd gotten approved were revoked.

Every step forward he'd taken had been met with an obstacle that sent him ten steps backwards.

Unbeknownst to him, Verse had used his long-reaching connections to make things difficult for Christian. Verse's plan had been to ruin the man and make sure the rest of his life was rife with struggle.

But when Christian finally reached out to us for help in saving his business, my plans changed.

"Somebody's fucking with me." He growled, swiping his foot across the ground and sending gravel flying in the air. "They're making shit hard and messing up my deals. Every business I have is being hit with bogus inspections, sanctions, and a bunch of other shit that's making my life difficult. I need this open by the end of the year because it's bleeding me dry." He huffed, reaching up to adjust the cap covering his bald head before swinging his gaze back to mine. "You think you can find out who's doing this?"

Instead of answering, my gaze dropped to the gun he held, not saying a word.

He knew how I rolled so he sighed, hurrying to his car and tossing it in the front seat before shutting the door.

"I got plans for this, Hakeem." He griped, closing the distance between us again. "I promised myself that I'd continue Big Tim's life work and that's what I'm trying to do. Even if it's not in Uptown, I know he'd be proud."

I merely hummed, keeping my gaze on him.

He blew out another breath. "You are one intense muthafucker, you know that?"

I did but remained silent, enjoying how he squirmed under the penetrating stare I fixed on him.

"You remember who I am, right?" Confusion settled on his features at my random question. "My past. My reputation." I hated talking, so I hoped the short phrases were enough to get my point across because I didn't want to lose my temper.

Not yet at least.

He smiled, thinking the reputation I'd mentioned would be used for his benefit. "They called you the *Reaper*. You trained under Travis Knight then worked as an... *enforcer* for him and his grandson Axel. Until you walked away to be a bodyguard for Verse Presley after getting revenge on the men who killed your brothers."

I remained stoic at the mention of my past. Of who I'd been before Verse pulled me out of the deep shit I'd gotten myself involved in. That Hakeem had been headed to an early grave because of his self-destructive behavior.

"*Allegedly*." I added.

He snorted before his grin turned calculating. "The experience you have will be perfect for whoever is fucking with me. I want them to *suffer*."

"Do you remember the details surrounding the way my brothers' murderers were killed? The way they suffered?"

He nodded. "That's exactly the skill I need so I can move forward and get this shit open."

"You were right when you said this community needs more outlets for the youth to focus their energy on so I'll make sure this center will be opened by the end of the year... but unfortunately, Christian, you won't be here to see it."

Ignoring his alarmed expression, I pulled out a pair of thin black gloves that I hadn't used in ages. With the same patience that had been instilled in me years ago, I slipped them on, keeping my gaze on his. "You hurt someone I care about."

His brows furrowed as I slowly closed the distance between us.

"You hurt a child. You violated her and had the nerve to call yourself our *uncle*." His expression fell and I could see the realization wash over him. "You thought an apology would be make up for what you did? For the pain and trauma you inflicted on her?"

This monologue was more words than I'd said all month but I needed him to know why I was here.

"You built a good life after leaving Uptown. You lived happily for twenty-plus years after what you did." I paused, tilting my head. "Of course, if I was aware of what you'd done sooner, that never would've happened. But I'm aware now, so... your time to pay has come. Whether you go out easy or suffer is completely up to you. Either way, this will be your last day on this earth."

Indecision flashed across his face before his eyes swung towards the car where he'd placed his gun. Finally, his gaze met mine again, going hard with determination.

Instead of annoyance at his decision, I smiled for the first time in probably five years. "I'm going to enjoy this."

BEFORE YOU GO...

Reviews are so important, especially for indie authors. They help fuel us to work even harder to provide the content you want to read as well as help other readers decide if they want to check out this project.

If you enjoyed this book (or even if you didn't), please consider leaving a review on Amazon and/or Goodreads.

K.

ALSO BY K. LASHAUN

All The Way Series
Between

Only Friends

Rewind Series
By Chance

Second Chance

The Things Unseen Series
In This Moment

To Be Loved

The Four Letter Word Series
Love's Truth

Standalones
Everything & More

Only Gift I Need

ABOUT THE AUTHOR

K. Lashaun is an adult contemporary author born and raised in the great state of Alabama. Her start in writing followed the typical blueprint for most authors — consuming an insane amount of book at an early age before turning that love of reading into a knack for storytelling.

She enjoys crafting imperfect — *unapologetically black*— feel good, love stories.

She has penned nine books to date with many more on the way.

K. Lashaun would love to hear from you. Click below to follow her on Instagram and Facebook or visit her website at www.klashaun.com

facebook.com/AuthorKLashaun
instagram.com/authorklashaun

Made in the USA
Columbia, SC
10 June 2025